For Jan
with much love
J x

Parallel Lines

BOOK ONE OF THE THREE LIVES TRILOGY

Jane McCulloch

Text copyright © 2014 Jane McCulloch
All rights reserved.

First published.

ISBN: 1503318443
ISBN 13: 9781503318441
Library of Congress Control Number: 2014921063
CreateSpace Independent Publishing Platform
North Charleston, South Carolina

For Toby's children

PROLOGUE

Dr Strutter arrived at his Wimpole Street consulting rooms in a state of considerable frustration. He was ten minutes late, and this in spite of having left his Hampstead home half an hour earlier than usual. Being a man of precise habits, the inadequacies of others, particularly those who ran the London Transport system, left him in as near a stressful state as he ever came to getting. As he explained in somewhat indignant tones to his receptionist, Mrs Maitland, "We just sat there, with no explanation, no announcement, for twelve and a half minutes."

He peeled off his raincoat, shook it and rolled up his umbrella. "Do you know, for one dreadful moment I thought I might end my days stifled amongst very indifferent company, and this thought, not surprisingly, left me a little agitated."

Mrs Maitland, who was used to his little ways, smiled as he continued,

"I particularly wanted to be here early today, to give myself a chance to sort through those papers you turned out of that old filing cabinet." He went towards his room.

Mrs Maitland called after him, "Shall I bring you a cup of tea?"

But Dr Strutter had already closed the door.

"I'll take that as a yes." she murmured to herself.

He stood staring at his desk and a shudder went through him. Its usual immaculately tidy appearance had been transformed into what looked more like the stall of a jumble sale. The polished leather surface, never usually disturbed by so much as a loose paper clip, was now lost beneath a mound of old papers and files. He gingerly picked up one or two documents from the top of the pile, giving them a cursory glance. Then he let them drop, rubbing his fingers together as if removing some imaginary dust. With a sigh he seated himself in his desk chair, staring in front of him with an air of distaste.

Mrs Maitland entered with the tea, and took in his look with a glance.

"I just don't know where to begin," he said in despairing tones.

She cleared a space for his cup and spoke rather briskly, "I think you will find that most of these papers can be disposed of. I could do that for you, but not until you are sure there is nothing there you want to keep."

Dr Strutter sighed again. "Thank you Mrs Maitland, but I must rise to meet this challenge myself. Bring in some large dustbin bags if you would be so kind. I will have a purge. It will be deeply cleansing."

As she was leaving the room he said testily, "I suppose my appointment book is somewhere beneath all this mess. Be so kind as to remind me when I have my first appointment?" "Eleven thirty." she replied. "Ah, that is good." said Dr Strutter. "I have two hour's disposal time, which I sincerely hope should be enough."

He took off his glasses and absentmindedly wiped them on the bottom of his tie. Then he picked up the top file.

Once started on his demolition work he made good progress. In fact, he had taken barely an hour, and had almost reached the bottom of the pile, when he caught sight of something that made him stop. It was a black note book.

The shock of seeing it caused him a quick intake of breath. With fingers, that surprisingly shook, he flicked open the cover and looked down at the large bold hand.

On the first page was written, **"First Session   November 21ˢᵗ 1978**

It was her notebook. Celia's. He had forgotten he had it. His eyes went down the page, reading slowly at first, then devouring the words at an almost feverish speed. After two or three pages he slammed the book shut, walked to the window, and stood staring out. A few moments later he returned to the desk and put the rest of the papers hurriedly into the black bags. He sat back and pressed the intercom.

"Mrs Maitland. Can you come in and remove the dustbin bags? Oh, and see to it I am not disturbed by any calls until my first appointment arrives."

Not for the first time Mrs Maitland was puzzled by the unpredictable behaviour of her employer, but she knew better than to question his demands.

After the departure of the dustbin bags, Dr Strutter walked slowly back to the window and stood for several minutes gazing down at the street.

Immediately the memories flooded back. It had been just such a grey, rain-soaked and deserted Wimpole Street the day she had arrived, all that time ago, in November 1978.

Did he want to remember? Well, it made no difference. He couldn't stop himself now.

The memories returned, unbidden, and with crystal clarity. He suddenly smiled as he recalled watching the large dilapidated Daimler being manoeuvred, with difficulty, into a space far too small for it. The gap hadn't even boasted a meter and the driver, judging by the jerky wheel movements, was showing definite signs of desperation. He had surmised, correctly, that the tall young woman alighting from the car was on her way to see him, and was obviously aware that she was late.

A few minutes later Celia Roxby Smith had come into reception and was shown into his room. He had at once been struck by her appearance. Her oval face was framed with shoulder-length hair of pale red-gold, and her complexion, although pallid, had a delicate flush on the high cheekbones. Even her figure seemed perfect, clad as it was in a clinging silk dress, obviously expensively cut, and in a colour that matched her eyes.

The whole effect was one of coolness, elegance and beauty. But what he remembered most was the look of sadness and desperation in those strange blue-grey eyes.

He returned to his desk, sat down, and after a few more minutes lost in thought, he opened the book once again and started to read.

The writing was fluent. Occasionally there were crossings-out and there were some charming misspellings. She had her own method of recalling it all, where she would write her own thoughts and reactions in a different colour pen, to distinguish them from the narrative. She also wrote in dramatic form, so that it read like a work of fiction. This gave him a far more informed picture of the sessions than he could have achieved had he merely recorded them himself.

On the title page she had printed: **MY SESSIONS WITH DR STRUTTER**

Then on the first lined page she had written: **FIRST SESSION November 21ˢᵗ 1978**

So he started to read her account. Celia's account.

She began…

"This is what I remember of that first session with Dr Strutter.

I have to admit, the day didn't get off to a good start. I reached Wimpole Street late and was already feeling flustered. Typically there was nowhere to park and as always when things go wrong I started muttering to myself like a madwoman. "Damn! Damn! Damn! What the hell am I doing?" and so forth. Yanking the gear lever, which was really stiff, and reversing into the only visible space, I almost shouted, "Stupid bloody car. Bloody London and I'm bloody late. I'm bound to get a fine. Oh God. More for bloody George to grumble about."

A quick glance in the driving mirror showed me that I was not looking my best. But then surely one didn't have to look ones best for a psychiatrist? Wasn't pale and interesting more appropriate? I didn't want to be here anyway. It was only because of George.

I flung a hairbrush through my hair, didn't bother with my face and pushed the car door open, with great difficulty. "Bloody heavy door." I was now at screaming point. I let it slam and locked it, making a mental note to tackle

George about getting a car I didn't have to fight a battle with the whole time. And now it had started to rain. No umbrella.

I ran across the road and stared at the myriad names displayed on the door. There he was. 'Dr Strutter, 3rd floor'.

Pressing the bell I gave my name. The door, after several pushes, opened. 3rd bloody floor and yes, no lift. I climbed the stairs grimly trying to compose myself for the ordeal to come. All right. I would give it one try and then tell George it was not worth the expense or the bother. A tight-lipped, neat little woman sat in reception. They're a special breed aren't they, receptionists? I've noticed that they always have that slightly disapproving look. This one quickly managed to imply that I was late.

"Ah yes. Mrs Roxby Smith. You can go straight in. It's the door opposite."

She took my coat and by this time I was really wishing I was somewhere the other side of the world or better still on another planet!

Dr Strutter opened the door just as I reached it. He held out his hand, "Mrs Roxby Smith? Do come in." I panted out my apology, I was sorry to be late, the traffic, nowhere to park and so on. His voice was calm. "Please don't worry. My next patient cancelled, so there is no problem."

He let go my hand, closed the door and indicated a dark green high-backed leather chair on one side of a marble fireplace. He then sat down in a similar chair facing me and waited.

There was silence and I could hear the clock ticking on the mantelpiece. My irritation began to mount. "No couch?" I asked after a moment, in what I thought were suitably mocking tones. He looked at me. "You would like to lie down? You may do so if you wish," and he pointed to a chaise-longue on the far side of the room.

Obviously no bloody sense of humour either. I knew this would be a disaster.

I shook my head, slightly embarrassed. "No, no. I just associate psychiatrists with couches, that's all. His tones were rueful. "Something of a cliché I think. Too many American films and TV programmes have given the wrong impression about us."

There was another pause.

"This is a very comfortable chair." I ran my fingers along the edge of the arms and added, "I do like leather chairs."

As he still didn't speak I made an examination of the room. It was nicely austere, certainly nothing to distract the patient. I liked the way the leather chairs and the desk had a really worn look. However this made me feel over-dressed and I wished I'd settled for something tweedy instead of tailored silk. My eyes came back to his.

This was ridiculous. Surely he should say something?

"Aren't you going to ask me questions?" He smiled. "What would you like me to ask you about?"

Oh really.

My annoyance bubbled up and overflowed. I said firmly, "I don't know. But I have to be here for a reason. I thought you'd want to ask me about dreams and that sort of thing."

"Would you like to talk about your dreams?"

Why was he being so unhelpful?

"No I wouldn't. Apart from the fact that I don't dream much, I have the greatest difficulty in remembering them." I paused, aware that I sounded fairly hostile.

"I don't think I'm going to be a very interesting subject, do you? I knew this was all a great mistake, my coming here." And for some reason I suddenly shivered.

He showed immediate concern. "Are you cold? I can turn up the heating."

"No thank you. I'm fine. A bit nervous perhaps. Doctors always make me feel nervous."

I looked across at him and then suddenly, unable to stop myself, I burst out laughing.

"Something amuses you?

How stupid was that? I now had to explain and make myself even more ridiculous.

"Well yes. I mean, it may sound rude, but a rather silly pun came into my head. You see I told a friend of mine I was coming to see you and she said, 'I've heard of Dr Strutter. - A Jung man of course." I was embarrassed now and finished lamely, "That's just it. You see, you're not."

"I'm not?" He was puzzled.

I said very quickly, "A young man. Or at least, not a very young man."

How could I have said that?

I clasped my hands together in an effort to regain my composure and fervently wished I could leave. "I'm so sorry. That wasn't funny at all. It's just that I don't know what you expect me to do or say."

I couldn't look at him after this, so I glanced towards his desk. There was an opened letter lying marooned on the tidy surface and instinctively I knew it must be about me, so I blurted out, "I don't know what you've been told, but it was all a stupid mistake."

"Mistake?"

"Yes. My overdose or whatever they called it."

Dr Strutter stroked the knees of his trousers and then said in his quiet, calm voice, "Perhaps you could tell me about the incident? About how it happened? I've read through your notes but they tell me very little. Just a suggestion you'd been suffering from bouts of depression...

I couldn't let that go.

I burst out, "You might call it depression, I call it Life!"

I know the interruption sounded rude but I felt a mounting irritation and almost shouted,

"Is that all they say? In their report about me"

Those calm tones again. "Basically yes. They thought we might sort out any problems that were making you depressed, by talking them through together."

I gave a mirthless laugh. "That would be fine if I knew what they were."

For the first time I made a proper examination of him.

I had to consider whether I could trust him. Was he going to be a friend? God know I was in need of an ally.

His appearance gave little away. I supposed he was in his late forties but difficult to tell. A rather ageless face. Nice voice though, soothing and calm, even if I had found it irritating at first. I had been told he was 'brilliant'. Brilliant. What the hell did that mean anyway? All he seemed to do was study me in silence.

I looked at my watch. Fifteen minutes gone already and nothing really had happened.

Suddenly his voice broke through the silence. "Shall we start with the incident?"

"The incident?" For a moment I couldn't think what he meant. "Oh the overdose."

I paused, "What do you want to know?"

He looked directly at me, "Why do you think it happened?"

Oh God. How could I tell him? How could I explain? He wouldn't understand. I didn't really understand it myself.

So I shrugged and tried to appear nonchalant.

"It's difficult to say. I suppose I was feeling depressed at the time, more so than usual. A bit 'low' as my mother would say. And on top of that we'd had a ghastly dinner party…" I paused again, uncertain how to go on.

Dr Strutter put his hands together under his chin. He seemed to have many little mannerisms like this. He'd already fiddled with his tie. Twice. But he suddenly seemed interested. "Ghastly? Why ghastly?" he asked.

I shrugged. "They always are really. I find dinner parties something of an ordeal. This one was more so than usual. All that panic and exhaustion beforehand, a lot of people I didn't want to see, eating and drinking far too much and talking about things I didn't want to hear. That, and the feeling they would never leave." I paused again, but he remained silent, obviously waiting for me to go on. "Well, probably because I was feeling low," I gave the word 'low' a nice hint of self-mockery, "I drank too much, far more than I usually do and then stupidly took a lot of aspirins."

It was impossible. Impossible to convey in a few sentences the awfulness of it all. He wouldn't understand anyway. He didn't know any of the background to it.

Dr Strutter leant forward. His voice became more insistent.

"Why was this dinner worse than other dinner parties?"

Worse? If only he knew. It had been the dinner party from hell.

I made an effort and plunged in with the outline of what had happened. I think I said something along the lines of…

"Well, for a start, I was in a fury with my husband George, over something he'd done. As a consequence I started drinking early, about five in the after-noon. I remember thinking about nine o'clock, this is disastrous, if I feel so terrible now what am I going to be like in an hour's time? So I went out to the kitchen and took four aspirins. I don't usually take so many, but on this occasion I felt I needed a double dose, so ignored the danger. Then I suppose I kept on drinking and when, in an hour's time the guests still hadn't gone, I took more aspirins. I have no very clear recollection of what happened after that, except I do remember taking more aspirins after the guests finally departed. By that time I didn't really know or care what I was doing. George found me collapsed on the stairs."

I broke off here and picked up my bag and desperately started looking for my cigarettes. I hoped to God he would let me smoke. Meanwhile I struggled on with my account. "Next thing I knew I was in hospital, stomach pumps, the lot. It was all very nasty and humiliating." My hands were now shaking so I said, "Do you mind if I smoke?"

He said politely, "Not at all." He fetched an onyx ashtray from the desk and waited while I stuck the cigarette into the holder and lit it. I inhaled deeply, felt better and continued, "Everyone just presumed I was suicidal. It was most annoying."

He was now definitely showing interest. "Who's everyone?"

"George, the nurses, the dinner party guests."

He leant forward again. "Is there any particular reason why your husband should have thought you would try to commit suicide?"

I couldn't answer that. Not until he knew more.

I think I looked away and just puffed away on my cigarette.

After another silence and to my relief he changed tack. "Which of your parents had red hair?"

This was rather a surprise. It seemed an odd sort of question but I was happy to answer.

"Neither. I inherited my hair, along with a great many other things, from my grandmother." I paused and told him quite truthfully, "Funny you should mention my hair. I've always hated it. I mean, if you're going to have red hair it should be flaming red, of the Titian variety, not pale and insipid, like mine. 'Flax on a distaff' my mother used to call it."

Dr Strutter again smoothed his knees and suddenly smiled. 'To me it is more of a red gold. I believe the correct term is strawberry blonde."

What a strange man he was turning out to be!

He ignored my look of surprise and continued, "You seem to be quite concerned with what your mother used to say."

That's psychiatrists for you! But this time he was definitely on the wrong tack and I quickly corrected him.

"I honestly don't know why I quoted her. Please don't get the wrong idea. It's not significant I assure you."

His next question did seem predictable. "Do you get on well with your mother?"

I removed the cigarette from the holder and stubbed it out giving me time to put together an adequate answer.

"Do I get on with her?" I considered this. "Do I get on with her? It's hard to say. We don't quarrel, but then again, we're not close. I'm probably too insipid, like my hair. She's rather a remote person and doesn't show affection. Perhaps she blames me for..."

Here I broke off.

I wasn't going to go down that route. Far too complicated.

I continued quickly. "My mother is actually a talented painter. She illustrates books. I've always admired her talent."

How did I manage to sound so detached, when I was really so angry?

"If I am honest, I think I despise her weakness in relationships. She lets people bully her, ride rough-shod over her. Even me. Which is quite ridiculous."

At this point Doctor Strutter managed a smile and relaxed back into his chair.

"It sounds as if you never expect people to find you interesting or likeable."

That was astute of him.

"I suppose not."

There was another silence. I stared at the wall and suddenly noticed the one picture in the room. "I like that water-colour. It's clever of you to have only one painting on your walls. Not much chance of your patients becoming distracted."

He smiled again.

It started me wondering if I could make him laugh.

"That painting was done by one of my patients. Are you interested in painting?"

My turn to smile. "Not particularly. I actually hate being made to look at paintings. It probably comes from being dragged round too many art galleries as a child. But there are one or two water-colours I do like."

He nodded. "Do you have any special interests?

At last, a straightforward question that I could answer.

"Music." I told him.

"Is that one of the things you inherited from your grandmother?"

The idea. It really made me laugh.

"No, absolutely not. When I said I inherited a lot of things from my grandmother, I was referring to those things that irritate. Whenever my parents were displeased with me they would say, 'You're just like your grandmother.' Poor lady. I never met her. She died soon after I was born but she certainly left a legacy of bad feeling."

He considered this and then asked, "Do you play an instrument?"

"Yes. The piano. Unfortunately I wasn't good enough to be anything other than a teacher and I would have loathed that. But I do get pleasure from playing, as long as I'm not asked to perform and inflict it on anyone else."

He nodded seeming to understand this. "But you enjoy listening to music?"

"It is my greatest pleasure in life."

What a relief. We seemed to be having a spontaneous conversation at last.

"Any particular composers?"

"Well the usual classical composers, Vivaldi, Bach, Corelli, Beethoven, Mozart, Schubert. Anything pre 1830 and the odd piece after, especially the English composers, Elgar, Vaughan Williams, Walton…"

It was all sounding rather highbrow.

"I like traditional jazz as well. And some pop music. Occasionally the really good ballad crops up."

It was at this moment I did something so crass, and so out of character, I almost can't bring myself to write it down. But this is to be an accurate account, so it must be recorded.

I asked him, "Do you know the number, 'Parallel Lines'? It's played a good deal at the moment. Some Irish group. The lead singer has a wonderful voice. You may have heard her?"

Well of course he hadn't, in fact he sounded quite apologetic. He explained that his only contact with the pop world was when he was telling his boys to turn their record players down.

Funny. I somehow hadn't expected him to have children. It was rather difficult to imagine him having a world at all outside his consulting room.

He was now watching me and it gave me the strangest feeling that he could read my thoughts. He had this sort of strange, intense look.

Anyway, I said rather quickly, "Oh I do sympathize. I don't know why everyone has to play their music with the volume up. But you ought to try and listen to 'Parallel Lines'. It's a really good song. I identify with it somehow."

I think that might have been a mistake but he didn't pick me up on it.

"Do you remember any of the words?"

"Oh yes." And I added almost boastfully, "You see, I have this useless gift. When I hear something just once or twice, it sticks. Consequently my mind is full of bits of nonsense. However, I find this lyric less nonsensical than most."

"Tell me some of it."

I was rather taken aback by this. "What, sing it you mean?"

"Sing or speak, whichever you prefer."

I replied almost without thinking, "Well I'll have to sing it. Lyrics sound a bit silly on their own without the music."

So I did. I still can't believe it. I sang to him.

"The Lines of Life are drawn
To the edges of the sky
It's the road we all are travelling
Never asking why.
And if you never ask girl, it's gonna be too late
You'll find you're with St Peter, outside the Golden Gate.

Breakaway. Don't stay behind the bars.
Keep reaching out, reaching out, reaching for the stars.
Breakaway, just Breakaway
From those parallel lines.
Those parallel lines.

Each year the same old story
The adding and subtraction
You're locked into a way of life.
You can't control the action.
But if you never act girl, it's gonna be too late.

You'll find you're with St Peter, outside the Golden Gate.
Breakaway. Don't stay behind the bars.
Keep reaching out, reaching out, reaching for the stars.
Breakaway, just Breakaway
From those parallel lines. Those parallel lines."

As I write it down now I still think those words have a special meaning for me.

When I finished singing there was a moment of silence. I was even more aware of the clock ticking. Embarrassed I said, "I do apologize. I don't suppose many of your patients make you suffer their singing." He smiled and before he could say anything I continued quickly. "There's actually a lot more verses but you get the gist. I know it's ridiculous but somehow that particular lyric just gets to me. What was it Noel Coward said? 'Nothing so potent as cheap music?' Well he was right."

Dr Strutter looked at the clock. "That's all we have time for today."

It seemed a bit abrupt. I was worried my singing might have been the last straw, but then he said, "Will you make an appointment with Mrs Maitland for next week?"

I was really surprised. "You mean, you want to see me again?"

"Yes I think it could be useful."

He got up, turned his back to me and walked to the window.

Mrs Maitland wasn't in reception, so I decided to ring her and not wait. I grabbed my coat and raced down the stairs, reaching the car just before a traffic warden.

I looked up and Dr Strutter was still standing at the window. I didn't think it would be right to wave, so I started the engine and left my illegal spot with all speed...."

Dr Strutter was so buried in the reading of Celia's black book that he jumped when he was interrupted by the loud buzzing of the intercom.
Mrs Maitland's calm voice informed him that his first appointment had arrived.
He closed the book and put it in the top drawer of his desk, there was no more time for it now but he would return to it later.

He suddenly smiled. Was Mrs Maitland tight-lipped? He'd never noticed it and would have to take a closer look. Crossing the room he opened the door for his next patient.

Just as he had done with Celia, all those years ago.

Chapter 1

CELIA'S STORY

The rain had almost stopped as Celia Roxby Smith, leaving Wimpole Street at speed, turned the corner into Devonshire Place and slowed the Daimler down to a more or less legal limit. In front of her there was now a free parking space and on the spur of the moment she decided to take it. For a few minutes she sat in the car, going over in her mind every moment of that first meeting with Dr Strutter. And it was while she was doing this that she came to a decision. She would write down an account of each session with him, and in this way would be able to go back over events, without having to rely on her somewhat faulty memory. It was a great idea. Hadn't it always been her intention to have a stab at writing? Well, this was the ideal way of making a start, and at the same time she would be killing the two proverbial birds with one stone by recording the sessions as well. Feeling pleased and excited she now applied herself to the job of organizing it. First she would need a notebook to write it in, and then she would require a quiet spot near Wimpole Street, where she could immediately put down an accurate account of each session, while it was still fresh in her mind.

She decided that a quick walk to Marylebone High Street would probably provide her with what she needed and putting all the spare change she had in the meter, she set out on her quest.

A few minutes later she had accomplished both objectives.

After purchasing a rather expensive large black leather notebook, she found an almost empty coffee shop, ordered a pastry and coffee, and settled down to her writing.

Once started, she worked away feverishly and had only just finished, when she realised her hour with the meter was up and she ran back in panic to the car. It would have been too galling, after her earlier luck, to have landed herself with a ticket now.

As she neared the Daimler, Celia saw the same traffic warden advancing towards her, but she reached the car before him. To have cheated him once was pleasing enough, but to have done it twice was positively exhilarating. Again she made her James Bond getaway and felt almost affectionate towards the old car as she pulled away fast into the London traffic. Perhaps she should keep the Daimler after all.

Once out of London Celia experienced a feeling of pure light-headed joy. The rain had completely stopped, the clouds had cleared, and not even the fact that she was driving back to George could dampen her spirits. She reached the outskirts of Oxford in good time and turning towards Woodstock it took her only ten minutes to reach the Civolds' imposing school gates. She drove slowly up to the Headmaster's House waving vaguely in a royal way at various masters and boys. Parking the car she let herself in at the front door. George was in his study, but came out as he heard her key in the lock.

"Oh, you're back," he said, and managed to sound cross about it. "Did you have a good drive?"

Celia threw her coat on the hall pew. "Yes it was fine," she told him and she went into the drawing room. Suddenly exhaustion overcame her and she flopped onto the sofa.

He followed her into the room. "Drink?" he asked. She nodded. George walked over to the drinks trolley, made a gin and tonic for her and poured a large whisky for himself. Then he sat down opposite her, and looked expectant. "Well? How was it?"

She braced herself for the interrogation that was bound to come. "Good, I think."

"What did he say about you?"

She felt a flicker of annoyance. "He's not that sort of doctor George. He doesn't give a diagnosis on the spot."

"Well I wouldn't know would I," he sounded sarcastic, "never having needed that sort of doctor myself."

She ignored this. "He was actually very pleasant. We just sort of talked."

"What about?" George's tone was sharp and she knew he suspected that they had talked about him. He wouldn't like that. Not George. Would that be guilt? Or paranoia?

She remained deliberately vague. "Oh very general things. I think he was just trying to build up an overall background picture."

George gave a snort. "Well I take my hat off to him if he manages to probe your shell."

Celia ignored this. "We talked about pictures, and music."

George got up and poured himself another whisky. "I would have thought we could have found someone in Oxford who could have done that, without all the time and expense of sending you to London."

"This was only the first session George. It's early days."

"So he wants to see you again?"

"Yes, next week."

He looked across at her. "Well if he can manage to put you to rights, I suppose it will be worth it."

This wasn't said with affection, but with a rudeness that would normally have made her wince, but in her present mood she let it wash over her. It was obvious George was irritated by the whole business and Celia knew why. He had no control over her in this. No control whatsoever. She put down her drink and stood up. "I'm a little tired George. I think I'll have a bath and then ask Cook to put something on a tray for my supper. Do you mind?"

She could tell George was about to say something really sarcastic and nasty, but then for some reason he decided against it.

"No. That's all right. I have to pop over and see Bill Mackintosh about the new time-table anyway. I'll take him out for something to eat, so I might be late back,"

Celia smiled to herself. She knew exactly what that meant. And what did it matter what time he came back? They had separate rooms now anyway and as long as she didn't have to endure a dreary supper with him, she didn't mind what he did.

After luxuriating in a long bath, Celia sat at her desk and opening her black book read over what she had written. Occasionally she made a correction, but there weren't many. Then she closed it and slid the book into the top drawer and carefully locked it putting the key in a jar on her bedside table.

Looking out of the window she noticed the moon was full. How strange, it was almost light as day. Even the ugly school buildings looked better in the moonlight.

She ran her hands over the leather surface of her antique desk. It had been a surprising wedding present from her mother and the desk, along with her piano, were her two most precious possessions, a source of continual pleasure. Like Natasha. She looked at the photograph of her daughter and smiled.

And now she had the black book. Her secret life. Her secret thoughts. Secret from everybody, especially George. She must ring Mrs Maitland tomorrow and make the next appointment.

A whole week before the next session and to her surprise, she could hardly contain her impatience.

SECOND SESSION   November 28th 1978

So there I was. Back in the green leather armchair, with Dr Strutter sitting opposite me. I was suddenly apprehensive so I asked, "Do you really think my being here is going to help?"

Today I found his calm tones had a soothing quality. "I think so. It sometimes can help, talking to someone in no way connected to you."

That was true. There had been nobody to confide in for such a long time.

"All right. So what do we talk about?"

He smiled. "I thought we might discuss that song. 'Parallel Lines' wasn't it?"

Oh God. I hoped he'd put that embarrassing episode out of his mind but he hadn't.

"Your reaction to it was very positive." He suddenly looked like a naughty schoolboy as he admitted, "I sent Mrs Maitland out to buy me a copy."

"You did?" I couldn't help laughing. "Well at least you heard the proper version."

"On the contrary, I enjoyed the way you sang it but I wanted to hear all the verses. The lyric obviously affects you in some way. Do you know why?"

Of course I did, but it was going to be hard to make him understand.

I hesitated before saying, "It's rather difficult to explain…"

"Try," he said.

So I took a deep breath.

"For quite a while I've had this strange feeling that my present life is running an almost exact parallel with a past life, just as it says in the song. I'm running between parallel lines and there seems to be no escape. My life has become predictable and the future holds no surprises. I can see it all mapped out in front of me. I'm caught in a trap. I desperately want to break out of these parallels and make my own life, but I don't seem to be able to…"

This wasn't making any sense.

"You see?" I said. "I knew it would sound ridiculous."

Dr Strutter put his hands on his knees and stroked his trousers thoughtfully.

"Not at all." He thought for a moment. "These parallels. Are they people, objects, events, coincidences?"

I made a helpless gesture. "Everything." And with a touch of the melodramatic I added, "This whole beastly mess we call *life*. The parallels are everywhere."

He gave a little smile and looked at me encouragingly. "Could you elaborate a little?"

"You mean tell you about them?"

He nodded. "Yes. I'd like to hear. And you might find it useful to explore the subject further."

I hesitated and wondered whether this would be a moment to have a cigarette while I thought how to start. Almost as if he could read my mind he got up and fetched the onyx ashtray.

I was definitely beginning to warm to Dr Strutter.

Once lit up I took the plunge. "All right. I'll try. But I'll have to give you some background first, otherwise the parallels won't mean anything."

Dr Strutter nodded, stroked his knees, sat back and waited for me to speak.

Once I started I found I couldn't stop. I must have gone for forty five minutes without a break. I began at the beginning and, as far as I remember, this is what I said.

"I was born, thirty three years ago, rather typically on VE night – a mistake from the start. My poor mother had a terrible time as everyone was out celebrating and my birth was virtually unattended. In fact she nearly died and took months to recover. It is probably part of the reason why we never really bonded."

I paused here and stubbed out my cigarette, although only half smoked. Too difficult to smoke and talk at the same time.

"From the very beginning my childhood was cold, both physically and emotionally. We, that is my parents and myself, lived in a large, bleak and dilapidated house in Holywell, Oxford. Recently they have stopped through traffic, but when we lived there it must have been one of the busiest roads in England with cars and lorries passing through day and night. Only at the back of the house could you get away from the constant roar and rumblings. Here there was a steep, untidy garden, with one glory, a magnificent mulberry tree, which spread its branches over the entire lawn. The garden was totally neglected. My parents just weren't interested. Occasionally, when it became hugely overgrown a student would be bribed to tidy it up, otherwise the garden was unused and unloved, except by me. That mulberry tree was wonderful. It became my secret hiding place and I would spend hours amongst its branches, reading, thinking, or watching my cousins who lived next door."

At this point I broke off. All this was rather new to me.

"I hope I'm not overdoing the background bit. But without it I don't think I will be able to explain the parallels."

He hastened to reassure me. "No, no. You must tell me everything you need to. Please go on. What about your parents?"

Dear God, my parents! But I had to take the plunge.

"My father, Bernard Maddington, was, well, still is, a historian. At that time he taught at a pioneer co-educational school about five miles outside Oxford. The school had actually been started by my grandfather and when Bernard returned from the war it seemed the obvious thing for him to take up a teaching post there. Unfortunately my grandfather died soon after that and the Governors felt my father was too young to take over the job of Headmaster. They appointed an older, rather conventional man from what my father called a 'fourth rate public school', which according to him was about as near the dregs in English education as you could get. He declared immediate war on this poor man, whom he nicknamed 'the Rabbit' and battle stations went on throughout my childhood."

I looked across at Dr Strutter. "I don't want to seem unfair to my father, but if I am to be accurate, the picture I draw of him will seem fairly brutal. I've sometimes wondered if it would all have been different if he'd been made the headmaster. It's impossible to say. As it was, most people conceded he had a brilliant mind, most considered him a good teacher, but alas, many found him eccentric, egotistical and extremely difficult. Scarcely a day went by when he wasn't in a rage about someone or something. We all suffered from his savage tongue, but I think the poor Rabbit suffered almost the most."

Dr Strutter leant forward. "Was he brutal to you?"

I thought he might pick up on that.

I hastened to reassure him. "Not physically. In fact he paid very little attention to me, something I was quite thankful for, as I found him rather frightening. I think I should explain I was a shy child, timid and inhibited, prone to stomach upsets and terrible nightmares. Not the sort of child my father wanted at all. I'm sure he'd longed for a boy, but as my arrival nearly killed my mother she was told to have no more children, so that was that.

From quite early on I can remember they had separate rooms, which I realise now must have put a considerable strain on their marriage."

Not a good idea to go too deeply into that subject!

"My father was good looking, in a rather Heathcliff sort of way, and this, combined with his fiery personality, meant that he never lacked female admirers."

Here Dr Strutter asked if it would have made a difference if he'd had more children.

Again, astute of him.

"Yes, I think it would. I actually wish they'd adopted another child and then I might not have felt so inadequate. As things turned out I was far from being a spoiled only child. On the contrary, I was very aware that I was looked on as a mistake and consequently always felt that way."

I hoped I didn't sound too sorry for myself but perhaps I am.

I took out another cigarette and Dr Strutter asked about my mother.

"Ah, my mother. Audrey. Well when I was a child she had two passions in her life, Bernard and her painting. She is a professional Illustrator and a very successful one."

He reacted as if struck by something. "Audrey Maddington! Doesn't she illustrate children's books? I seem to remember them, charming pen and wash drawings."

I nodded. "Yes, that's her. Thank goodness that side of her life was rewarding, because her relationship with my father definitely wasn't."

Was I being fair? It was important that I was fair.

"From my earliest recollection he treated her pretty badly, that is in private. There was hardly any show of affection between them and she bore the brunt of all his rages. But in public it was different. He would pay her great attention and actually boast about her, saying things like, 'My wife Audrey is having great success with her exhibition.' Or, 'I know I am biased but there really is nobody to touch my wife when it comes to children's book illustrations' and so on and so forth. It was pretty sickening."

Dr Strutter asked me if I was aware of this behavior as a child.

"I don't think so, not when I was young, although I remember being bewildered by his sudden changes of mood. By the time I was ten I began to hate it and now I find it absolutely nauseating. It's all so hypocritical. And my mother plays up to it in public as well. To those who don't know, they appear to be the most devoted couple"

I wonder if Dr Strutter knows anything of the strain and stress involved, when the public face has to mask a private hell. Probably not. I'm sure he has a very well ordered life, but who am I to make judgments? How can you ever tell what goes on beneath the surface?

He noticed my hesitation and asked, "Did your father give you the same sort of treatment? Did he boast about you as well?"

I gave a mirthless laugh. "He really didn't have much to boast about when I was young, but later, when people started paying me compliments, he certainly joined in, which I found equally awful."

Dr Strutter smiled at this. "He was forced to notice that the ugly duckling had turned into a swan, yes?"

"Something like that." I knew this was a compliment but felt a little embarrassed, so said briskly, "Anyway, to go back to my parents. My mother always blamed Bernard's awful behaviour on the war. Invariably she would say, 'Poor Bernard, he doesn't mean it you know, it's because he had a bad war'."

Dr Strutter immediately asked, "And did he have a bad war?"

"Difficult to tell. He certainly enjoyed dining out on all his old war anecdotes which were repeated with great regularity. He was taken prisoner after Dunkirk and spent three years away. He managed to escape and received a decoration. He loved that 'war hero' bit. He certainly never gave the impression of having suffered greatly. Not like being in a Japanese prison camp." I hesitated. "I suppose you think that is being unfair but I truly think Bernard had quite a good war, if there is such a thing. In a strange way it was probably one of the most fulfilling times of his life."

I looked to see if Dr Strutter was going to make any comment, but as he didn't I continued. "What I have come to realise is that the war had a disastrous effect on their marriage. You see, almost immediately after he returned, my mother became pregnant, and that was of course followed by the big disappointment of my arrival. They never had a chance to settle into a proper relationship and so they quickly drifted apart."

Dr Strutter seemed to be mulling this over. He suddenly asked, "Was your mother a beautiful woman?"

I had to smile at this. "No, definitely not beautiful, although from the early photographs, particularly the wedding, she appeared almost pretty. I don't know how soon in the marriage she gave up bothering about her looks, but I only remember her looking a mess. Occasionally Bernard would say, 'For goodness sake Audrey, do something about your appearance, we have so-and-so coming over.' Then she would make an effort, which was almost worse. Without the paint-covered smocks, her skinny frame and unruly hair looked all the more dowdy and her attempts to wear make-up were disastrous."

I paused here for a moment because I wanted this account to be scrupulously fair.

"I think I ought to add that in spite of her appearance, there was something about her that made you look at her; a sort of vulnerable, child-like quality. This might be the reason she never seemed to be short of male admirers. Perhaps they felt protective towards her. Whatever it was, there'd always be a steady stream of visitors to her studio."

Once again, Dr Strutter leaned forward, as he seemed to do when something particular struck him. "Did your father mind these visitors?"

I laughed. "Bernard? Good heavens no. He was just rather scornful. 'Audrey's Fan Club' he used to call them."

"Did you always call your parents by their first names?

"Yes." I shrugged. "They didn't seem to be the mummy and daddy sort of parents. By the time I reached boarding school it was too late to change and this of course made me even more of an oddity. But I'll get on to that later. I really have to go back to the house in Holywell, because somehow it greatly added to the bleakness of my childhood. That house was never really a home. If anything, it was even more neglected than the garden. For some reason, which I could never fathom, my parents behaved as if we were paupers. This can't have been the case. My father had his teaching salary and earned good money from writing text books, and then there was the added income from my mother's painting. Yet the economies were endless. And most of them were ridiculous. Apart from my father's study the place was virtually unheated. After my third attack of tonsillitis, they were persuaded to let me have a single bar fire in my bedroom, but there were terrible scenes if I left it on for too long. There would be similar scenes if a light was left on. This I found torture. As I told you, I suffered from nightmares and was frightened of being left alone in the dark and begged for the landing light to be left on. But no, the cry would go up, 'Who do you think has to pay the electricity bills? Do you think we are made of money'?"

I gave a laugh. "You're not going to believe this but another extraordinary economy was with the loo paper. Audrey would save the tissue paper wrappers off the oranges to use instead. If those ran out we had to resort to the pages of the calendar on the wall before fresh supplies were found. Many's the time you would find the month down to September when we were only in March."

A slight exaggeration but it made him smile.

I was beginning to enjoy myself so made a mental note to stick more closely to the facts.

"The only really civilized room in the house was my father's study. But no-one was allowed in there, except by invitation. On those few occasions, it was something of a treat, to sit in front of a roaring fire and feel warm at last. The study had wall to wall books, a large desk and one armchair from where Bernard would bellow for attention. 'Audrey I want more coffee.' 'Audrey I can't find my papers on Charles 11'. To which her reply would always be, 'just coming Bernard' and she'd leave the studio to attend to his needs."

I broke off here as my voice was becoming a little tired. "Would it be possible to have a glass of water?"

"Of course, of course."

Mrs Maitland was summoned, a glass of water brought and after I had taken a few sips I felt restored. He seemed concerned. "Do you need a break?"

I explained I was not used to so much talking and said again, "I hope this isn't too boring for you." He was quick to answer. "Not at all. I also think it is useful for you, to recall your childhood, especially if it provides the background to these parallels."

He glanced at the clock. "It is almost time, so I think it might be a good moment to stop and pick it up next week."

I was almost disappointed at this, but of course it was sensible. There was too much background to fit into one session. Maybe it would take two or three. George would grumble about the expense, but I really didn't care about that.

The end of the second session.

SESSION THREE   **December 5th 1978**

This time we plunged almost straight in, because no sooner had I sat down than Dr Strutter asked me a question.

"We were talking about your childhood and I wondered, as it appears to have been somewhat bleak, if you were fed properly?"

I gave a laugh and told him that for the first few years of my life I basically lived on boiled eggs and cornflakes. Poor man, he began to look in shock. He took off his glasses and wiped them on the bottom of his tie. Another of his little mannerisms I noted.

I quickly explained. "My mother had no idea how to cook, even the most basic things. Bernard mostly ate at school, but early on in the holidays he noted the dire situation and a series of housekeepers were engaged. None of them were very satisfactory and the standard didn't improve greatly. I felt it safest to stick to cereal and eggs.

As for the decoration in the house, it was as drab as the contents. The carpets were so worn they were a hazard and the paint and wallpaper were faded and stained."

Dr Strutter seemed surprised, "Wasn't that odd, if your mother had such an eye for beauty in her illustrations?

Clever of him. That had always puzzled me as well. Another cause of my impatience with Audrey.

"Yes, it never ceased to amaze me, but she showed as little interest in the house as she did in her appearance. If she had come from a poor background I might have understood, but both my parents were from fairly wealthy families. At the start of their marriage they had been well provided with wedding presents and they'd also inherited some good pieces of furniture, but these became smothered in general household junk. Nothing was ever thrown away. There were newspapers everywhere. They had been given some good china and glass too, but this was kept hidden away in a cupboard and never used. For everyday use we had a basic service of chipped pale green. To this day I have had a particular loathing for anything in that shade of green."

At this point I took out a cigarette and while lighting it, a thought suddenly came to me. "Do you know, I am inclined to think that all this rejection of comfort and luxury may have had something to do with my father's fierce brand of socialism. He was very left wing, bordering on being a Communist."

Here I gave a laugh. "He actually thought it a great joke when he asked the cook to put a pastry hammer and sickle on the pie crust. His passion was for all things Russian. Come to think of it, our drab existence greatly resembled what I imagine life was like in the U.S.S.R. However, I really suffered from this drabness. I dreamed all the time of a beautiful life, filled with princesses, and princes, and flowers, and jewelry. I treasured the few beautiful objects I could find in the house. One of these was in the neglected china cupboard, an eggshell tea service, so delicate you could see the light through it. I would get the pieces out and study the patterns and characters for hours. They're probably still there, gathering dust."

I knew I was going into too much detail and made a conscious effort to stick to the main story.

"As I think I said, my two cousins lived next door with their widowed mother, my aunt Dolly. She was the person I loved most in the world and without her I think my childhood would have been almost unbearable. It was difficult to believe she was Bernard's sister, as she was totally different in looks and character. Plump and placid, she had wispy hair drawn back in a bun and skin that had a weather-beaten, leathery look. She also had a funny breathless way of speaking which gave the impression that she was vague, even a little stupid. But this was far from being true. Dolly had a quick mind and an observant eye."

I took the cigarette out of the holder and stubbed it out. Dr Strutter was still listening intently. He was certainly a good listener. I don't think I could have talked in this way to anyone else.

"Dolly was very shrewd and I know she didn't miss anything that was going on, particularly on our side of the fence. Oh and her clothes. They were completely individual and I suppose a bit eccentric. She made them out of beautiful soft materials and colours, so it looked as if she had just stepped out of one of those Dutch oil paintings. Bernard viewed her appearance with scorn and would say, 'My poor sister always resembles a sack of potatoes.' But I thought she looked wonderful. Best of all, she worked in a large Oxford bookshop and when I wasn't escaping to my room, or hiding in the mulberry tree, I would be sitting in the children's section of the shop, pouring over the new arrivals. It didn't matter to me that I had no toys, which I didn't, as long I was able to spend time among the books. Of course my final escape was to Dolly's kitchen. It was a haven compared to ours, which was cold and bare, with lino flooring and chipped brown tiles around the sink. In Dolly's kitchen there was a huge dresser covered in brightly coloured pieces of pottery and a great stove that yawned up delicious cakes, jams and homemade bread. In the middle of the room there was a large refectory table. This would be covered with the bits of patchwork, needle-point, geranium plants, magazines, recipe books, bowls of fruit and jugs of homemade cordial or wine. It was a treasure trove and I would sit for hours, telling her the latest development on the 'home-front' or learning how to knit dishcloths or make chocolate fudge. She had endless time for me and endless patience."

Dr Strutter asked, "Did your aunt have a good relationship with your parents?"

I considered this. "Well, yes, in a way. The great thing about Dolly was that she was the only person who wasn't frightened of Bernard. For instance, when someone suggested I should take up piano lessons, and Bernard had gone into one of his predictable rages about paying for them and the ghastly noise he would have to endure, Dolly told him firmly it would be money well spent and I could practice on her piano so as not to disturb him. And he gave in without a murmur."

Dr Strutter considered this. "So it was Dolly who redeemed your other-wise bleak childhood?"

I nodded. "She certainly helped, but in spite of this I think I was a very lonely child. My first ten years were basically spent in solitude. I lived in a complete fantasy world and this can't have been healthy."

There's certainly no room for fantasy in my present life! I'm in the real world now all right. Perhaps that's the problem. Perhaps I should go back to my daydreams.

I smiled at Dr Strutter. "I really must have been a cranky child. I had these imaginary brothers and sisters and these became totally real to me. My idea of heaven was to be in an ordinary, utterly conventional family, who ate chicken and baked beans, who had a Ford Consul, with parents called Mummy and Daddy, who dressed their daughters in pink taffeta and gave their children cuddly toys and shiny bikes. They'd be taken to Sunday school and be allowed to bring their friends home for tea and chocolate biscuits."

Doctor Strutter was smiling. He was seemed amused by my account but as he made no comment I continued.

"I actually did try bringing a friend home from school once. There wasn't any tea, Audrey was in the studio painting, and Bernard came into the room in one of his 'Rabbit' rages. The poor girl was so frightened, she burst into tears and had to be taken home. The same year I was invited to a smart children's party, but Audrey had failed to take in the fact that it was marked Fancy Dress on the invitation. In fact, I didn't possess a party frock, so I had gone in an ordinary jumper and skirt. My humiliation was complete when some mother asked, 'Oh Celia, have you come as a Refugee'?"

Dr Strutter laughed at this.

What a triumph! I could actually make him laugh.

"As you can imagine, after that I refused all invitations and my isolation was complete. Is it any wonder I preferred my daydreams and fantasy world?"

He didn't answer this so again I carried on.

"After a little while I began to find it difficult to distinguish between my own life and my imagined one. This landed me in a great deal of trouble when I went to boarding school, but that comes later."

I took a sip of water and Dr Strutter asked, "Didn't you say you had two cousins? Surely you could have spent time with them?"

At the thought of Wal and Luke I put down the glass of water with a bang.

"No I could not! My entire early life was endangered by those two fiends. In fact, my love for Dolly was in direct ratio to my hatred for Wal and Luke. Their father had been killed in the war, which is why Bernard suggested to Dolly she move in next door to us. This could have worked well in theory, but in practice Wal and Luke grew up to be girl-haters, and a much younger girl cousin whom they considered to a sneak, cry-baby and a coward, was most definitely their enemy. Wal was three years older than me. He also had red hair, but his was carrot-coloured and stood up on end. He was very precocious and even an unbiased outsider could tell he was in need of parental discipline. But Dolly's gentle approach was useless and both boys were completely out of control. Luke was a year younger and more like Dolly to look at with his round face and dark hair. There the similarity stopped. If anything, he was even more devilish than Wal. My suffering at their hands had no end. In summer I would be pelted with mulberries. Wal would threaten to chop off my hair, Luke would threaten to tie me up, throw me into the cellar and there leave me to be eaten by rats. I believed every word they said and was so frightened by their threats I obeyed their every command."

I paused.

I knew I was dithering. I wasn't sure whether to tell him the anecdote, just as an illustration. I finally decided to and hope I did the right thing.

"I could give you an example of their persecution methods."

I was obviously looking anxious but he nodded encouragingly so I plunged in.

"One day they asked me, 'Where's Mum'? This surprised me as I thought they knew she was giving tea to members of the Women's Institute. On hearing this, Luke said, 'Go and tell Mum that Wal is having a wank under the table'. I hesitated, immediately sensing a trap. So they repeated the request with the usual threats of what would happen to me if I didn't do as I was told. In total innocence and fear of their cruel punishments, I carried out their command, and of course the result was disastrous. Dolly's tea-party was ruined. The boys listening outside split their sides laughing and in total bewilderment I was sent home, although I am sure Dolly knew who had masterminded the incident.

In the end it seemed easier to avoid Wal and Luke altogether."

I looked at Dr Strutter. It was difficult to tell what he was thinking.

His voice showed no emotion as he asked about my schooling. "I am assuming you were sent to good schools?"

"You'd think so, but on the contrary, it was erratic to say the least. I was sent to one local school after another. At the end of each term Bernard would test me and then go into one of his rants declaring my progress was unsatisfactory. Dolly and Audrey would then be sent to search for another school, putting me wherever there was a vacancy in the class. Consequently, my early education lacked continuity and was quite inadequate and I never really recovered from it. The constant change of schools, with all the different systems of teaching, made me look backward and unintelligent.

Finally Bernard insisted on an IQ test and to everyone's surprise, I came out surprisingly high. This just convinced Bernard that I was a lazy and difficult pupil and this situation might have continued throughout my school days, but for a stroke of fate. My mother was suddenly commissioned to do some book illustrations which took her abroad to Italy. Bernard was completely unable to look after me by myself, so there seemed no alternative but to send me to boarding school. The only consolation was that at least I wasn't sent to Bernard's school. His rages were bad enough at home, I couldn't have endured them at school as well. Instead, after a great deal of grumbling over the expense, I was packed off to a large boarding school for girls, perched high up on the South Downs and there I was to remain for seven years."

I broke off and looked at the clock. "I'm about out of time."

Dr Strutter smiled. "It seems that might be a good place to stop anyway. We can continue next week."

I gathered up my bag. "There is a little more background to give you first and then we can move on to the parallels."

"I look forward to it," he said in his polite way.

As always he left his seat and walked over to the window, and as always I looked up, but I didn't wave. It just didn't seem right somehow.

The end of my third session.

Chapter 2

The traffic out of London was worse than usual that day, perhaps due to Christmas shoppers, and consequently Celia arrived back rather later than she had intended. George came out of the front door the moment he heard her car. He looked at his watch in a meaningful way, and his voice had more than just the usual irritation. Something had definitely annoyed him.

"You're very late. What kept you?"

Celia climbed wearily out of the car. "Sorry George. The traffic was heavier than usual coming out of London."

George gave a thin smile. "The traffic. Why is the traffic always the excuse?

For once Celia didn't ignore his sarcasm and spoke more sharply than usual.

"It's not an excuse George. That's what happened. Where else did you think I was?"

George shrugged. "How should I know? You might have been buying up Harrods. I really have very little knowledge of what you do with your life."

Celia sighed. He just couldn't resist the veiled dig. "Well I'm sorry to disappoint you George. It was the traffic. Anyway I'm not all that late."

She started to walk into the house. George didn't move.

"I have been struggling with your builders for the last half hour. They seem to think I would know what shade of colour you want for the drawing room. This whole redecoration thing is entirely a whim of yours and I want to make it clear I will have nothing to do with it. I don't have the time."

Celia again said a little wearily, "Yes, I know that. There really shouldn't be any need for you to be involved."

"No there shouldn't," he said severely, "but that tall lanky one…"

"Ron" Celia said.

"Ron" George repeated the name with distaste. "He was bothering me with pathetic pleas for advice. Can you please inform him that I have no idea what your colour schemes are, and have no wish to be involved."

With the delivery of this salvo George marched back into the house and into his study, slamming the door.

Celia took off her coat and went into the kitchen. Ron and Joe we sitting drinking tea and didn't appear at all fussed by her lateness. Ron was tall and lanky with hair that stuck out in tufts. Joe was short and round with a balding pate. Oxfordshire's answer to Laurel and Hardy she often thought. Joe was smoking a roll-up. Oh dear, another black mark from George. He disapproved of smoking, except of course for cigars.

She sat down. "I'm sorry to be late back Ron. Has there been a problem?"

Ron looked surprised and said cheerfully, "No problem Mrs Roxby Smith. I just didn't know what time you'd be back and we wanted you to choose the paint. Me and Joe can pick it up in the morning."

He spread out the colour card and it took a mere three minutes to sort out the problem.

As they were leaving, Celia said, "Ron, it would be best if you didn't interrupt Mr Roxby Smith in his study. He's rather busy with School Reports just now."

Ron looked puzzled and said indignantly. "I didn't. I just asked him what time you was coming back. I wasn't sure if we should wait. When Mr Roxby Smith came into the kitchen to ask Cook for a cup of tea, I thought I'd ask him then that's all."

He added with a sniff, "I know better than to go into his study."

Celia smiled inwardly, reflecting that Ron's language would have been a good deal more ripe if he hadn't been talking to her. Really, George was the limit. So much for the 'struggle with the builders' and the 'constant pestering.' The man was becoming absurd.

She said apologetically, "Well, I'm only out on Wednesdays, so the problem of my not being here shouldn't arise again."

Ron shot her a look of what she took to be sympathy and knew exactly what it implied. How on earth had she managed to get herself hooked up with a bear like George?

She often asked herself the same question.

As she sat at her desk that evening she decided it would probably be better to forgo the coffee shop in future and come straight back, thus avoiding the rush hour traffic and George's petty fuming. The Session would still be quite fresh in her mind if she wrote it up the same night so it wasn't such a big sacrifice. All that she would basically give up was a Danish pastry and a little time to herself. But wasn't it typical of George to complain about the painters? He had resented their arrival from the start. Yet hadn't he always reproached her for not taking an interest in anything to do with their lives together? She had thought he would be pleased at the transformation of the dreary drawing room. But no, it seemed to be a constant source of irritation.

Perhaps he might like it when it was finished, but she didn't expect miracles. You didn't win with someone like George.

She stared gloomily out of the window and thought about her time at the session.

Was it really of value, telling him all this stuff about her past? It might be best to get through the background as quickly as possible and move on to her theory about the parallels. She didn't want to bore the poor man, however much George was paying.

One more session of background. That's all it should take.

A shiver went through her. It was a bit upsetting talking about her past anyway.

Perhaps she shouldn't go into so much detail? It really wasn't necessary.

Looking down at the black book she decided not to go over what she had written that afternoon and putting it away in the drawer she slammed it shut and carefully locked it.

FOURTH SESSION   December 12th 1978

I was amused to notice that on this visit a glass of water and the onyx ashtray were already in place beside the armchair.

Dr Strutter stroked his trousers in the now familiar way and said, "I believe you were going to tell me about your schooldays."

I took a sip of water and nodded. "Yes, I'll make it as brief as I can.

"That is fine. Please go ahead."

His hands were on his knees and for the first time I noticed how beautifully manicured they were. I also noticed he had one broken nail and he must have been aware of it too because quite often during the session he would rub it with his thumb as if it was an irritation.

Right. Schooldays. I plunged in.

"I know this must seem like a terrible tale of woe, but I am trying to be honest and tell you how it really was. I'm not trying to gain your sympathy or anything. My childhood was pretty awful but I feel quite detached from it now."

I looked to see if he would comment but as he didn't I started at a brisk pace.

"Boarding School. I arrived at Ferndean in 1955. It's difficult to convey the horror and bleakness of the place. I can't think why my parents chose it. I have since realized there were smaller schools where I would have been far happier. This was one of the largest girl's boarding schools in the country. The buildings were ugly, red-brick and Victorian. They were also cold and impractical. The houses were we lived were about half a mile away from the main building and we walked back and forth four times a day.

This was exhausting for me, especially for the first few terms when I had little physical stamina, owing to the lack of nourishment I'd been given as a child. Indeed the school doctor was so appalled by my skinny appearance and pale complexion, I was put on extra milk and extract of malt. However the school meals were entirely made of 'stodge' so I soon became a more normal weight."

"Stodge?"

"Yes, terrible leaden sponge puddings, you know, that sort of thing."

I gave a shudder and made a face which made him smile. "Please continue."

"You will understand that the first ten years of my life had left me totally unprepared, in every way, for the rigorous regime of a girl's boarding school.

From the moment I arrived I was a total outsider. Ferndean was an utterly conventional institution. The girls all had the same backgrounds, looked the same, talked in the same way and had the same interests. It was utterly alien to me. Without wanting to be, or even trying to be, I was different. Someone with a stronger character than mine might have made the most of this. But to me it was total misery."

I paused again, "I don't know how great your knowledge is of teenage girls?"

He smiled. "I have two boys."

"Well lumped together teenage girls are a pretty horrendous bunch. At that time it seemed to me they only had two interests, boyfriends and film stars. My two passions, reading and classical music were just not party of their world. If I'd even had an interest in lacrosse or horses there might have been a glimmer of hope. As it was I soon realized I was doomed. Added to this I had none of the right equipment. Audrey had gone into despair and bewilderment over the School List and had quickly given up. So I was dispatched with various bits of uniform from all the other schools I had been to. If it hadn't been for Dolly I'd have had no name-tapes either. This motley assortment was crammed into Bernard's dilapidated old army trunk."

Dr Strutter was looking amused. "It seems you were destined to look like a refugee your entire childhood."

This made me laugh. "I suppose it does seem funny now, but at the time it was tragic. I regarded with envy the other girls in their smart grey tweed suits, waiting for Matron to inspect their impeccable layout of clothes on their beds. When she reached mine, she looked at it with growing disbelief. 'It's straight off to the School Shop with you in the morning my girl.' This was spoken with fierce disapproval, but in spite of this I felt I had to protest. I could just see an outraged Bernard when he received the bill. So I told her nervously that I wasn't sure we could afford a whole new set of clothes.

'School regulations my dear' she told me sternly. 'If you're a pupil at this school the rules say you have to wear the uniform.' She must have noticed my look of panic, because she added, 'Perhaps we can find you some second-hand uniform.'

I think this was kindly meant but only encouraged sniggers from the other girls who had been watching the whole scene with growing fascination."

I paused and took another sip of water. This whole school episode made me shudder.

"The worst was still to come. One of the required items on the list has been a blanket or eiderdown. As I pulled out Bernard's old grey army rug, the girls could contain themselves no longer. They fell onto their beds laughing. I put it back in the trunk and slammed the lid shut. I'd rather have died of cold than endure another moment of their mockery. I remember feeling a dull sort of anger I as looked round at the assortment of satin quilts and mohair blankets, which lay on all the other beds in the rooms. There were fluffy animals too and photographs of family and home. I had nothing. It all seemed terribly unfair."

I looked across at Dr Strutter. He said nothing but his face had a sad, slightly shocked look. I was rather pleased that my story was affecting him. It made me realize the full extent of what I had endured.

"Inevitably the first year was the worst. After that I developed a thicker skin. It might have helped a little if I had been sent letters from home. But I wasn't. As far as I can remember, I think I only received one postcard from my mother during my first term, sent from Italy. Oh, and because she was in Italy I couldn't go home at half-term like all the other girls but had to stay in the school house by myself, which the awful Housemistress thoroughly resented."

"Couldn't Dolly have helped?" Dr Strutter asked.

I shook my head. "Sadly not. She had taken a job in the wilds of Yorkshire during term time. I think she was some sort of Matron at the boy's school where Wal and Luke were being educated, to help out with the fees."

He nodded. "What about the school-work? Was that a struggle as well?"

I smiled. "Strangely that was not a problem. There were certain subjects, Maths, Physics and Chemistry, where I had to work hard to keep up and these I dropped as quickly as I could. But in History and English I was at the top of the class and although they were not wonderfully taught, I took pleasure in these lessons. No, it was in my relationships that my life became a minefield."

I took out a cigarette and didn't immediately continue with my saga. I had tried for so long to put those days from my mind, it was going to be difficult to dredge it all up again. However, I couldn't stop now. A couple of puffs and I continued.

"All new girls were put through a cross examination. 'Where do you live Celia?' That one was easy. Oxford. Not much excitement there. The most popular girls were the ones whose parents were posted abroad for some reason, usually the Foreign Office or the Army. They came from exotic places and had life styles I'd never dreamed of.

The questions continued, 'What did my father do?' I told them he was a teacher and added that he was also a writer. At last there was a flicker of interest. Then came the 'status symbol' question. 'What sort of car do you have?' I knew at once that this carried huge importance and I thought sadly of our ancient battered Morris. At this point my wonderful fantasy world came into my head. Almost before I knew it I told them we had a 'Ford Consul'. Bullseye. Gasps all round. 'Wow, is it the new model?' I nodded. 'Gosh, what colour?' I told them cream. For the first time in my life I found I was the centre of attention. I was in full flight now. I told them I had two older brothers and somehow the names Wal and Luke didn't sound good, so my imaginary brothers were named Rupert and Benedict. There were more gasps. How could I stop now? Of course they went to Eton. It had all been so easy."

Was he shocked by this? He was very silent and his expression was inscrutable.

"I had found a way of making my existence bearable and for a short while I was something of a star. Then I became overconfident, with disastrous results."

I put out my cigarette, stubbing it out slowly to give myself time.

"Strangely it came about in the one area where I could have remained truthful. Music.

It had been quickly noted that I had some music talent, thanks to Dolly and the piano lessons. I also showed an enthusiasm for all things musical, and this was to be the cause of the trouble. Among the books I had brought with me to the school was a collection called "The Childhood Lives of Famous Composers."

At some point I had the idea to take these books to the Musical Appreciation Class so that the teacher could read them to us. Each book was illustrated with pictures and extracts from the relevant music.

I basked in the glory of having brought the books to the teacher's attention.

It should have been enough, but it wasn't. I foolishly boasted that I was able to play all the music in the books. It gained me admiration but unfortunately someone had passed on this information to the teacher, Miss Cotter, a prim, bitter old spinster, of which there was a plentiful supply at Ferndean."

I took a large gulp of water.

"On that fateful day, she finished reading the book and then, to my horror, she said

'As we have some time left, Celia can play to the class for the rest of the lesson'.

I shook my head and protested but she firmly pointed to the piano stool and then, quite deliberately turned to one of the most difficult sonatas, pinned back the pages and waited. I stared miserably at the notes. I had learned some of the easier sonatas but to sight-read what was in front of me was an absolute impossibility. I started to panic. I remember I flushed red and started to sweat. My hands felt like lead and my heart was beating really fast. I was also aware that twenty-four pairs of eyes were trained on me.

At last, after what seemed like an eternity, the bell rang for the end of class. Miss Cotter said in her clipped voice 'Class dismissed'. I remained rooted to my seat. She closed the book with a bang and handed it back to me. Her voice was withering and cold, 'I hope this has taught you a lesson Celia. Your piano teacher tells me you have a talent for the piano, but I knew you couldn't possibly play all the Mozart pieces in the book. I trust you will be more careful about what you say in future.'

Miserable and humiliated I took the book and went out of the room to face the hostility and mockery I knew was to come. On my desk was a large sheet of paper which said, 'CELIA MADDINGTON IS A LIAR.'

After that the bullying began."

This was hell. I hope to God it would be therapeutic.

I looked at Dr Strutter, "You probably don't have much knowledge of the kind of bullying that girls can inflict. With boys it is physical violence. With girls it is something much worse; whisperings, malicious innuendoes and cruel practical jokes."

I shuddered. "You probably won't believe this but I can remember to this day the names of my chief persecutors. I sometime wonder what has happened to them and whether they have any guilt about the suffering they inflicted. I mean, they must have known that most nights I cried myself to sleep."

I had worked myself into an anger and needed a moment to calm down.

Dr Strutter was looking at me sadly. "What happened after that?"

I gave a wry smile. "Well, after the music incident it didn't take long for all my fabrications to unravel. My beautiful fantasy life had been built on very feeble foundations and these soon began to crumble. No cream Ford Consul arrived on Speech Day but instead a battered old Morris which emitted huge clouds of exhaust fumes as it came down the drive. No elegant mother alighted from the car, but Audrey, disheveled and dowdy. No Maddington brothers were found at Eton. No amazing present arrived on my birthday, in fact it was usually forgotten altogether and of course no designer dress appeared for the school dance, but a rather bizarre creation of Dolly's. Indeed, no boyfriends arrived to partner me either. I spent most of the evening in the cloakroom so that no-one would notice I had nobody to dance with."

I tried not to sound too sorry for myself and said briskly, "So you see, once again I found myself isolated."

Dr Strutter stroked his knees and sounded almost annoyed, "You were not only isolated, you were completely alone."

I thought about this. "Yes, in a way, but I wouldn't be honest if I didn't point out that my life at Ferndean wasn't all misery. There were two major compensations."

At this he smiled. "I am very relieved to hear it. What were they?"

"Well, the first was definitely the school library which was extremely well stocked. Every spare minute I had I would spend working my way through the glories of Baroness Orczy, The Bronte's, James Hilton, Dickens, Galsworthy and so on. I remember 'The Forsyte Saga' took me half a term to finish during which time I found it difficult to concentrate on anything else."

Dr Strutter's glasses yet again found their way to the bottom of his tie where he polished them. "And the second compensation?" The glasses were returned to his nose.

"The second compensation was the school choir. In general Ferndean was not a school that was interested in the arts. Their idea of the perfect girl was one who was average in the classroom, who had a tidy appearance, a healthy appetite and who excelled at lacrosse. At the end of her days at the school she would take a secretarial course, or go to cookery school or study flower arranging and then quickly get married and become a pillar of her local community. It was obvious from the very first day that I in no way fitted into this category. It was also obvious that Music and Drama were subjects that were tucked away and almost forgotten. The school orchestra, if it could be called that, was only brought out on Speech Day for the briefest of moments, during which it emitted the most awful excruciating sounds. The frail and elderly lady who was entrusted with the music life of the school, and also my piano lessons, had been fossilized for years. Indeed, I always felt she might expire before the end of an orchestral piece with the weight of the baton!"

That amused him.

"Happily this situation was redeemed by a Miss Wilson. Unlike all the other teachers, she was young, pretty and just out of college. Officially she was part-time, giving private clarinet lessons, but she also took over the choir. She somehow managed to involve the school choir with the local Choral Society, which was a very good one. Every term we would take part in one of the great choral works. I lived for those concerts. They were the highlight of my life. During the seven years at Ferndean I must have sung in most of the Oratorio repertoire. On several occasions we even embarked on secular works, including a couple of Gilbert and Sullivan's. If this had been taken away from me I would never have been able to endure Ferndean."

I glanced at the clock. There was not much time left. It was obvious I would not get to George today. However I had to finish the school saga, so I pressed on.

"Inevitably, there was one terrible evening when my life in the choir was threatened by my Housemistress, Miss Ellis. She was a particularly nasty specimen of womanhood. There was rumour of a boyfriend who had been killed in the war, which no doubt added to her bitter and warped personality. She had been in the WRACS during the war and still behaved like a sergeant-major. There were a favoured few among the girls and I most certainly wasn't one of those. She made no secret of the fact that she disliked me intensely and whenever possible made an example of me. I can still hear that voice.

'Celia Maddington! Your clothes are a disgrace.' 'Celia Maddington! Your deportment is deplorable!' And so it went on. Hardly a week went by without me being given a serious reprimand. I became so used to it I could almost ignore it. But not that night."

I lit a last cigarette and blew the smoke out slowly.

"On that particular evening I was summoned to her room. That meant that it was serious.

I was asked to sit down opposite her with a desk between us. She looked at me with distaste before saying, 'I gather you missed lacrosse practice today. Why was that?'

I told her I had been at choir practice and her reaction to this was one of disbelief and shock. If I had told her I was on the Game she would have been less surprised.

I tried to explain that we had extra choir practices at the moment because of the performance the following week. Her sharp foxy nose twitched with annoyance. She proceeded to give me a long lecture about loyalty, not just to the school but to the house. I can remember it word for word. 'Let's take your appearance Celia. It is a disgrace. Your uniform is always ragged. I noticed the hem was down on your school skirt. It will be mended before tomorrow please.' You could tell she was enjoying herself. 'Your hair is always untidy. It will be cut short next holidays otherwise I will take you to the hairdressers myself. What were your posture marks last term?' She fired the question at me like a pistol shot. I told her I didn't know. 'Well you certainly won't get a posture belt if you sit like you're sitting now. Straighten your back!'

On and on it went and I punctuated everything with 'Yes Miss Ellis, No Miss Ellis,' until she finally went in for the kill.

'Now, about the time you are giving to music and choir, we really should be cutting down on that.' I began to be filled with foreboding. 'This house,' she went on, 'this house has an impressive array of games cups, but this won't go on unless we all put our backs into it. The house captain tells me you have no interest in games.' She thumped her fist on the table. 'This will not do. I shall talk to the music staff about you giving up the choir'."

I stubbed out my cigarette.

"Well, I immediately fell into paroxysms of sobbing as I shrieked hysterically, begging her to reconsider. For once the woman seemed startled by the effect she'd had. She pushed a box of tissues towards me and told me to stop crying and pull myself together. But my sobs went on. Finally she said, 'Very well, if you are so keen on this choir I will let you continue for the moment.

But I insist you attend all lacrosse practices in the future. Is that understood?'
I nodded and made my escape before she changed her mind.

After this no mention of my leaving the choir was ever made again. However, I was careful in future to fulfil all my lacrosse duties, loathe them as I did. The smell of linseed oil still makes me gag!"

I paused, exhausted. "I think that just about sums up my school days."

I must have been looking anxious because he said, "Is something worrying you?"

"Not really." I hesitated. "It's just that I thought I would have finished all the background by the end of this session and I still have a bit more to bring it up to date."

The meeting with George – 'a bit more'! I suppose it was one way to describe it.

Dr Stutter said in his calm way, "That is no problem. Will you be able to finish it in the next session?" I nodded. "Good, then we can just fit in one more before the Christmas break and start on the parallels in the New Year."

I stood up and realized I towered over him. I am after all nearly six foot. In spite of his small physique and quiet, calm voice, he did have a strangely powerful presence.

I reached the car and for once he wasn't looking out of the window.

The end of my fourth session.

Chapter 3

"Celia! Celia!"

George was bellowing from the bottom of the stairs. She opened the door of her bedroom and walked out onto the landing.

"What is it George?"

"Can you turn that infernal racket down? I can't hear myself think." He started to walk back into the study. "What is it anyway?"

"Samuel Barber. A piano concerto," she replied.

"Who?" He was still bellowing and really the music wasn't on that loud.

"Samuel Barber. An American composer."

George snorted. "Well if you must have something on, play some English music. And keep it low. I am trying to write my end of term speech."

Celia tried to sound contrite. "I'm sorry George. I didn't mean to disturb you."

She started to retreat when he shouted again "Have you done those Christmas Party invitations? I left the list on the kitchen table at breakfast."

She turned back. "Yes I saw it. I'm just doing the Christmas cards and then I'll do the invitations."

"Right. Well they need to go out today." The study door slammed.

Celia sighed, walked back into her room and took out the Samuel Barber cassette.

She toyed with the idea of putting on some Elgar but then rebellion set in and she put on Stravinsky instead. George wouldn't know the difference anyway. He was a complete Philistine when it came to music.

A sense of listlessness swept over her as she returned to her desk.

She picked up George's party list and her eye ran down the names. No surprises there. How depressing. There was nobody there she really wanted to see. They were either teachers who she saw most days anyway, or George's ghastly 'county' friends.

She stared at it angrily. This was meant to be a *joint* party, yet George hadn't even consulted her. She would like to have invited Dolly and her husband Tinker, maybe even her parents, as a sort of goodwill gesture. But George would never have countenanced that suggestion. She pulled out the invitations that had been printed especially for the occasion. "My Wife and I... blah, blah, blah..." It was awful and vulgar. She had been quite prepared to write them out herself, but there was no hearing of it.

Celia let out a sigh. Christmas was going to be an awful ordeal. The only good thing was that the drawing room looked greatly improved, the decorating having turned out to be a great success. She decided in the New Year she would start in on the rest of the house. In fact she had already asked Ron and Joe back. George would be told when it was all organized and that was that.

Pushing the Christmas cards aside, she made a start on the invitations. It was stupid to put it off, as there would be no peace if they weren't in the post that afternoon.

She picked up her pen and started to write, thinking grimly, 'Roll on next Wednesday and my escape to London'.

FIFTH SESSION   December 18th 1978

After the usual breakfast arguments I set out for London.

The wet, misty weather had given way to freezing conditions and the drive was rather hazardous, but I somehow managed to arrive on time and was shown into Dr Strutter's room by a smiling Mrs Maitland. I think she might be warming to me.

Today I noticed the fire was lit. He seemed a little guilty about this, saying that a fire wasn't really necessary as he did have central heating.

I told him I loved fires and indeed the whole winter season as well.

He shook his head, "As soon as winter starts I find myself longing for sunnier climes."

And to prove the point he rubbed his hands together as if trying to get life back into them.

What a strange man he is.

Anyway, he was obviously keen to start because he looked down at some notes on his knees and said, "We seemed to reach the end of your school days last time. Did you go to University?" I quickly put him straight on that. "No, no university."

No bloody money for that. No bloody encouragement either.

I stretched my hands towards the fire, thinking how best to explain.

"You see I emerged from that dreadful school without any clear idea of what I wanted to do with my life. I could see the look of exasperation this indecision drew from my parents and I was also well aware that I compared very unfavourably with Wal and Luke, both of whom were hideously bright. Wal had just finished his National Service, most of which was spent in Cyprus and which he claimed he actually managed to enjoy.

He was studying law and well on the way to becoming a successful lawyer.

Luke had managed to escape National Service because it had just been abolished. He went straight from school to Cambridge, on a scholarship and this in spite of being expelled from two schools!"

I lit a cigarette and noted that both the ashtray and the glass of water were in place by my chair.

"I found Wal and Luke as obnoxious as ever, perhaps even more so with their added conceit and self-assurance. I hated their affected voices, the endless witticisms, the awful wisecracks. They asked me to their parties, Dolly probably insisted, so I reluctantly went along."

I stared at the fire, remembering the horror of it all.

"Didn't you enjoy the parties at all?"

I shook my head vehemently. "No. It was more of an endurance test. I never had the right clothes and I would stand silent and awkward in a corner, terrified if any of their clever friends actually tried to talk to me. I usually made my exit as soon as it was politely possible."

I did sound pathetic. But then, I WAS!

I gave a laugh which I hope didn't sound too bitter.

"Bernard, of course, adored their company. They would talk and drink, sitting up to all hours. The next morning it would be, 'Wal said this...' or 'Luke informs me that...' until I felt I could scream. It wasn't that I was jealous of them, I really wasn't. I just knew that if they hadn't been around I might not have looked so hopeless."

Dr Strutter nodded as if he understood this.

"I think we were only a week or two into the holidays when the inevitable question came up. 'Well Celia, what plans do you have? You can't sit around here for the rest of your life.'

This was a question that was asked on a daily basis until my mother nervously pointed out that it was only the holidays and I should be allowed to enjoy that. To which Bernard replied acidly, 'My good woman, I'm well aware that it's the holidays which is precisely why she should be making up her mind what to do in order that she can start some sort of training in the Autumn.' Then with a withering glance in my direction he added, 'Although it beats me what that could be, and after spending a fortune on that awful school as well'.

My poor mother was torn between her desire to be fair and her fear of Bernard's reaction. She begged me to come up with some idea, if only to calm him down."

Dr Strutter leaned forward. "Couldn't Dolly help?"

I nodded. "Well, of course, I took all my woes to her and she listened to my endless moaning. I told her I knew Bernard wouldn't want to spend any more money on me, so what was I supposed to do? I added that I felt that both my parents would have really liked me to disappear in a puff of smoke.

At this she said told me sternly to stop feeling sorry for myself. But my wails continued.

I said crossly, 'It would be different if I was like Wal and Luke, winning scholarships everywhere…' She interrupted me at this point and to my surprise she said, 'Good heavens, you're much nicer than those two horrors!"

Dr Strutter smiled. "Well that must have pleased you."

"Well, yes. It surprised me and I just hope she meant it."

He said firmly, "I'm quite sure she did."

I suddenly felt I might be irritating him, so continued briskly. "You were right about one thing. It was Dolly who found the solution for me.

We were sitting one morning in the kitchen drinking frothy coffee, her latest invention, when she leapt to her feet and with breathless triumph shouted, 'I have it! I have the answer to your problems.' I asked her what on earth that could be and she shouted, 'Music!'

Now one thing Ferndean had done, was to kill off for ever my daydreams and life of fantasy. My feet were now so firmly on the ground I almost went the other way in my efforts to be truthful and realistic. So I told Dolly, firmly, that my musical abilities were not enough to give me a career. My protestations made no difference. Dolly was in full flow. 'You might not be a concert pianist Celia, but you are very good and quite good enough to qualify as a teacher.' I told her I would be a hopeless teacher but again she was not to be put off. 'The qualification would be useful and you could do a secretarial course at the same time.' Her voice came out in little excited gasps. 'With that combination you would find endless outlets in the Arts world, there's the BBC and music libraries, or working in a piano museum or a music agency.' She was waving her arms around excitedly. 'Endless opportunities. I can't see even Bernard objecting to that.' But of course he did. 'And who my dear girl, is to pay for this wonderful idea of Dolly's? It's typical of my sister to think of you doing two courses, when most people would have been content with one.'

In the end, after much shouting and argument, a compromise was reached. I would do two courses in Oxford, cheaper from home, and as my contribution towards my keep I was to help with the housework and type the occasional letter. Luckily the latter was not called upon as Bernard had a very efficient secretary and it soon became apparent that typing was not one of my greatest talents.

Jane McCulloch

So, for two years I worked very hard at the piano and struggled with the typing and shorthand." I paused. "And it was during this time that I met George."

"Your husband?"

I nodded and lit a cigarette. I couldn't do this bit without smoking.

Oh God. The explaining of George.

"It seems strange, looking back on it. Without being aware of it he walked into my life and just took it over. In fact, I only have the vaguest recollection of our first meeting.

I remember Bernard saying 'Oh good, Lenin is coming over.' When my mother looked puzzled he explained it was George Roxby Smith, the new history master. He went on, 'I call him Lenin because of his Russian appearance. I like him. You'll like him. Extraordinary fellow. Knows everybody. Very ambitious. His family has an estate in Norfolk. He's asked me up for the Boxing Day shoot.'

Audrey said, 'I didn't know you could shoot Bernard.' My father sounded impatient.

'I don't, but I'd damn well like to have a try.'

That was so typical of Bernard. One of my mother's relations had a shoot but he'd always despised it in the past saying it didn't go with his socialist principals.

I soon learned that everything to do with George met with approval from my father.

Bernard was certainly right about George's Russian appearance. He was short and stout with a high forehead, narrow eyes, close together, and a pointed beard. The resemblance to Lenin was uncanny, especially as the first time I met him he was wearing one of those Russian fur hats. On that day I was summoned down to meet him and we were formally introduced. It was part of George's charm that he immediately made you feel that he really wanted to meet you. I remember he took both my hands and held on to them.

'So you're Celia. I've heard so much about you. You're studying music aren't you?'

I felt embarrassed. I'm sure Bernard had made it sound as if I were about to make my debut at the Wigmore Hall."

Dr Strutter smiled at this. "How old was George when you first met him?"

36

It wasn't difficult to work out, George being ten years older than me, so I told him twenty eight.

"After that first meeting I began to see a great deal of George. He and Bernard started working on a text book together. Bernard reveled in these visits. He would shuffle about in his old corduroys and scruffy sweater, dispensing very large drinks. George would look equally casual, but in contrast, he'd be quite immaculate in expensive tweed trousers, linen shirt and cashmere cardigan. They made a good double act. George kept Bernard amused for hours with endless anecdotes of the famous and Bernard made a good audience. 'Oh the bliss of it. The sheer bliss of it,' he would wheeze, scattering ash all over the floor. Even Audrey emerged from her studio to listen and occasionally gasp, 'Oh George, that can't be true. You've made it up.'

I have to admit, I also enjoyed George's visits if only because it broke up the unbearable tension in the house. For once Bernard was happy to sit back and let someone else have the floor and from the outset George was kind and attentive to me. Even flattering. He'd say admiringly, his narrow eyes fixed on me, 'I think Celia resembles one of those beautiful Botticelli women. The Primavera. Yes, definitely the Primavera.'

'Does she by God! And Bernard looked at me with fresh interest because everything George liked and admired, Bernard did as well and I suddenly fell into that category."

I paused here because I was actually embarrassed about admitting the next bit.

"I usually minded if people listened when I played the piano. But not George. In fact, I think I probably showed off, playing the flashy pieces to impress him. He told me I should take my talent seriously and go to the Royal College or Academy with a view to becoming a concert pianist. This was nonsense and I protested, 'I'm really not good enough George'. He instantly replied 'Oh, but I think you *could* be.'

I wasn't. But of course I was flattered and pleased by his interest.

He also took a great interest in my appearance and under his guidance I became transformed. A hairdresser was summoned who turned my straight hair into something that resembled the style of Lauren Bacall. He then started to supervise my wardrobe. Looking back I realize he must have spent a fortune on me. I was worried about this at first, but overheard my parents discussing

George's finances. It turned out that his family, with the estate in Norfolk, were not landed gentry at all, but had sold out after making a fortune from some sort of new soft drink. George was very rich indeed. 'Nouveau riche' sniffed Dolly, who from the first had disliked him. 'His family is trade, which is why he is such a terrible snob.'

Whatever he was, he had worked a miracle with me. For the first time in my life I began to have a little confidence, even if it was only in my appearance.

I could see the effect I had on people as I walked into a room and I'm afraid to say, I loved it."

My God! First I'd described myself as a bloody waif, now as a show-off!

I lit another cigarette and noticed he was smiling and he said, "Svengali had worked the miracle and turned you into a swan."

Svengali? Was I George's Trilby? I hadn't thought of that.

I blew the cigarette smoke towards the fire and collected my thoughts.

"Well, the swan was suddenly finding life exciting. We dined out a great deal. George knew about food and wines. To me, at that time, it seemed he knew about everything and he was certainly good company. There were concerts, theatres, the opera, parties. And unlike the Luke and Wal parties, I really enjoyed them. George made me feel a social success, so I suppose I became one."

Dr Strutter leant forward. "Weren't you aware that all this attention was leading somewhere?"

This made me pause for a moment, trying to remember exactly how I'd felt. I needed to be honest.

"I suppose at the back of my mind I vaguely felt that George wanted something more from me, but at the time, I was too happy to feel more than a little unease."

I laughed. "Far more unnerving was the behavior of my father, who started to flatter me in public. He would say things that would make me cringe. 'Do you know, George Roxby Smith thinks Celia should become a concert pianist. I'm a lucky man to find I have such a talented daughter.' Worse still were the remarks about my appearance when he would say in terrible arch tones, 'I think Celia is looking particularly ravishing tonight, although as her father I suppose I shouldn't say it.' It was all bewildering. To have been ignored for nineteen years and then suddenly find myself the centre of his attention.

Bernard said, 'You should be flattered Celia. George is an extremely eligible bachelor. He could have any woman he wanted, but seems to give all his attention to you.'

Dr Stutter spoke again. "Did you find George attractive?"

I considered this. "Well, he wasn't good looking in a conventional way but he did have enormous charm and personality. Oh, and energy. I think that's what I found attractive, and of course the fact that he took such time and trouble over me. It was seductive somehow. He was certainly good to be with, always the life and soul of any gathering. The cry would go up, 'George has arrived!' Nervous hostesses would greet him with relief as if his very presence ensured success."

I stubbed out my cigarette and was tempted to throw it into the fire, but instead put it in the ashtray.

"You have to understand this was all very odd and new to me. I suddenly found myself pushed into the limelight. Everyone accepted me as George's girlfriend. Even Audrey noticed it and said in her quaint way, 'I think George is really fond of you Celia.'

I tried to play this down and assured her he liked visiting her and Bernard.

Audrey looked coy, 'In the beginning maybe. Now I think he comes to see you.'"

I took a sip of water and considered carefully how to put things clearly.

"There was, however, no danger of George sweeping me off my feet. Charmed and excited I may have been, but I recognized in George very early on, a man who never made an impulsive move. His every action was carefully calculated, down to the last penny he spent on me."

I spoke slowly because I wanted Dr Strutter to understand this.

"He is probably the most organized and disciplined person I have ever met, and the most ambitious. He is always in control and his mind always guides his heart, never the other way around."

I gave a hollow laugh. "Looking back on it I realize his wooing of me was conducted like a military campaign and he didn't make one mistake. For my twentieth birthday Bernard uncharacteristically gave a dinner party. Admittedly all those invited were his friends and age-group, except for George, but I was pleased to be given a birthday celebration at last and it was a surprisingly good evening, no doubt partly due to the case of champagne, brought by George as my birthday present. Halfway through the meal he proposed a toast. 'To the beautiful and talented Celia. A happy birthday and a successful life.' He paused and then went on, 'I, too, have cause for celebration tonight.' Another dramatic pause as everyone waited expectantly. 'I have been offered the position of headmaster at Civolds Prep School.' Another pause for maximum effect, 'And I have accepted.' There were noisy congratulations and more champagne. Bernard was particularly effusive. 'My dear boy that is wonderful news. Congratulations. I've heard it is a school with a great deal of potential and in a good area too, so near to Oxford. I have no doubt in your hands it will undoubtedly flourish.'

Of course, I was uneasily aware that this announcement somehow involved me and my fears were realized a week later when George proposed."

I looked across and to my amusement Dr Strutter was nodding, almost as if he had anticipated this.

"The whole thing was conducted in a very old fashioned way. George actually asked my father for my hand. Bernard couldn't agree to it fast enough and was delighted. It was the perfect solution to all the problems I had presented for so long. He therefore became infuriated when I started to dither and he told me in stern tones that I'd be a fool not to marry George and then delivered a warning that sounded more like a threat. 'The man won't wait forever. You should accept him quickly before he moves on to someone else.' It was no good turning to my mother for advice either. She had become ridiculously starry-eyed about it all, re-living her engagement to Bernard which was probably the happiest time she ever spent with him.

As I sat trying to make up my mind in that cold, drab kitchen, watching Audrey prepare yet another inedible meal and listening to Bernard bellowing demands from the study, I thought grimly that almost anything would be better in comparison.

However, that was hardly grounds for marriage.

Sadly the one person who I might have tuned to for advice was not around. Dolly was away for two months visiting relations in Australia. This actually proved to be disastrous. She didn't arrive back until two days before the wedding by which time it was too late to back out.

So alone with my dilemma I sat day after day, wrestling with my future. I thought I could be a good wife for George if only because George thought so too. He would have considered it very carefully before proposing. Obviously my main asset was that I would be a help in his new job. He knew the school would look more favourably on a headmaster who had a wife. This may sound cynical but I had no illusions about his feelings towards me and if I'm honest I also knew I wasn't in love with him, not in the romantic way I had always understood love to mean. This was not a 'Jane Eyre' or 'Wuthering Heights' situation. What was it that Byron said about Caroline Lamb? 'Her imagination was heated by novel reading.' That summed me up completely. I had lived with romantic novels for the last ten years and I knew my feelings for George did not come anywhere near this category. So if romance and passion were out, what about sex? My thoughts turned to panic and I finally decided to tackle George on the subject."

This part of the narrative required a cigarette break. I stared at the fire trying to work out the best way to proceed, almost hoping Dr Strutter would say something, but he didn't, so once again I ploughed on.

"You have to understand my knowledge of all sex matters was practically nil, another of Ferndean's failures. Apart from some vague information imparted from novels and the odd film, I virtually knew nothing. I finally plucked up courage and asked George nervously if he thought we'd be all right physically together. After all, apart from the occasional good night kiss there had been no other contact. George brushed my fears aside with his usual confidence. 'We'll be fine. I've no worries on that score. Try not to anticipate problems that aren't there.' Unsurprisingly I didn't find this very reassuring and I continued to dither. Finally Bernard exploded. 'I find your behaviour towards George quite appalling Celia. For God's sake put the poor man out of his misery. He needs a wife before he takes up his headmaster's duties. I've a good mind to tell my secretary to put it in The Times and have done with it.' I knew this was no idle threat.

I was finally worn down and said yes, and had the dubious satisfaction of having pleased both my parents for the first time in my life. With enormous relief and positive enthusiasm, they embarked, at George's instigation, on organizing a large and ridiculously grand wedding, which was thankfully financed by George's family.

Bernard seemed to have only two grumbles about the whole things, one was having to wear morning dress and the other was having to invite the

Rabbit. Otherwise he beamed goodwill over the entire proceedings. Audrey, to my great relief, put the entire wedding into the hands of experts, which of course, George provided. A famous designer was found for the wedding dress and the trousseau. The bridesmaids and pages, of which there were far too many, were all related to George. The invitations, service, flowers, reception, were all organized with great speed and efficiency by George. I remained throughout the entire preparations in a state of limbo, saying yes to everything. I watched impassively as each room gradually filled with presents. In fact, I had only one worry and that was that Bernard would remain sober long enough to walk me up the aisle in a straight line.

So the day arrived. The Cathedral was packed with representatives from the academic world with a few left-wing politicians on one side, and a motley assortment of George's relatives with a scattering of minor celebrities on the other.

Dolly did her best to give me courage before the ceremony. 'Oh duck,' she said, 'you do look terrible' and she poured a large glass of cooking brandy down my throat. I noticed her eyes were full of tears as she sniffed, 'It's extraordinary how similar this wedding is to Bernard and Audrey's. Oh dear me yes, in every way.' I knew she wasn't happy about the marriage and made it very plain how much she disliked George. 'If only I had been around we could have talked it through,' she wailed, adding in a doomish way, 'I do hope you know what you are doing my love.'

Her words had an ominous ring. Halfway up the aisle, I knew with terrible certainty I had made the most terrible mistake. If I have been one of my heroines I would have done the sensible thing and left him at the altar. But I wasn't brave enough for that.

We had a whirlwind honeymoon, doing a tour of the Burgundian monasteries, taking in a good many restaurants on the way. Two weeks later I was installed in the Headmaster's house at Civolds, larger and colder even than Holywell."

There was silence for a moment and once again I was aware of the clock ticking.

"And you're still living there?" he asked at last. I nodded.

Still there. But not in the same bed thank God!

He took off his glasses and wiped them on his tie. "So if I am not mistaken we have reached the point when we can start on your parallels?"

"Well, yes, if you think that's a good idea."

He made no comment but stood up and walked to his desk. "We have Christmas to get through," he said with a wry smile, "and then I go away for a week. Can you ask Mrs Maitland to make an appointment in three weeks?"

As I reached the door I said, "I hope you manage to enjoy the Festive Season."

Because I knew I bloody well wouldn't!

End of fifth session.

Chapter 4

Two days before Celia was due to have her next session, she decided, on a whim, to drive over to Oxford and visit Dolly. Time was hanging heavy on her hands. Natasha had returned to school the day before and the decorators weren't due back for another week. She informed George of her plan at breakfast, only mentioning a visit to her parents and not to Dolly, who for some reason he'd always considered a bad influence. "Is that a wise move?" he asked, looking over the top of his paper. "You know a visit to your parents always ends up leaving you depressed."

This immediately put her on the defensive. "I don't think it does really, but as you know, they aren't the easiest people in the world." She hesitated, "Actually I feel guilty that we didn't have them over at Christmas. I am their only daughter after all."

George snapped his paper shut. "All that Puritan guilt will do you no good at all Celia. You should get your famous London doctor to do something about it." He stood up.

"Anyway, Natasha went over to see them last week. They probably enjoyed a visit from her a good deal more than they would one from you."

In spite of having schooled herself not to react to George's barbed remarks, this one made Celia gasp. "That is an awful thing to say."

He was unrepentant, "My dear Celia, I am only telling you what you know to be true. Those damned parents of yours are the reason I'm paying out so much in medical fees. In my opinion they have a lot to answer for."

Celia opened her mouth as if to say something else and then changed her mind. There was no point in telling George anything when he was in this mood. He kissed the top of her head with a perfunctory gesture. "Well don't tire yourself. You're only just over that cold."

This latter remark was not sympathetically made, but more of a reproof. He suspected Celia had used her cold as an excuse to get out of a New Year's Eve party she hadn't wanted to attend. And he was right. She sighed, another reason for Puritan guilt. Was there no end to it?

She watched him make his royal progress over to the main school and thought grimly that this particular frog definitely hadn't turned into a prince.

The weather overnight had become icy cold and the countryside looked more like Siberia than Oxfordshire. Hoar-frost covered the trees and bushes along the roadside and it felt as if she was driving through lace. A pale watery sun was doing its best to start a thaw but not really succeeding. She was thankful to be in a coat that resembled something Napoleon's armies might have worn during their retreat from Moscow. It was a new purchase and actually thanks to George. After a long line of tasteless gifts, he had taken the hint and given her money for Christmas. With it she had bought a trench coat with fur collar and lining. She had thought at the time it might be excessive for England but now it had come into its own.

After parking the car she walked with extreme care on the ungritted, icy pavements to Holywell and was soon warming herself by the Aga in Dolly's kitchen.

"It's like hugging a bear," Dolly remarked, as she removed Celia's coat.

"Great isn't it? A Christmas present from George."

Dolly's eyebrows went up, "You do surprise me," she said wryly, "and how is the horrid little man?"

Celia laughed, "About the same. Do try and be a little more charitable towards him."

Dolly looked almost cross. "I don't have that much Christian charity in me. After all he did drive you into taking an overdose."

Celia frowned "Dolly! It wasn't an overdose as you very well know. It was a stupid accident. And I've told you before, I don't want that ever mentioned again."

Dolly looked contrite. "I know darling, but it was George drove you to it and you must understand I worry about you."

"Well you mustn't. I'm fine. She hesitated. "I'm even seeing a doctor."

Dolly sat down suddenly interested. "What sort of a doctor?"

Celia now wished she hadn't mentioned. it. "Well, you know, a shrink. He's apparently quite famous in shrink circles."

Dolly's eyes lit up. "Darling how too exciting. Do you lie on a couch? You must tell me everything. I've always wanted to know. What does he do?"

Celia shrugged. She didn't want to talk about Dr Strutter to anyone, not even Dolly.

"He doesn't really do anything, just listens while I talk. But it's good to get out of the house and escape to London once a week."

But Dolly wouldn't let it go. "What's his name? I am sure Tinker would know him. He knows everybody."

Celia smiled. Tinker and Dolly had now been married nearly twenty years and she still had the same extreme adoration for him as on the day they met.

She said, "I expect he would. Where is he anyway?"

Dolly looked exasperated. "If you'd only given us more than five minute notice of your impending visit, it might have been possible to re-arrange the diary. As it was we couldn't. Tinker has a lot of book-binders over from Hanover, poor love. They take up all his time. I've hardly seen him for the last week. He was very sorry to miss you. Can you come over again, when he's not so busy?"

She nodded. "Of course." Dolly patted her hand and went back to the Aga.

Celia looked at the bulky outline of her aunt with affection. She'd hardly changed over the years, except for a few flecks of grey in the wispy hair. She stirred a pot vigorously.

"I hope you're hungry. You're as thin as a rake and I'm determined to fatten you up, even if I only have one meal in which to do it."

Celia sat back, relaxing in the warm atmosphere. It was all so perfect, from the trailing geraniums and coloured pots on the dresser to, the large pans of delicious smelling food on the stove. She thought sadly that she had never learned to cook. In fact, from the first days of their marriage, George had surrounded her with people who 'did'. He probably didn't think she was capable of producing a decent meal.

"I'm having the house decorated," she said suddenly.

Dolly turned round in surprise. "Are you? That's good to hear. I haven't seen the place for some time but as I remember it had a cold, drab look. With your sense of style you should make a definite improvement."

Celia laughed. "Oh really Dolly. What do you mean 'sense of style'?"

"You just have it ducky. Look at the way you look? Wal was only remarking the other day that you were the most elegantly dressed woman he knew. Even in that huge coat you managed to look as if you'd come off that thing models walk up and down on."

"Cat walk."

Dolly said, "That's the one."

Celia felt greatly surprised. "Wal said that?"

Dolly nodded and went back to her cooking. "Tell me about these improvements."

So Celia described how she had removed all the awful pale green paint and replaced it with very pale yellow, also changing everything else, the curtains, the sofa, chairs.

"I got rid of the lot. It's a complete transformation. You should come over and see it."

Dolly slammed a lid on the saucepan. "I will darling, when the horrid little man is out."

Celia laughed. "He was actually quite good about the re-decoration. He resisted at first, but now it's done he likes the results. And to be fair, he's always been very generous with money."

This drew a snort from Dolly. "It's easy to be generous with money when you have lots of it. And despite all his family pretentions of owning land in Norfolk, we all know how that came about. From a soft drink they invented, that's where." She sniffed. "I bought it for the grandchildren once and it left a terrible orange mark round their mouths. I dread to think what it did to their insides."

Celia laughed but decided to change the subject. "How are things next door?"

Dolly sat down again and sighed. "Much the same. Your mother is very busy with a new book assignment. I expect she told you about it?"

Celia shook her head. "No, but Natasha did. She went over to see them last week.

She and Audrey get on very well, chatting about drawing and painting."

Dolly smiled. "I know. Audrey adores that child. She also thinks your daughter has a definite talent in the art direction."

Celia nodded. "Natasha really is rather remarkable. I don't just mean her drawing and painting. She has the ability to get on with everyone, even Bernard."

There was a moments silence as Dolly said, "So, are you going in to see them?"

"I think I have to. Not that they will want to see me."

Dolly took her hand. "Darling Celia. What a strange person you are. You always think the worst of yourself. Can't you understand? They do love you in their own funny way."

She hesitated before saying, "And you are a difficult person to show affection to you know."

Celia said a little huffily. "Am I? I don't see why."

Dolly let go her hand and laughed. "Of course you are, you're terribly prickly."

She paused and sighed. "I just wish you could fall properly in love. A really passionate affair is what you need."

Celia looked shocked and said a little crossly, "How very Barbara Cartland of you. I am sure a passionate affair is just what I don't need. My life is enough of a mess already, without adding adultery to it."

Dolly gave her a strange look but all she said was, "If you say so."

Some hours later, and rather reluctantly, Celia left the warmth of Dolly's kitchen and made her way next door. She rang the bell and immediately heard her father shouting,

"Audrey! Audrey!" Her father was shouting from his study.

Shades of George. Those parallels again.

After a moment her mother called out from the studio, "What is it Bernard?"

"There's someone at the door."

"Well couldn't you answer it?"

"I'm busy."

There was silence. 'Don't mind me,' Celia muttered to herself. 'I'll just freeze to death on the doorstep while you decide who is to let me in.'

The door was cautiously opened by her mother, who looked shocked at seeing her.

"Good heavens, Celia! Were we expecting you?"

"No. I'm sorry. It was a spur of the moment decision to come into Oxford. I won't stay long. I just thought I'd drop by to see how you are."

There was no 'lovely to see you'. Instead Audrey rather grudgingly said, "Well you'd better come in."

Her usually skinny frame was smothered in layers of assorted jumpers, so that she looked almost rotund. As Celia stepped inside she quickly realized the reason for this and decided to keep her coat on. The temperature in the house didn't seem to differ greatly from the outside.

"It's Celia," her mother called out to Bernard and he came to the doorway of his study.

He had a grumpy, distinctly unwelcoming expression. "Were we expecting you?"

Celia explained that she unexpectedly had come into Oxford and thought she'd call in, now privately wishing she hadn't. Bernard was only wearing one cardigan which indicated his study was very much warmer than the rest of the house.

She followed him. "Close the door. I don't want to let the draughts in. I have to think of the heating bills." He turned to his wife, "Audrey go and make some tea."

Her mother left and Celia sat down. That familiar smell, a mixture of menthol and cigarette smoke, brought memories flooding back, most of which she'd have preferred to forget.

"Natasha came over to see us last week." Bernard sniffed, "It's just as well we had a visit from her, otherwise we'd have thought you'd all emigrated."

She knew this remark was mainly aimed at George who now went out of his way to avoid seeing them. She said rather lamely, "I'm so sorry. Things are always busy at the School over Christmas, it's difficult to get away."

Bernard looked at her over the top of his glasses but said nothing. There was a tap at the door and Celia let her mother in with the tea things. As the watery tea was poured out of the chipped teapot into those pale green cups, Celia thought of the contrast between this house and Dolly's.

"Natasha came to see us last week." Audrey said, handing her a cup.

Celia felt exasperation. What was this? Did they think she didn't know what her own daughter was doing? "Yes, I do know," she said a little crossly, adding, "She was very impressed by your new assignment Audrey."

For some reason Audrey looked nervously at Bernard and then said quickly, "Bernard has a new commission too, haven't you Bernard? Tell Celia about it

Her father scowled. "I'm finding it a damn nuisance, but the money is good. It's a biography of George 1V."

Celia tried to sound encouraging. "That sounds interesting Bernard."

He burst out, "Well it would be, if the damn publishers would let me get on with it, but they are always interfering. Can't keep their noses out of it. Anyway, I'm only doing it for the money."

"More tea Celia?" her mother asked.

She shook her head and after a little more desultory conversation she made her excuses and left.

As she climbed into the car she realized that her parents hadn't asked one single question about her, or her life. If Dolly was right and they did feel affection for her, they had a funny way of showing it. Worse still, bloody George was right again. She did feel depressed after seeing them. She yanked the car into gear and moved out into the Oxford traffic. Suddenly she thought of Dolly's remark about her needing a passionate affair. It set her wondering what that would feel like. Was it really what she needed?

Little flurries of snow had started up and the traffic was moving slowly. She mentally pulled herself together. A love affair wasn't going to happen anyway, so it was best she put the whole idea out of her mind.

A few miles out of Oxford she started to shiver and realized she was feeling feverish. Sharp little daggers stabbed at her throat when she swallowed. By the time she reached home she knew she was ill and thought gloomily it was a judgment on her for lying to George earlier about her cold. The next day the doctor confirmed she had a severe throat infection which was likely to last at least a week.

Reluctantly she rang Mrs Maitland and postponed her appointment with Dr Strutter.

SIXTH SESSION   January 26ᵗʰ 1979

I was a little nervous about this session. Five weeks had elapsed, mainly due to the wretched throat infection that just wouldn't clear. It had given me time to think and I had come to the conclusion that I was looking on these visits to London merely as a means of escape from life with George. It was hardly going to be a permanent solution to my problems.

"How is the throat?" he asked, looking concerned.

"Much better," I replied, "although it gives out if I talk too much."

"Let me know if you are feeling tired."

I nodded. "And you will be pleased to hear I'm cutting down on the smoking. A sort of New Year Resolution. Not totally serious. Just cutting down."

He smiled and waited for me to begin.

I said a little nervously, "I'm not really sure where to go from here."

"What about starting on the parallels?"

I told him I wasn't sure where to start.

"Why not the point where you first noticed them?"

Clever man.

"The funerals." I said, "I think that's when I first became aware of them."

I suddenly longed for a cigarette but didn't think he'd be impressed at my giving in so soon, so I took a deep breath and plunged into the first parallel.

"It must have been about 1969. I'd been married for four years, difficult to say whether happily or unhappily. Life had taken on an immediate routine. Civolds is a school set in a series of buildings that take up a good deal of the small village. Everyone in the village seems to be involved with the school, which makes it quite claustrophobic at times. Anyway, there I was, married, and Natasha our daughter was born one year after the wedding." I hesitated. "I was rather delicate after a difficult birth and kept to myself for a while. This rather irritated George. He...I...well, to be honest, the sex was never very wonderful." I looked across at Dr Strutter, but as he said nothing I stumbled on. "As I think I explained, I'd had no previous sex experience at all, so I didn't know what to expect..."

This was awful.

I took a deep breath. "At the beginning George was quite patient, but he was also very demanding and I'm afraid that after Natasha was born I came to dread the sex bit of our marriage. I knew it was what was expected of me, so I complied whenever I thought it necessary, but I also knew George realized that I didn't enjoy it. Luckily most of his energies were poured into the school, or so I thought. Bernard had been right about one thing. George was a good headmaster and this rather old fashioned establishment began to thrive under his care. I helped as much as I could, entertaining parents, appearing at school functions, having the senior boys over to tea and that sort of thing.

I know it all sounds a bit boring, but on the whole I think I was pretty content. Anything was better than my previous life.

So, to the funeral. It was just after Natasha's third birthday that we received the news that one of George's relations had died. It was his great aunt and I had rather liked her. She was witty and sharp, often making shrewd observations. For instance she'd remarked on first meeting me, 'George will always do the right thing. It's typically clever of him to marry you.' Her death didn't exactly come as a shock, she'd been ill for some time, but George seemed terribly upset by the news. It was therefore something of a surprise when he announced he couldn't make the funeral. He said almost airily, 'Sorry darling, I have the accountants coming over and I simply cannot put them off.'

I felt a rising panic. George's relations were a frightening bunch and I didn't want to do this on my own. I asked him to put the accountants off. After all she was his great aunt and everyone would expect him to be there. George became very irritated by this and said, 'Don't be silly Celia. I agree one of us must go. If I can't, then you must. We work as a team, don't we?' I particularly hated it when he addressed me like the boys on Speech Day. He continued briskly, 'you don't have to stay long. It's a funeral, not a party.'

The day arrived and reluctantly I loaded Natasha into the car. It was very cold and everything was covered in white frost. I turned on the car heaters and some music and began to feel more relaxed. Perhaps it wouldn't be so bad after all.

It was at this point Natasha started to scream. This was very unusual because she was a good car traveler and generally just fell asleep. Not that day. Nothing would console her. After an hour of trying everything; drinks, singing, telling her stories; I stopped the car and lifted her out, still screaming. She was burning hot. I undid the buttons of her dress and revealed a cluster of angry red spots. Chicken pox. It had to be. There was nothing for it but to abandon the funeral, turn the car round and head for home.

The return journey was quieter, as Natasha exhausted, at last fell asleep. She hadn't woken when we arrived back, so I lifted her out of the car and carried her up to bed. I then went into the bedroom to ring the doctor."

I paused here and took a sip of water.

"I was quite unprepared for what I saw next. George was wrestling naked, in the arms of a woman I immediately recognized as the new matron. I had been so quiet going in they didn't notice me, so to get their attention I said, 'George, I'm back'. It was a fairly stupid remark in the circumstances but I was in shock. So were they. Both lay there speechless. I left the room and went downstairs. It wasn't until after I had rung the doctor that the full impact of what I had just seen, really hit me. My heart started pounding and I felt violently sick. It wasn't really jealousy, more a feeling of humiliation and betrayal.

I heard someone running down the stairs and then the front door slammed. A few minutes later George came into the room.

I said rather sarcastically, 'I assume Matron has gone back to the nametapes.'

He ignored this and said coldly, 'I didn't hear you come in.'

'Obviously not.' I replied with equal coldness.

His face had a pinched, angry expression. 'Is there some reason for you not being at the funeral?'

Indignation flooded through me. 'Natasha has chicken-pox. Or at least I think she has. I was trying to ring the doctor from our bedroom when I found you and...' I broke off. 'The doctor's on his way now.'

George walked over to the window and stood with his hands behind his back looking out.

At last he said, 'Yes, well, it's unfortunate you returned when you did. I apologize.'

He turned round to face me and added, with pompous severity, 'I do hope you are not going to make a big issue out of this Celia. I assure you it meant nothing and you know how much I dislike scenes.'

You had to admire him. There he was calmly lighting a cigar as if nothing had happened. It was then I noticed his eyes. They were hard and cold. Basilisk eyes. I had the nasty feeling that I was at last getting to know the real

George. I asked if there had been other women, since we were married. He just shrugged and said he supposed there had been a few. This shocked me even more. It was the callous way he made the admission.

He continued, 'They mean absolutely nothing, so I don't think this line of questioning is going to be very helpful.'

I felt a surge of anger. 'It may not be helpful to you George but as your wife I think I have a right to know.'

He looked genuinely surprised. 'Why? Much better if you don't. It doesn't affect us.'

I had reached boiling point. 'What do you mean it doesn't affect us?' I exploded. 'It affects me. It affects bloody me.'

George looked at me with distaste, then at his watch. In an ice-cold voice he said,

'I have to go and see the accountants. Try not to be so bourgeois about this Celia. If I may offer you some advice, I think you will find it best if you put the whole incident out of your mind. But if you *are* going to think about it, just ask yourself why this has happened. It's not difficult to understand. I'm only human and it is not as if you are over enthusiastic in the bed area of our life.' And with that he left. He hadn't even inquired about Natasha. I was shaking with rage and indignation. Why did he have to address me like something out of a Jane Austen novel? However, his parting shot about me being bourgeois had really gone home. And it was at that moment the parallel struck me. It was just too similar to ignore."

I took a gulp of water to restore my croaky voice and Dr Strutter asked, "Do you mean that in that moment you realized your marriage resembled your parents?"

I hoped he didn't think I was looking for marriage counseling and hastened to put him straight.

"No, it wasn't that, although our marriage is similar to my parents in that we all lead separate lives. No, the parallel is far more specific than that."

He persisted. "You mean that incident, which you have just related, resembled a previous experience?"

I nodded. "Yes I do. It was quite uncanny. Do we have time?"

"I think so. How is the voice?"

"It will last if I keep drinking water." I collected my thoughts.

"It's a little difficult to work out the exact date, but it must have been about 1951, because I think I was six when my mother's father died. He was a rather formidable military man, who I found rather frightening." I sighed. "As you will have gathered, I was a pathetic child who found almost everything frightening."

Dr Strutter smiled, but didn't say anything, so I continued.

"My grandparents lived in a large old manor house and my cousins had informed me that it was haunted. They told lurid tales of a wailing woman dripping in blood who wandered up and down the corridors at night. And of course I believed them and was terrified. The three cousins also lived in the manor. My uncle ran the estate which consisted of a series of farms. Oh God, how I hated those farms. I took no pleasure in country pursuits. They seemed completely alien to me. I found the animals smelly, dirty and frightening and I was terrified of being stuck on the back of a pony. At least in Oxford I had the safe haven of Dolly's kitchen. There was no safe haven in the manor and the three cousins were almost as bad as Wal and Luke. So my heart sank when I heard my grandfather had died because I knew it would mean a trip to the manor for the funeral.

'I don't think I want to go Audrey,' I nervously told her, 'Church makes me feel sick.'

After several pleadings to be left at home, her patience ran out. 'Of course you must go. You loved your grandfather didn't you?' What could I say? I nodded miserably.

She added kindly, 'And as a special treat Mark and Judy have asked up to stay on over the weekend so you can have a holiday with your cousins.'

My heart sank. This was the worst possible news. 'Is Bernard coming with us?' I asked.

Audrey shook her head. 'No he can't spare the time. He has the end of term reports to write.'

I felt desperate enough to appeal to Bernard. 'Please Bernard. I don't want to go to the Funeral. Couldn't I stay here with you?'

He looked alarmed and spoke sharply. 'Of course you couldn't. I wouldn't have time to look after you.'

Realizing it was hopeless I resigned myself to my fate.

On the morning of departure I remember Bernard was in an unusually cheerful mood.

I heard him singing 'Take a pair of sparkling eyes' in the bath and that was always a sign of good humour. He also gave me sixpence pocket money."

I'm afraid at this point I weakened and took out a cigarette. Dr Strutter made no comment but I think he smiled.

"The journey was terrible. I was not a good traveler in cars, but this could have been something to do with my mother's driving, which was erratic in the extreme. She actually considered it a virtue never to change gear and more often than not jerked along with noxious fumes seeping out from an over-heated engine.

On this particular occasion, the drive, combined with my nervous state, soon turned my face to a nasty shade of green. It wasn't a long journey but by the time we arrived at the church, even Audrey noticed I was looking far from healthy. She advised me to take a walk around the churchyard before going in. I was promptly violently sick over the back of a tombstone. It took two more attacks of vomiting to convince my mother she should take me home. By this time I was weeping and shaking and working myself up into a state. I overheard my mother moaning to my aunt, 'Honestly Judy, I really don't know what to do with the child. The slightest thing upsets her and then she has these vomiting attacks. The doctor says it's quite common, especially with an only child. Apparently she will grow out of it, but she shows no signs of that. And it isn't as if she doesn't see other children. There are Dolly's boys and the children in her class, but she remains withdrawn in her own little world. And she has all these phobias that make her feel sick. You wouldn't believe it, church, music, films, parties. Anything can set her off. There's no end to it. And the nightmares. Well it makes Bernard so annoyed. I tell you Judy you don't know how lucky you are with your three. They're so normal.'

Normal! They were fiends.

I remember Judy telling my mother she ought to be pleased to have such a quiet child compared to her three noisy hooligans. Then to my horror she added, 'Why don't you change your mind and stay? It will do her good.' For one terrible moment I thought my mother was going to say yes. Then to my relief I heard her say in martyred tones, 'Bless you Judy, but I think it best if I go back. Once she starts on one of these bouts it takes her a while to get over it. You have the house full. I'm sure you don't want a sick child as well.' I knew Audrey was disappointed at not staying and I did feel guilty about that.

I said in a small voice, 'I'm sorry Audrey. About being sick.'

She said briskly, 'Well it can't be helped. But you must try and get over these states. You are too old for them now.' She yanked at the gear lever with a screeching noise. 'When we get home you can go straight to bed and lie down. I'll ask Mrs Baker to make you some soup.'

Mrs Baker was a sour-faced woman with suffering written all over her, but she was definitely the best of a long run of cooks, so I ignored her moans and grumbles.

We arrived back at about five. It was cold and dark. Obediently I went to my room and climbed on to the bed. I had just closed my eyes when I heard the most terrible noise and commotion coming from my parent's bedroom. Bernard was shouting, Audrey was screaming and there was a third voice that I recognized as Diana Morgan, my father's secretary. I was fond of Diana. She came to the house a good deal and went out of her way to be kind to me, bringing me cakes and sweets. With a child's perception I noticed Bernard was usually a good deal more pleasant when Diana was around. Not that day. Now he sounded angry as the volume of noise increased. I got out of bed and opened the door. I could hear quite clearly. Diana said, 'I think I should go Bernard.' Bernard shouted, 'No. You stay. Audrey must go.' Then everyone started shouting at once.

A few minutes later Diana came out of my parent's bedroom. It's strange but I didn't find this at all odd and said cheerfully, 'Hello Diana. I've been awfully sick.' She looked flustered and upset, but managed to say quite kindly, 'Oh Celia, I'm so sorry. Look I can't stop now, but I'll see you another time when you're better, all right?'

She ran down the stairs and out of the house. I remained hovering uncertainly, as the row continued. My mother's voice was high and whining, 'It's gone on long enough it has to stop. I can't bear it. How could you do this to me Bernard?' She started to cry.

Bernard said, 'Stop that crying Audrey, you'll only make yourself ill.'

On and on it went, until finally I heard my father say, 'Stop your dreary moaning and take your middle-class morality to someone else.' This made her completely hysterical and she started screaming. Then there was the sound of a slap followed by silence.

I knew something dreadful had happened but didn't know what. I climbed back into bed and lay staring at the ceiling. After about an hour Mrs Baker arrived with a bowl of soup. She spoke quite kindly. 'My, oh my, you do look pale. Now, when you've had this soup, Celia, your father wants you to have a bath and then go downstairs to see him in his study. Can you manage that?'

I told her I could and she said, 'That's a good girl. I'll be off now.' And she left.

After my bath I went downstairs to my father's study and knocked on the door.

'Come in,' he called out. The study door was heavy oak and had a wrought iron handle which I found difficult to operate. It therefore took me some time to let myself in and Bernard could barely hide his irritation. 'Ah, there you are Celia. Come over here and sit down.' I removed some books off a footstool, sat on it and waited. He peered at me over the top of his glasses. 'Are you feeling better now?' I nodded. 'Yes thank you Bernard.' He said sternly, 'You must try and grow out of this silliness you know.' I nodded again. 'I'll try Bernard.' 'Very well.' He paused and then spoke in gentler tones. 'Now Celia I want you to know that your mother is going away for two weeks to stay with Mark and Judy.' This surprised me. 'Why?' I asked. He looked irritated at this interruption. 'Because she is tired and exhausted that's why. She needs complete rest.' He paused. It was obvious he wasn't finding this easy. 'This means you and I have got to manage on our own. Do you think we can?' I wasn't at all sure about this but dutifully replied, 'Yes Bernard.' 'Good. Now tomorrow you will go back to school. Mrs Baker will be here to give you tea and cook your supper. I don't think there should be any problems.'

There was a strange smell in Bernard's study. A combination of tobacco and cough drops. When he wasn't smoking Bernard was always sucking some form of boiled sweet. There was a bowl of them on his desk but throughout my childhood I never remember him offering one. I would have liked one at that moment, but instead I said, 'Will Diana come over and see us?' He looked very startled at this. 'I don't know. Why do you ask about her?' I wriggled on the uncomfortable stool. 'I just thought she might come over while Audrey was away.' From Bernard's expression I realized I had wandered into forbidden territory, so I concluded quickly, 'I like her. She gives me sweets and cakes.'

He looked relieved. 'Well that's very kind of her.' I changed the subject. 'Will Audrey be back for the holidays?' His patience had run out. 'I expect so' he said wearily. 'Now no more questions. Run along to bed, but don't go into your mother as I expect she'll be asleep.' I got up and put the books back. 'Goodnight' I said. 'Goodnight Celia.'

He went back to his reading. I hesitated, not knowing whether to kiss him or not. I didn't usually but tonight seemed different somehow. So I did. I think he was touched, because he patted my hand and said, 'Run along, there's a good girl.'

I think I was probably closer to my father that night than I have ever been since."

I took a large gulp of water and knew I was close to tears.

Dr Strutter waited a moment before commenting. "Very interesting. And you say there are more parallel incidents like this?"

I nodded. "It was George's comment about me being bourgeois that brought back the memory of my father saying the phrase 'middle class morality'. It started me thinking about the two events. They were so similar, even down to the bed situation. I moved out of George's room a week after the funeral and my mother never shared a room with Bernard again."

Dr Strutter absorbed this information and then stood up. I knew we had gone over our time, so I quickly crossed the room. "I'll see you next week if that's all right?"

'Most certainly.'

He walked to the window and was still there when I reached the car.

The end of the sixth session.

Chapter 5

Celia eased the car into top gear and put her foot down. As she sped through the Oxfordshire countryside she sang softly to herself, "Breakaway, just breakaway From those parallel lines, those parallel lines"

She shouted out the last line as she overtook a startled lorry driver and felt the urge to call back to him, 'Don't worry, I may appear mad, but I'm on my way to see my shrink!'

And she laughed out loud. This sense of release was new to her and over the last week she had felt almost happy. Even George had noticed it as he looked at her over the breakfast table, "This psychiatrist chap seems to be doing you some good. You definitely seem more relaxed."

She was quick to reassure him. "Oh I am George."

"What exactly does he do?"

This made her immediately evasive. "Nothing really. I talk and he listens."

George immediately became sarcastic. "You talk? My God! He must be a miracle worker." She let that pass as he persisted, "So, what do you talk about?"

"Oh a bit of everything," she remarked casually and then saw his eyes narrowing, which they always did when he was annoyed, so she quickly added, "Well childhood mainly."

He snorted. "Anybody could have told you that was the root of your problems."

Celia remained silent as he added ominously. "Let's hope this expensive man can work a total miracle and return our lives to normal again.

She knew exactly what he meant by that. 'Normal' to George meant them sharing a bed again. She also knew she would never give in over that. Sharing a bed with George was definitely out of the question.

Feeling he had made his point George folded his paper and informed her he would be back late. "I'm seeing one of the masters for supper".

She looked at him and couldn't decide whether that was true or not. It was quite possible he'd be seeing some woman, of which she had lately learned there had been quite a few.

He stood up and delivered his parting shot, "I hope this psychiatrist fellow gets some quick results. It's costing me a small fortune."

This last remark was rather unusual for George and a little worrying. One of the few advantages of their bleak marriage had been a complete lack of financial problems.

He was positively generous to her and had always encouraged her to spend money on clothes and now there was all the re-decoration, which it had to be admitted, was working out to be very expensive. So why this remark? Were there really money worries, or was this one more little game of George's?

Of one thing she was certain, she was in no hurry to give up on the sessions.

A glance at her watch showed her she was making good time, so she slowed down a little. George would not be happy if she was brought up on a speeding charge.

Suddenly Dolly's remark about her needing a passionate affair came into her head.

This had shocked her at the time and from Dolly of all people. It was complete nonsense of course. Celia sighed. Why, oh why, did everyone think sex was the answer to everything? Good God! From her experience she could tell them it bloody wasn't. So why on earth would she need an affair? What was the point of getting involved with another man? She had quite enough trouble with the one she had already. It was ridiculous. Dolly must have been reading too many romantic novels, or she had reverted to the sixties, with all that drugs, sex and rock and roll.

Of course she'd missed out on that era, being incarcerated in Civolds for the entire time.

Celia pulled a cigarette out of her bag, lit it, and her mood immediately lightened.

Here she was, on her way to her seventh session.

She now looked forward to these session days with a fevered impatience. The week in between couldn't go fast enough. She loved the drive, the freedom of getting away from Civolds and then, she actually enjoyed the time with Dr Strutter. It had become a challenge to get a little more from him than the occasional mannerism or wry smile.

If she raised a laugh, as she had managed to do on a couple of occasions, she counted it a triumph.

Another look at her watch. She was now running late and in a panic put her foot down.

All this day-dreaming had to stop and oh horror, Mrs Maitland would no longer smile at her if she wasn't on time.

SEVENTH SESSION   February 2nd 1979

Having stupidly dawdled on the journey I was a little late, so only a watery smile from Mrs Maitland today.

Dr Strutter waited for me to get settled into my chair and then asked, "Is this going to be another parallel?"

I nodded. I had thought this one through during the week and I said, "Yes, I thought I'd do a holiday incident next."

He picked up the ashtray. "Are you smoking today?"

I smiled and took the ashtray from him. "I'd better have it just in case."

He sat down, took up his listening position and waited expectantly.

No social chit-chat today, so I plunged straight in.

"As I think I told you, after the funeral episode, George and I led separate lives, in private anyway. I can't begin to tell you the relief of having a room of my own, although I did feel the odd pang of guilt. I know George would have liked another child and I sometimes worried about Natasha being the only one. Even so, I couldn't have gone back to sharing a room with him, let alone a bed. He seems reconciled to it now and I know there are other women in his life."

Dr Strutter lent forward, "And does that worry you?"

I shook my head. "No it doesn't. Not after the initial shock anyway. It seems only fair in the circumstances and I don't pry. It somehow works, although I know it's strange."

"And Natasha? Has it affected her?"

I thought about this. "I honestly don't think it has. Inevitably she and I have been thrown together a good deal, but I really enjoy her company. She's not at all like I was as a child, timid and withdrawn. On the contrary, she is happy and outgoing, with a tremendous self assurance. I was worried George would find it difficult to communicate with a daughter, being surrounded by so many boys, but when he does see her he is both affectionate and indulgent and she is one of the few people who can stop him from being pompous."

I paused, wondered about a cigarette and then decided not.

"I was determined Natasha should have plenty of opportunities to mix with children of her own age. For this reason we spent most of our summer holidays with George's brother, who lived in the family house in Norfolk. This was the rather grand house, built in the Georgian style, which George's parents had built when they made all their money from their soft drinks business. It was set in extensive grounds about a mile from the sea. They had sold off the shoot some years back, which I think had left them with plenty of money."

I broke off and apologized for giving him so much background and so many names of relations, but without this the parallels wouldn't make sense. He smiled and said he quite understood.

"Paul, George's older brother, couldn't be more different in character. They're opposites in almost everything, especially when it comes to bringing up children. Paul believes children should grow up free from discipline, able to express themselves in front of adults without inhibitions or fear. This was anathema to George, who of course believes in discipline. In the method of rearing children Paul was totally supported by his wife Maddie. This anarchic method of bringing up children also meant that the house was always untidy and there were endless breakages. Unlike George, Paul didn't worry about possessions, except for his books which were in a library and the one room in the house that the children were not allowed to use. Everywhere else in the house there were scenes of destruction and most of the antique furniture, china and glass, so carefully collected by George's mother, had been broken, chipped or smashed, to be replaced with more serviceable modern items. It was a horror to George to see the family valuables gradually being destroyed and this, along with the children being out of control, meant he did not accompany us on these visits."

I looked at Dr Strutter and smiled. "This lack of parental control did lead to some bizarre situations and could be fairly exhausting." He murmured, "I can imagine."

"There were four children, Danny the eldest, Lavinia, known as Livvy and twins Meg and Fred, who were a year younger than Natasha," I made a mental calculation, "who on this particular holiday must have been about six. Paul's wife Maddie had a wonderful quality of gentle vagueness. I never heard her raise her voice once and I sometimes thought being with Maddie was like sitting in a field of clover. However, the consequence of this passivity was that the children did more or less what they like liked.

'My feeling is,' she would explain after Danny had kicked a football through the glass door of the drinks cupboard, 'my feeling is that they will meet with enough pain and unhappiness when they grow up, without having grief all through their childhood. They're not willfully bad,' she would add clearing up the broken glass, 'just a little thoughtless.'

This sort of incident was a daily occurrence, but it was mealtimes that proved to be the most testing when it came to this method of child-rearing. It was nearly always Danny who started things off. I remember one lunch time very clearly. Danny began, 'Mum, did you know Livvy's been thrown out of the Brownies?' To which Maddie replied, 'No I didn't. Why's that love? Danny doubled up with glee and shouted in triumph, 'She said *fuck* to Brown Owl'. All eyes turned to Livvy who shouted 'I never did.' 'You did so' Livvy shouted even louder, 'I said *fart* not *fuck.*' Maddie intervened in her usual quiet way, as if really interested. 'Why did you say that Livvy'? Livvy now red in the face and near to tears said, 'Well Sally Matthews farted and was trying to pretend she hadn't. Anyway I don't care. I hated the Brownies.' Maddie was immediately sympathetic. 'But I thought you liked them love. Weren't you an Elf? What was their little rhyme?' Livvy muttered sulkily, 'I'm a helpful little Elf, helping others not myself', amd then she wailed, 'But Brown Owl wouldn't let me be an Elf because there too many, so I had to be a Pixie and I hate the Pixies.' Danny, now in full triumph, shouted at the top of his voice, 'We are known as little Pixies, helping people into fixes!' and he roared with laughter. 'Out of fixes you stupid boy!' screamed Livvy. Danny banged the table with delight. 'Into fixes if you were one.'

It was all too much for poor Livvy. 'You are a horrid, beastly boy,' she said, calmly emptying her macaroni cheese into his lap. Well, you can imagine the uproar. Maddie mopped up Danny and merely commented, 'Oh Livvy love, was that necessary? Danny go and clear yourself up and be a good boy, don't tease your sister so much.'

Meanwhile Paul would be trying to control the twins down the other end of the table,

'Fred, leave Meg alone. She can feed herself. Fred! I said leave Meg alone. Fred!'

Every mealtime was like this and generally ended with Paul saying wearily, 'Pack it in kids.' And the children would chant in unison, 'Pack it in kids' and think it the greatest joke. I always left the table feeling I had been in the front line of a battlefield."

Dr Strutter was smiling. "And how did Natasha take all this?"

"Quite honestly I think she rather enjoyed it and reveled in the drama of it all. It was so different from her life at home and she got on well with the cousins, particularly Livvy, who is still her greatest friend. There was only one minor crisis when she found a bat flapping around her bedroom, but Danny obligingly squashed this against a family portrait with his tennis racquet."

Dr Strutter laughed. What a triumph!

I rummaged in my bag and managed to locate my cigarettes.

"And you" he asked.

"Oh, I think I was just pleased to be away from Civolds and see Natasha so happy. Apart from mealtimes I had plenty of free time. Paul and Maddie were well off and could afford plenty of domestic help, so my time was my own. They had a beautiful Bechstein piano which somehow had escaped being trashed, so I made good use of that. On warm days I would drive the children to the flat, bleak beach, with the uncomfortable pebbles and cold grey sea. I'm afraid that bit of the Norfolk coast isn't my favourite part of the world, but the children didn't share my qualms about the beach and spent their time happily making irrigation systems and dams, or playing cricket. I managed to read a great many books on those holidays, taken from Paul's well stocked library."

I paused and took a deep breath. This was the part I preferred to forget.

"Towards the end of that particular holiday, the weather changed from sun and blue skies to wind and driving rain. The excursions to the beach were no longer possible. Penned in and pent up, the children soon became restless and irritable. There was no television in the house, Paul and Maddie deliberately didn't have one, which in general met with my approval, but on this occasion it might have been a good diversion.

On this particular day, after they had been extremely quarrelsome, Maddie suggested they play hospitals. 'You know loves,' she said in her vague way, 'doctors and nurses. Natasha and the twins can be the patients.' She provided them with slings and bandages and we left them to it.

This seemed to be an inspired idea and for a while total peace reigned. Then Danny came into the room, white-faced. 'You must come quickly' he said and there was panic in his voice. 'Something is wrong with Natasha.' We rushed upstairs and into the children's playroom. Natasha was lying on the floor with her eyes closed, very pale and taking short rasping breaths. The other children stood round, silent and shocked.

'What happened?' we both shouted.

Gradually we learned that they had decided to give Natasha an operation. In administering the anaesthetic they had put pillows over her head. 'Like the gas mask they used when I had my teeth out.' Danny explained. They had meant no harm but obviously pressed the pillows down too hard and almost succeeded in suffocating the child. They let go when she started struggling and fighting for breath.

Although she was winded and a bit shocked there was no real harm done.

Natasha soon recovered and rather enjoyed all the fuss that was made of her. The only ill effect was the nightmares. For a few months afterwards she would wake in the middle of the night, screaming and fighting for breath."

I looked down and noticed my hands were shaking. Dr Strutter stroked his knees lost in thought. After a while he said, "And you have a parallel to this?"

I pulled out another cigarette, knowing it would be necessary for this one, and flicked my lighter. "Yes, it was the nightmares that made me think of it."

I had a few quick puffs and then plunged straight in.

"It was about a year after my grandfather's death around 1952. My mother sat at the breakfast table reading a letter, making little murmurs of 'how nice, how very nice',

Finally Bernard growled from behind the newspaper, 'Nice! Nice! Can't you ever find a word other than nice?' He barked at me, 'What is the proper usage of the word nice Celia?' I was prepared for this one. 'Exact, Bernard.' 'Quite right,' he said and somewhat surprised he went back to his newspaper. I don't know why he should have been surprised. 'Proper usages' were one of Bernard's obsessions and I was well schooled in them.

On this occasion Audrey was not to be put off by Bernard's growls. 'Listen dear, Mark and Judy have invited us to stay with them in Scotland.' Bernard scowled. 'Scotland? Why Scotland?' My mother replied, 'They've taken a house for August. Isn't that lovely?' She looked at the letter again. 'In Perthshire, by a loch. We'll be able to swim.' Bernard shuddered. 'The thought of swimming in a Scottish loch is enough to freeze the blood, and there are more mosquitoes up there than in a Burmese swamp, and before you wax lyrical on the subject Audrey, you can count me out!' My heart sank.

I could see the storm clouds gathering. She must have known what was coming, but still pretended to be surprised. 'Oh Bernard why? It'll be lovely.' He replied firmly, 'I have my book on Charles II to finish in August and I wouldn't get any work done if I came with you. You and Celia go. You'll enjoy it.' With that he left the breakfast table.

I knew that wasn't the end of it. My mother would never let it go. Day after day she would tackle him on the subject and I would position myself so I could hear.

It was always an ominous sign when Audrey's voice became shrill and whiney.

'You think I don't know the real reason why you won't come with us, yet you always have a reasonable explanation Bernard. You must think I'm some kind of fool.' Bernard's voice became icy, 'Frankly Audrey I don't give a damn what you think.'

My mother's voice went up a notch. 'What do I tell Mark and Judy? They will expect you to come with us.' My father was becoming angry, 'You can tell them what you bloody well like. Start with the truth, that I am writing a book in order to earn some money. We don't all inherit farms and run estates.'

But my mother was like a terrier with a bone and she just couldn't let it go. She made her final plea, "You really should come with us, if not for me, then for Celia's sake.' I couldn't really blame my father for exploding. 'Don't be so bloody ridiculous. My absence won't make the slightest difference to Celia and you know it. I shan't be going Audrey, so there is no point in going on with this.'

My mother changed tack. 'You've already made other plans haven't you?'

'No Audrey,' he said wearily.

Then the tears arrived. 'There's someone else I know there is. You can't wait to get rid of us.' On and on it went until my father finally shouted 'Enough!' and went into his study and locked the door. I could never understand why Audrey kept on with her allegations. It only ended in Bernard's fury and her tears."

Dr Strutter looked at me. "Were her allegations correct?"

I thought about this. "Nobody knows exactly, not even Dolly. I did ask her about it. Obviously there had been the affair with Diana, but whether being caught that one time put him off future indiscretions, I've no real idea. I actually rather doubt it and there were endless rumours. He was an attractive man and had a reputation of being a womanizer. My mother obviously thought he did." I gave a rueful smile. "I wouldn't really have blamed Bernard, for having affairs I mean. His relationship with Audrey was pretty joyless."

I thought about another cigarette and decided against it.

I was going to kick the habit even if it killed me!

"Anyway, I knew my father wouldn't come with us, no matter how much my mother pestered him. I didn't mind this at all. The really disastrous news was when Audrey decided to take Wal and Luke. I immediately made my protests and was told very severely I was being selfish to want to deprive them of a holiday. Mark and Judy had plenty of room and were happy to have them.

I miserably thought that I now had five enemies instead of three.

My other three cousins consisted of two boys, David and Adam, and the youngest, a girl, Sarah, who was a year older than me. She might just as well have been a boy because she was fierce and tough, despising anything remotely 'girlish'. Beside her I appeared a weakling. Reluctantly I resigned myself to my fate.

The train journey seemed interminable. Wal and Luke, the worms, were on their best behavior in front of Audrey and played endless games of snap, with only the minimum of cheating. Judy met us at Edinburgh and we piled into the large Estate car. It was a long winding drive, made longer by the fact they had to keep stopping for me to be sick. This in no way increased my popularity.

At last we arrived at a large Gothic house, on the edge of a loch, surrounded by mountains. My worst forebodings were immediately realized. To the others it was heaven. To me it was dark, damp and frightening. They spent their days happily running wild on the moors, climbing trees, fishing and bird-watching. I stayed behind, knowing full well they didn't want me with them. I was quite content to stay out of danger, in my bedroom, reading. However the grown-ups noticed this and were worried. I heard July say to her boys, 'Darlings, you really must try and include Celia in your expeditions. She's getting very left out.' David spoke. He was the eldest. 'Sorry Mum. We would take her with us but she just doesn't fit in. She's always feeling cold, or sick, or worrying about getting her dress muddy. You should hear what Wal and Luke say about her.'

Judy's voice sounded brisk and I had the feeling she didn't greatly care for them.

'I wouldn't pay too much attention to what those two tell you. Quite honestly, it's difficult for Celia. She has no brothers or sisters and leads a very quiet life. It's left her lonely and she finds it difficult to mix with other children. It's why we invited her up here, to be with you all. She's a very sweet little girl really, just a bit shy. Do try.'

And to give them their due, they did. The next morning I was presented with a large pair of Wellington boots and told, 'We need you Celia, to help us dam a stream'

For one blissful, happy morning I helped David and Adam build this dam. David said, 'Well done Celia. You're doing really well.' I was flushed with success, but I should have known my happiness would be short-lived. I had reckoned without Wal and Luke. One of them came up behind me and pushed me into the stream, the other kicked in my side of the dam. I watched tearful and helpless as water poured over my entire morning's work. They jumped up and down, shouting their taunts. 'She'll cry now. You watch. Cry baby. Cry baby.' I shouted defiantly. 'I'm not. I can put the dam back. I've got...I've got magic in my fingers. I will magic it back.' Wal looked at me in disgust. 'Just listen to her. Magic finders indeed. You're cuckoo, that's what you are. Always making things up.' 'She's cuckoo,' echoed Luke. Humiliated I walked away and sat on a little hillock by myself. I could hear them talking. David said, 'Why did you do that you two? She was perfectly all right. You didn't have to ruin her dam.' Wal said, 'She could have built it up again. She didn't have to start blubbing. If it had been Sarah she wouldn't have cried.' 'No, I'd have hit you.' she said, and gave Wal a thump which caught him off balance and he fell over. Luke looked on admiringly. 'Sarah's pretty good for a girl. I wish she lived next door to us instead of cissy Celia'.

David looked at his watch, 'Come on you lot, it's time for lunch. We'd better be getting back.' I trailed behind, at a safe distance. David joined me. 'You shouldn't get so upset Celia. They only do it to tease. They wouldn't bother if you didn't get so upset.'

'I know,' I said, adding, 'I wish I was like Sarah.' David gave a mock groan. 'No, you don't. Sarah can be a real pig and you're much prettier. Come on, I'll race you to the house.' He let me win and instantly became my hero. As long as he was around, the others left me alone.

I looked across at Dr Strutter who remained his usual impassive self. I decided against another cigarette and to speed through the next bit as fast as I could.

"Towards the end of the holiday there was a sudden and unexpected heat-wave. The old swimming pool at the back of the house was filled. I would paddle around quietly at the shallow end, while the others made a great deal of noise and splash at the other.

One day, the thing that I most dreaded, happened. I was left without David's protection. He'd gone shooting with his father. That afternoon I took special care to keep to myself and stood quietly at the shallow end of the pool hardly daring to make a movement. Suddenly I noticed the four of them talking. I knew by their furtive looks in my direction, that they were plotting something. Before I had time to make my escape to the safety of the house, they had jumped into the pool and had me surrounded. Then they started splash me. 'Please don't,' I cried, 'I don't like water on my face.' This of course made them splash all the more. I made a dash for the edge and tried to crawl out, but Luke caught me by the legs. Wal said nastily, 'So, Celia doesn't like water on her face. We'll soon see about that.' And with this he ducked me under the water. I came up spluttering and choking. I could see their faces laughing as I gasped for air. I was absolutely terrified and had just opened my mouth to cry out, when they ducked me again. And again and again. They took it in turns.

I don't remember a great deal after that. I gather that when I didn't come up for air they panicked and dragged me out. Then, realizing I was half-drowned they ran for help.

Judy luckily knew how to administer artificial respiration, but I learned later they thought they had lost me. The children of course were punished and they all trailed in shame-faced and apologized. It had probably given them quite a fright as well. Certainly Wal and Luke made sure they didn't step out of line for the rest of the holiday. I was kept in bed for a few days and fussed over. It wasn't the days that were the worry. It was the nights. I had this recurring nightmare and would wake up screaming and fighting for breath. That nightmare has never left me. I still have it occasionally."

I stopped talking and suddenly felt faint.

Dr Strutter looked alarmed. "Are you all right? You've gone a little pale."

My voice came out in strange gasps. "Yes. I think so. It's just that I've never spoken about that incident before."

I took a gulp of water and then noticed the time. "I'm so sorry. I've gone over my time again.

"That's quite all right. You did arrive a little late." He was still looking anxious.

"You seem to find it distressing to talk about these parallels. We could talk of other things and come back to the parallels later on?"

I said with a braveness I didn't feel, "No, I would like to continue. In any case I think that was the worst one to describe, the others will be easier, and I think it might be helpful to have got it out of my system at last"

"That's a good way to think about it." He paused. "You are recounting all this extremely vividly. Have you ever thought of writing it all down?"

I felt a little embarrassed as I admitted that I did write down the account of every session immediately afterwards, while it was still fresh in my mind.

He seemed to approve of this. "So do we have another parallel next week?"

I nodded, gathered up my bag and quickly made my exit.

For once I didn't even look up at the window, but went straight to the car. It took a few moments to calm myself before I could face driving home.

The end of the seventh session.

Chapter 6

Almost immediately after her February 2nd visit to Dr Strutter, a crisis started at the school, which soon developed into one of major proportions. It started slowly enough with one House going doing down with 'flu. But as February moved into March, the 'flu virus spread from house to house, and it was not only the children who became ill, but the staff as well. Celia began to dread the telephone ringing at breakfast with news of yet more cases. In the circumstances she didn't really feel she could leave the sinking ship for her London visit. So she rang Mrs Maitland, explained the situation and cancelled her appointments until further notice.

About ten days after this, George came out of his study and declared, "That's it. I've just taken another call. I'm going to have to close the School and send everyone home until we're over this damn thing."

Celia was immediately sympathetic, "Surely there must be enough teachers to cover?"

George shook his head. "It's no longer logistically possible. That was Mrs Lacey, to say she's now gone down with it, and there simply is no one to take her class."

He looked more harassed than she had ever seen him.

"What does Mrs Lacey teach?

He sat down on the hall bench, "English, but it's not that so much. I can cover the English classes myself. She is a form teacher and her class have an hour every day at a time which nobody else can cover."

Celia thought for a moment. "What happens in that class?"

George looked a little annoyed and said wearily, "Oh, just general topics," adding a little crossly, "Is this questionnaire leading somewhere Celia, because I have rather a lot to do."

"Couldn't I help?" she asked tentatively, "I mean I know I'm not a qualified teacher, but I am sure I could hold the fort for an hour on general subjects?"

George considered this surprising proposition. Finally he said, "Are you sure about this? Thirty ten year old boys is quite an undertaking if you are not used to dealing with them."

She inwardly smiled and thought that they couldn't all be as bad as Wal and Luke.

"Yes, I'm sure," she told him and fervently hoped she wouldn't regret it.

Next day, rather to her embarrassment, he insisted on introducing her to the boys, which he did in typically pompous fashion.

"My wife has kindly offered to take this class, so I do not want to hear any reports of bad behavior. Is that understood?"

Thirty pairs of eyes stared at her as they said in unison, "Yes, sir."

George smiled benevolently at Celia. "All right darling. I'll leave you to it."

He then, uncharacteristically, kissed her on the cheek, before abandoning her to her fate.

Celia cleared her throat and plunged in. "As I haven't seen most of you since you came to tea as new boys, I am going to find it difficult to remember your names, so it would be kind if you gave them to me, when you answer questions." The eyes were still staring at her. "Can someone tell me what you usually discuss at this time?" A hand shot up. "Yes?"

A rather skinny boy with ginger hair stood up. "William Hornby, Mrs Roxby Smith."

"Yes William?"

"We tackle all sorts of subjects, usually it's something Mrs Lacey has thought of. It can be current events," he added helpfully.

"Thank you," she said, "although I'm not sure I'm up to current events."

One or two of the boys smiled at that. She went on, "I thought we might discuss the lives of the great composers." Celia thought she detected a flicker of interest, "and I'm going to start with an English composer called Sir Edward Elgar." That would please George she thought. "Does anyone know anything

Elgar composed?" There was a pause, then a couple of hands shot up. She pointed to a cheeky looking boy with a very freckled face sitting in the front row.

"Michael Hanbury-Watkins. I think he wrote 'Land of Hope and Glory'. I heard it on the last night of the Poms."

There was general laughter at this. Celia decided to ignore his little joke but did give him a smile. "Yes, it is played at the last night of the Promenade Concerts which take place in the Albert Hall London. The music comes from one of his Pomp and Circumstance Marches. Does anyone know anything else he composed?"

Another hand went up. "Nigel Fellowes. I think he wrote Nimrod, Mrs Roxby Smith."

Celia felt pleased. This was going better than she expected. "Well done Nigel. Do you know where 'Nimrod' comes from? The boy shook his head. "Well, it comes from Elgar's 'Enigma Variations'. She wrote this on the blackboard. 'It's an interesting piece of music and it's very different. Do you know why? This time no hands went up.

"Well I will explain..."

The hour went by so fast Celia was surprised when the bell went.

George irritatingly came back to collect her. He dismissed the boys and after they had gone he asked, "Well, how did it go?"

She suppressed her irritation. "It was fine. In fact, I enjoyed it."

He looked relieved at this. "Do you think you could carry on for a bit?

She had no hesitation in telling him she could.

It was actually well into March before the School returned to normal. By this time Celia had covered all the composers she knew anything about, and was just beginning to wonder if she should start doing some research when George gave her the reprieve. He seemed genuinely pleased as he thanked her and said her classes had been something of a success. Praise from George? That was a surprise. And she was surprised still further when he said, "Would you like to go out to dinner tonight, by way of a thank you?"

It would have been churlish to turn down the invitation so she agreed. He looked pleased and told her he'd book a table for eight o'clock.

Of course, being George it had to be a very smart restaurant and, being George, he seemed to know a great many people there. It was rather obvious he was a regular visitor. On looking back later, it seemed to her that this was an isolated night, one oasis of calm, amidst the wreck of their dysfunctional life together.

Just as he had in the days before their marriage, he made sure she had a wonderful time. He was charming, attentive, and appeared genuinely amused by the accounts she gave of her classes. As they reached home she felt warmer towards him than she'd done for years.

"Thank you George," she said on the landing, "That was a lovely evening."

As she went into her bedroom she glanced back and he was still standing there.

His face had a strange expression which she couldn't quite read. What was it? Longing? Frustration? It was difficult to tell.

She went quickly into the room and shut the door. A feeling of panic swept through her as she realized he had probably imagined she would weaken and sleep with him again. But she couldn't do that. She just couldn't. It made her feel sick to even think about it.

As she climbed into bed the thought came to her that there were plenty of women who liked having sex with George, so why did he need her? It had to be about possession. She was his wife and therefore it was her duty to share his bed. Possession and control. But how could he be so old fashioned? It was like something out of the "Forsyte Saga."

And then she had another thought. Maybe George was right and she *was* sexually frigid. A feeling of despair swept through her. If that were the case the situation between them was hopeless and there was no solution. For George the only answer was for them to take up a physical relationship again. For her, the only answer was for that not to happen. It was deadlock.

Could Dr Strutter find a way through all this? She didn't think so, but as she drifted off to sleep she was certain of one thing. She wasn't going to stop the London visits, at least not yet.

But once again the fates stepped in.

It might have been that George was suffering from exhaustion after the 'flu epidemic, or it might have been because Celia hadn't given in to his obvious desire for her to return to his bed, but whatever it was, the uneasy truce built up while Celia had helped out with the teaching, soon began to disappear. Breakfasts once more became a battleground and George vented his anger on anything and everything, his prime target being the builders.

"How much longer are those damned workmen of yours going to clutter up the stairway? Travelling round this house has become a constant hazard."

Celia looked suitably apologetic. "It shouldn't be much longer now George. I'm afraid it was all delayed when I had to put them off because of the 'flu epidemic."

This didn't mollify him in the least. "You should probably have cancelled them altogether. It's a mine field out there."

Celia knew it was only a matter of time before he lost his temper completely. The balloon finally went up when some paint appeared on his academic gown. Although Celia cleaned it off so that no mark was visible, George's fragile patience was at an end.

"The moment term finishes Celia, I am out of here and I won't be returning until those damned builders have gone."

In view of all this, she felt it might be tactful to put off a return to Dr Strutter until after the holidays and reluctantly she rang Mrs Maitland to explain the situation.

Then, to mollify George she suggested they go away on a family holiday but when she put this to him he looked a little shame-faced and was rather over-profuse in his apologies. "Oh Celia, I really am sorry. I have made arrangements to go and stay with an old friend of my mother's over Easter. It's a duty visit really, but I though it a good opportunity to see her as she's getting on and very frail. She lives in Ireland which means I will be away a little longer. I rather assumed you would be needed here to oversee the decorating and of course look after Natasha."

He sounded nonchalant but Celia was under no illusions. 'An old friend of his mother's?' A likely story. He had obviously made some arrangement to be with his latest mistress. She didn't mind for herself, but was rather shocked at this cavalier attitude towards his daughter.

She said reprovingly, "I think Natasha might rather mind not seeing you."

He considered this and sounded almost contrite. "You are right of course. I'll treat her to a weekend in London before she returns to school. Ask her to choose a show and my secretary will book the hotel and the seats."

Celia was puzzled. Why this sudden complete division of parental care? Was this his punishment to her for not returning to his bed? If so it was very childish.

However, there was nothing for it but to arrange a separate holiday for Natasha and herself. She rang Dolly for advice. "Venice" was the prompt reply. "It is the most beautiful city in the world. Tinker and I were meant to go last year but we had to cancel when he was ill."

Celia had an inspiration. "Why don't you both come too?"

After consulting with Tinker it was quickly agreed and arrangements were made.

When Celia told George of the plan, he merely snorted and said, "I pity poor Natasha, being saddled with your dotty relations."

She didn't even bother to rise to this.

EIGHTH SESSION   May 13th 1979

It seemed a very long time since my last session. I'd returned from Venice only to find the good doctor had gone away.

"We always take a cottage on the edge of Dartmoor at this time of year," he explained. "My wife likes to walk and I indulge in my passion for bird-watching."

I told him it sounded very peaceful and felt a twinge of envy.

No such domestic bliss for me!

He flicked a bit of imaginary dust off the arm of his chair and said, "Do we have another parallel today?

"We do." I hesitated, "I think this will probably be the last one."

He seemed surprised at this so I explained, "I could tell you a great many, but I think you have the gist by now." I hesitated, "And to be quite honest I feel rather a fraud. There's nothing really wrong with me. I just enjoy coming here and talking."

He gave me one of his long, scrutinizing looks. "That may be more helpful than you realize. Talking about your past can make it easier to come to terms with what has happened. The events themselves don't really matter anymore. What matters is the way you learn to deal with them." He smiled. "Are you losing faith in your parallels theory?"

I tried not to sound indignant. "Not at all, in fact, the more I tell them, the more I become convinced about them. I'm not even bothering about the minor parallels, only with the main ones." I hesitated. "It's just that I don't want to waste your time."

He sounded quite sharp, "You're not."

I don't know what made me ask the next question.

I suddenly blurted out, "Dr Strutter, do you find me strange?"

The poor man looked quite startled and asked in what way did I mean 'strange'?

The words came out rather fast, "Well George says he has never met any-one so detached in his life and in a way I think he's right. I'm aware of it myself. It's just that I don't seem to be able to express my emotions. It's not just sexual, I don't feel involved or touched by anything. Even with Natasha, the most important person in my life, I don't show outward affection. What I think I mean is that I am not as tactile as other mothers are. Even Dolly says I am difficult when it comes to emotional issues."

I didn't mention here that Dolly's solution to my problems was to have a passionate affair!

I finished with a flourish, "And George says it's like living with an iceberg."

Dr Strutter considered this for a long time before he said, "A great many people find it difficult to express their emotions. It doesn't mean you are any less passionate or feel things any less deeply. You just don't let your true feelings rise to the surface."

He gave me a gentle smile, "The fact that you suppress your feelings has a lot to do with your childhood. You have been somewhat bruised and are afraid to expose yourself to hurt again." His expression changed to one of a frown. "Have you tried to explain to your husband how you feel?"

I gave a mirthless laugh, "Good God no! George thinks you are sorting me out."

Realizing that must have sounded rather rude I said quickly, "I'm sorry. That came out all wrong. You see, George doesn't really want to be bothered with me. Some time ago I suggested that as he found me so unsatisfactory it might be better if we separated. He told me that was absolutely out of the question and that he hadn't provided for me all these years for me to walk out of the marriage now. He added it would be harmful to both him and the school and that was that. He didn't even mention Natasha. Anyway, it's not going to happen, so it's not really relevant." I shrugged, "To be fair, he has always provided for me and been pretty generous, although I feel that is not just for my benefit but because it reflects on him if I look good. I am now just part of a package."

Dr Strutter was frowning so I apologized. "I'm sorry. I quite understand I'm not here for marriage guidance. Shall I start in on the parallel?

He nodded, leant back in his chair and waited.

"This last one is quite appropriate, because it is what brought me to you in the first place."

He looked interested. "Ah yes. Wasn't it the 'ghastly' dinner party."

My God! He didn't forget a thing.

"Yes. That dinner party."

I reached for my cigarettes. I was going to need to smoke to get through this one.

"As I think I explained, George and I lived this rather strange life, entirely based on routine. It was all fine as long as nothing broke the surface calm. However, about two years back, a change came over George which began to make my existence more difficult. He became irritable, on edge, and although not a heavy drinker, the whisky intake certainly increased. He was also frequently away. I never enquired where. To have done so would have invited hostility, or a lie, or both, so there didn't seem much point. It wasn't a particularly pleasant way to live, but in order to keep the status quo I maintained a low profile. George would inform me of his daily plans over breakfast and on this particular morning he said, 'I need to have some people over for dinner tonight, after the Governor's meeting. Can you tell Cook it will be about eight people?' His face wore the sort of expression which invited no comment, but in spite of this I ventured, 'Am I allowed to know who is coming?' Irritated at having to give me information he snapped out the list, 'Dr Farrant and his wife, Keith Jackson, Sarah Lodden, and possibly Bill Mackintosh and his wife. I'll ring you during the morning to confirm.' And with that he left.

I went over the list in my mind. Dr Farrant the school doctor was all right, affable and conscientious. His wife I found rather tiresome, although she was harmless enough. Her conversation tended to consist of descriptions of her latest kitchen gadgets or problems with the au pair."

Dr Strutter was smiling but didn't interrupt.

"Keith Jackson, the new school bursar I disliked from our first meeting. He was the worst kind of social climber, very smooth and conceited. However, George obviously rated him highly, so I kept my opinions to myself. I also noticed they spent a good deal of time together and always seemed to be up to some kind of scheming, like the conspirators in 'Julius Caesar'. Then there was Sarah Lodden, the Honourable Sarah Lodden. Now I really did like her. A large, formidable lady in her fifties, she ran the local madrigal group, which for some reason I had joined. The madrigal evenings were hilarious, terribly English somehow. The first time I arrived Sarah had said in her great booming voice, 'So glad you could come. There's boiled eggs in the kitchen and madrigals in the drawing room.'

That really made him smile.

81

Sarah's house was quite bizarre, full of chintz and bits of India. I think her ancestors must have been in the Raj. There were dogs everywhere, and cats."

I paused and asked, "Do you like animals?"

He seemed a bit startled by this sudden question. "Well I like dogs. We actually have a rather large mongrel called Gustav."

Now why wasn't I surprised by that!

"Well I like dogs too, but Sarah Lodden's animals were rather too numerous and smelly to be fun. Anyway, I assumed the reason she had been invited to this particular dinner party was because she was on the Board of Governors at the School. This was only one of her many community duties. She was also joint Master of the local hunt, a J.P on endless committees and had a tendency to refer to people as 'jolly good chaps' or as 'good eggs', which made George wince, but I found it amusing."

I thought about another cigarette and then decided against it.

"Halfway through the morning George rang, sounding even more abrupt than usual. 'You will have to be at your tactful best this evening Celia. This Governor's meeting is going to be damned difficult, so dinner afterwards could prove a little tricky.'

I asked, 'Why tricky? In what way?' He didn't disguise his irritation. He hated giving me explanations so his voice was sharp. 'We have a few serious problems to sort out, that's why. It's nothing that need concern you. My secretary will ring you with the final guest list a little later on.' He rang off before I could make any further inquiries.

A few minutes later the telephone rang again. It was Sarah Lodden booming down the line. We exchanged pleasantries and she told me she was 'in the pink' and then there was a long silence. Just as I thought we had been cut off, she burst out, 'Would it be possible to come over and see you?' I was a little puzzled, 'Aren't I going to see you tonight?' She sounded harassed, 'Yes indeed my dear, but I need to see you before. Can I come over in about an hour?' I told her it would be fine and she rang off. Then George's secretary rang to say that Bill Mackintosh, the classics master, would definitely be at the dinner, but as he was coming straight from the meeting, his wife would not be with us. So I rang Fiona Thornton, one of the younger and prettier matrons, to ask her to make up the numbers. I happened to know she'd had a fling with George. Far better, I thought to invite one that I knew about, than one I didn't.

Sarah Lodden arrived an hour later, looking flustered and unlike her usual bluff self. It was pouring with rain and her hat, which was pork-pied in shape, now resembled a limp cabbage leaf and she gave off a smell of warm, damp dog. I hung up her sodden clothing and led her into the drawing room. She looked bear-like and awkward.

'Celia, my dear, I'm so sorry to land on you like this. It's a fearful imposition.'

I assured her it wasn't, and was about to offer her refreshment of some kind when she launched into what sounded like a prepared speech. 'Oh my dear, you must forgive me but I'm going to have to speak very frankly. May I be quite open with you?'

I nodded. It was all rather intriguing. Sarah blustered on, 'We have a dreadful problem before us.' I told her I knew that it was going to be a 'tricky evening' as George had warned me. Sarah said grimly, 'Tricky would be an understatement,' and then asked, 'You know nothing more?' I shook my head. 'I try to involve myself as little as possible in school politics.'

Sarah was clearing her throat a good deal and now looked even more embarrassed and uncertain. 'How long have you and George been at the school my dear?'

I made a quick calculation, 'Well Natasha is eleven, so it must be twelve years.'

She gave a watery smile. 'Good heavens, it seems no time at all since we were welcoming the child bride.' I winced slightly at this but let her continue.

'You must know what a jolly good job you have both done.' I quickly told her it was George really and she patted my hand. 'No my dear, it is you as well. You must never underestimate your contribution. The poor old school was a bit in the doldrums before you two arrived. Now it appears to be doing well, lists full, boys getting through their common entrance. There are no complaints on that score.'

She paused again and fiddled with the damp gloves in her lap. I asked her if she would like a drink of something. By the look on her face it seemed she would need something a good deal stronger than tea, but she again declined the offer, saying she couldn't stay long. As she hesitated I said, 'Has there been some complaint about the school?'

Her lips were pursed, 'Not complaint exactly, but of course with one scandal the whole picture could alter.' I was surprised, 'Why should there be a scandal?' She looked at me, 'Oh my dear, this is quite appallingly difficult. Forgive me, but I do have to ask the next question. Are you and George happily married?' I wasn't at all sure how to answer this but luckily she went on, 'Outwardly all would appear to be well, but appearances can be deceptive can't they?' She hesitated, 'You see there have been various rumours.'

The poor woman looked so flustered and upset I tried to help her out. 'You say there are rumours?' She nodded and asked, 'You really don't know of any?' I told her I hadn't heard anything specific. By now she was contorted in an agony of embarrassment, so I tried to help her out, "Look, I do know there are other women in George's life.'

There was another long pause, 'Why don't you tell me what is worrying you Sarah? I'd much rather know.' She hesitated and then burst out, 'My dear you must believe me, the last thing I want to do is to pry into your private life. I simply loathe gossip, but when it affects the school…' She paused and then asked, 'Do you know Bill Mackintosh, the classics master?' I replied that I knew him slightly, and that he was coming to dinner tonight after the meeting.' She looked astonished, 'Is he really?' I asked why that surprised her. It was then that she finally came out with it, 'Because your husband is having an affair with his wife!'

She instantly became apologetic. 'Oh my dear, do forgive me, I so dislike having to tell you all this, but the fact is, Bill's wife moved out a couple of months ago. She rented a cottage in Wallingford, the next village to me. I've seen George's car there several times. However, Bill doesn't know that his wife's removal from his house had anything to do with George. I suppose he just thought there was a general breakdown in the marriage.' She broke off panting and completely out of breath.

Of course! Suddenly everything fell into place. It now made sense. I had often wondered about the frequency of George's visits to the Mackintosh's house. Poor Sarah looked almost tearful. 'I am so sorry Celia. This must come as a terrible shock.'

I shook my head. 'No, it doesn't actually, but I can't see how this affair affects the school.' Sarah sounded indignant now. 'Well it wouldn't have, except…' She faltered, obviously trying to put things as tactfully as possible. 'I'm sorry to have to tell you this my dear, but George has one or two enemies. I suppose such things happen in a close-knit community. However, I'm afraid this has now had dreadful consequences. You see, some time ago there was a disagreement between George and Johnson, the deputy head. Do you know Johnson?' I nodded. Our paths had crossed but I didn't know him that well. However, his name was often mentioned because George disliked him intensely and made his dislike fairly obvious. I told Sarah I knew he'd been at the school a long time. She nodded. 'Indeed yes. It must be well over twenty years.' I said, 'Our very own Mr Chips.' Sarah beamed. 'What a lovely way of putting it. He's a good teacher but not very assertive I'm afraid, and to be honest, rather stuck in his ways. We were all aware that relations between George and Johnson had not been good for some time and in the past year they have barely been civil to each other.' She gave a sigh, 'So it didn't alto-gether surprise me when I heard that Johnson had brought George's affairs to the attention of the Governors.' I was a bit stunned by this. 'Affairs? In the plural?'

Sarah looked deeply uncomfortable. 'I'm afraid so. The name of a matron, Fiona Thornton, I know was mentioned.' At this I burst out laughing. 'I'm sorry Sarah, you are not going to believe this. I've asked Fiona Thornton tonight, to make up numbers, because I was rung by George's secretary and told that Bill Mackintosh's wife wouldn't be coming.' Sarah was aghast. 'Oh my dear. How can you take it all so calmly?' I tried to reassure her, 'I'm sure it will be all right. George thrives on difficult situations. He knows how to wriggle. He should have been a politician. Please tell me everything, it's far better that I know.'

The damp gloves in her lap now resembled a piece of string. She took a deep breath. 'After Johnson's complaint, the Chairman talked to George. That was about six weeks ago and I was away so I'm not sure what was the outcome of that conversation. I'm sorry to say I returned to something much worse. Oh it's all so nasty and vindictive.' She looked at me. 'You presumably know the bursar, Keith Jackson?'

I groaned. 'Don't tell me he's involved as well.' Sarah nodded. 'I'm afraid so. He's now made a formal complaint against Johnson, accusing him of inde-cent behavior with one of the boys.' She paused dramatically. I was aghast. 'Has he grounds for this complaint? I mean is there any proof?' Sarah looked sad, 'Apparently so. George is backing him. That is what tonight's meeting is all about.'

There followed a shocked silence. Finally I asked, 'What will happen?'

'At the best Johnson will leave quietly at the end of term. It's a formal complaint and has to be taken seriously.' 'And the worst?' She struggled as she put on her gloves, 'Johnson will fight it out. The school will become involved in a terrible scandal and the stories about George will come out.' She again patted my hand. 'I'm so sorry my dear. My one object in coming here was to warn you of what might happen. It would be so awful if it came as a complete shock.'

I told her I was very grateful. The poor woman looked exhausted.

'I do so hope this trouble can be averted.' She looked at me nervously, 'My dear I wonder if it would be possible for you to talk to George about these indiscretions? Perhaps if you could be firm with him…' her voice trailed away. Inwardly I gave a mirthless laugh. I knew anything I said would have little effect on George, but I did my best to comfort her, 'I'll try, but I doubt it will do much good. George doesn't really listen to advice.'

She looked at her watch. 'I've taken up far too much of your time. Let's hope our worst forebodings aren't realized.' And with that she bustled off down the drive."

I definitely needed a cigarette break here but as Dr Strutter still made no comment, I carried straight on.

"Left to myself I was in no doubt of the grisly truth and the more I thought about it, the more depressed I became. It was obvious Keith Jackson and George had conspired against the unfortunate Mr Chips Johnson, to get George out of a hole, and then on the flimsiest of evidence, had turned the tables on the man. It was clever. Affairs were one thing, but what could be worse for a boy's prep school than to have one of the masters under suspicion for seducing the boys? It could only have been worse had Johnson been a member of the clergy.

Feeling somewhat shaken by the afternoon's revelations, I wandered over to the drinks trolley and almost without thinking poured myself a large brandy. I drink very little and brandy never, but on this occasion it was the first bottle that came to hand.

By early evening the combination of brandy and depression had brought on a pretty bad headache, so I took some aspirins, swilling them down with another large brandy.

My headache eased, but my depression increased. It was bad enough having to endure a loveless marriage, but to be disillusioned as well was almost more than I could bear.

Until now, my admiration for George in his professional capacity had helped me endure the relationship. Now even that was in jeopardy. He might have fooled the Chairman but he didn't fool me. Not any more. Oh no, my eyes were well and truly opened. It is what I had feared most. That I would end up despising him. So I poured some more brandy and for good measure took more aspirins in case the headache came back.

The Cook came in to say she was leaving and that everything was prepared. I waved an airy hand at her and received a very odd look in return.

George arrived home about seven thirty, with Bill Mackintosh. I peered at the poor old cuckold. I was beginning to feel decidedly odd. George followed me into the kitchen.

'Bill and I are going to the study to talk before the others arrive. Is everything in order?'

I pretended to busy myself with kitchen affairs and waved a wooden spoon.

'Fine. Just fine.' George looked at me more closely. 'Are you feeling all right Celia? You look rather flushed.' I grinned foolishly. 'I'm wonderful. Absolutely wonderful. Don't you worry about me George.' I swayed towards him. He seemed more like Lenin than ever. He picked up the brandy glass and smelled the contents. 'Good God! It's brandy!' I nodded and said admiringly, 'Clever George. Brandy in a brandy glass.'

He slammed down the glass. "What the bloody hell's the matter with you? You don't usually drink brandy? Are you drunk?' I looked shocked. 'Absolutely not.'

He looked unconvinced. 'Well I certainly hope you aren't. Tonight of all nights.'

He threw the remainder of the contents of my glass down the sink. 'I've had a bloody awful day Celia and I don't want it getting any worse, which it will do if you appear drunk in front of my dinner guests.' I waved a reproving finger at him.

'*Our* dinner guests George. *Our* dinner guests.' He took no notice of this and said pompously, 'I suggest you make yourself some black coffee and drink as much of it as you can.' With that he strode out of the room.

In sheer defiance I poured myself another brandy.

I honestly don't remember much about the dinner. In my befuddled state I decided it would be best if I didn't speak at all, so I just smiled at everyone, Malvolio-like. They were mostly too pre-occupied with their own conversation to take much notice of me, although one or two strange looks came my way. At some point someone asked if I was all right and before I could say anything, George hastily explained that he thought, 'poor darling Celia might be going down with 'flu.'

Luckily two girls from the village came to serve and clear the meal away. Juggling with plates, knives, forks, not to mention vegetable dishes, might have caused my downfall.

So I sat, silent and grinning, and just when I thought I was going to fall forward onto the table, George stood up and made an announcement.

'I know you will all be pleased to hear that from next term Bill Mackintosh will take on the job of assistant headmaster. There were murmured congratulations and Sarah Lodden shot me a significant look. I tried to focus on George and said, 'I didn't know Mr Johnson was leaving?' George looked annoyed. 'Well he is, at the end of term.'

I stared at George. 'Why?' I persisted. 'I mean, I'm very glad for Bill, but Mr Johnson seemed like our own special Mr Chips. You know, at the school until death do him part.'

I was aware that several faces round the table wore rather startled expressions. George looked furious and in a clipped voice said, 'You will have to cast someone else as your Mr Chips Celia,' and before I, or anyone else, had time to say anything he said,

'Here's to you Bill. The very best of luck.' We all obediently drained our glasses.

I somehow managed to make my way to the kitchen muttering something about organizing coffee. My head was pounding so much I could hardly bear it. So I took some more aspirins and tried to think clearly. Clever George. He must have persuaded Mrs Bill Mackintosh to return, to be at her husband's side in his important new job. She'd still be near George, although they'd have to be a good deal more discreet.

So George was happy and Bill was happy to have her back and the Governors were happy not to have a scandal on their hands. So everyone was happy. Except poor Mr Johnson. Clever, clever George.

I really was beginning to feel extremely peculiar. The room kept coming and going and apart from the headache I now had a terrible feeling of nausea. George came in, took one look at me and picked up the coffee tray himself. I could hear him making my apologies.

Luckily everyone left soon after that. Dr Farrent told George that I should take a couple of aspirins and if I wasn't better in the morning he would come in and see me.

After the last guest had left George returned to the kitchen and said in icy tones, 'I suggest you go straight to bed Celia.'

I clung on to the table. 'Where is Mrs Mackintosh George, that's what I'd like to know?'

He looked both astonished and angry. He came across the room and shook me.

'There are a great many things I'd like to know. Why was Fiona Thornton invited?

I said in injured tones, 'But George, I thought you liked Fiona Thornton. I thought you liked her very, very much.'

He was seething now. However the combination of fury, guilt and rage seemed to have rendered him speechless. I went on savagely, 'I'll tell you why I invited Fiona Thornton. I invited her to keep poor Mr Mackintosh company. Didn't know where to find Mrs Mackintosh.' He shook me again. 'Someone's been talking to you. Who's been talking to you?' I staggered back and clutched a chair. 'Clever, clever George. You have it all arranged don't you? Even for poor Mr Chips Johnson.' I waved a hand airily, 'Hello Mrs Mackintosh. Goodbye Mr Johnson.' George, apoplectic with fury managed to splutter, 'Go to bed Celia. I'll talk to you in the morning when you have sobered up.' And he left the room.

All I remember after that was going towards the bathroom to find some more aspirins.

The corridor came towards me and hit me on the head. There was a terrible pain and I seemed to be falling a long, long way down. Next thing I was in hospital."

I looked at Dr Strutter. "You see? It wasn't suicide at all, just a hopeless accident, although at that moment I honestly wouldn't have minded if they hadn't brought me round."

He was silent for a while, stroking his trousers and lost in thought. Then he asked,

"Did you ever talk to George about that evening?

I gave a hollow laugh. "No, there didn't seem much point. I expect he thinks I have forgotten all the events that led up to it. But I haven't. My eyes have been well and truly opened and he knows that I know all about him." I added, "There is not one jot of affection or respect left. Not after that night"

I know I sounded angry, so pulled myself together and tried to speak more calmly.

"Anyway, the doctors recommended I get help and George readily agreed. It added to his kudos. I could hear him telling people about my state in hushed tones, 'his poor sick wife on the verge of a nervous breakdown.' I'm sure he came in for a good deal of sympathy. Ironic isn't it? No matter how the odds are stacked against him, George always wins."

The clock ticked away. Finally I said, "Do you have any comment to make?"

With an almost infuriating calm he said, "I think any discussion can wait until I've heard the other half of the parallel."

I felt very tired and not a little deflated. He must have noticed this because he stood up.

"I think that's enough for one day and we're out of time. I will see you next week."

He was of course right. I couldn't have gone on.

I walked speedily to the car and didn't look back.

The end of the eighth session.

Chapter 8

It did not really surprise Celia that her plan to see Dr Strutter the follow-ing week was immediately sabotaged. Mrs Maitland was very pleasant and understanding as always, but Celia felt embarrassed by the number of cancel-lations she'd had to make. In the end she told Mrs M she would make a new appointment as soon as she could, and left it at that. But it was suspiciously odd the way George always seemed to discover some event she had to attend on a Wednesday, the one day she reserved for London.

She stared at the calendar on the kitchen wall and found that Wednesday, June 12th was absolutely free, a virgin space amongst the other heavy mark-ings. With some trepidation she rang to make an appointment and then wrote in large letters, 'CELIA IN LONDON'.

As she entered the kitchen on the morning of the 12th she found George staring at the entry. He swung round as she came in. "I see you intend to go to London today."

With all the patience she could muster she said, "Yes George. It seemed the only spare Wednesday before the summer holidays."

He took no notice of this but went straight on, "I presume then, that you had forgotten the House Cricket Tournament?"

"The what?" she asked somewhat bewildered and he repeated it, as if she were a rather stupid child. "The House Cricket Matches. You will be missing them?"

She stammered out, "Well yes, I suppose I will. I can't remember it having been an important date before. And it wasn't on the calendar."

George sat down and opened his paper noisily to show his annoyance. "That's a pity. A lot of the boys will be very disappointed you won't be watching them."

Clever George. She was once more in disgrace and made to feel guilty.

Breakfast continued in silence. As he got up to leave she said, "I'm really sorry about the cricket matches George. I didn't know about them when I made the appointment. It will be the last time I go up to London this term."

He frowned, "So you intend to go back to this man in the Autumn?"

Celia felt uncomfortable, aware that it was costing George money and she hadn't actually asked him. "I don't know yet. We'll see how today goes."

He gave a curt nod. "Well no doubt you will keep me informed."

The atmosphere between them was now so bad, it was a relief to go for a walk or take a drive, just to get away for a while. George wouldn't think of a separation, so she just had to put up with her life and accept it, warts and all.

She eased the car out of the garage and immediately thoughts began to fill her mind like scattering confetti. Flutter, flutter, flutter.

She began to ask herself questions.

Why, for instance did she feel so restless? She couldn't put all the blame on bloody George, or even being stuck in the bloody school. No, it was something more than that.

She wrestled with this for a while and finally decided it could well be due to the fact that she was brought up in the Fifties. It was a theory she'd considered before and it was beginning to take root. Of all the decades in the twentieth century, surely the Fifties had to be the least exciting? It was a decade that had somehow been lost between the Second World War and the 'Swinging Sixties'.

She changed gear and moved on to the motorway as her ideas began to take shape.

So what had happened in the Fifties? There had been Korea and Suez and the fear of the nuclear bomb. Wal and Luke had gone on CND marches, but she had been considered too young to take part and in any case she didn't have enough stamina.

Bernard had ranted and raged about the Cold War, the Berlin Wall, and the invasion of Hungary, but she had schooled herself not to listen to his outbursts. Even the happy events seemed doomed to indifference. Hadn't it rained all day during the Coronation? And the Festival of Britain was really very tame when you looked back on it.

There was no getting away from it, the Fifties had been grey and ugly and she had spent them in a little bubble of drab isolation. By the time all the fun of the Swinging Sixties came along she was incarcerated in marriage and the school.

She smiled to herself as she overtook a large lorry. The excitement of the Sixties had certainly passed her by. Quite frankly she couldn't have told a drug from a dishwasher. As for 'Flower Power' and 'Sexual Liberation', they would never have been allowed within the walls of the enclosed fortress of Civolds.

She moved into the fast lane.

It wasn't exactly that she was longing for a life of drugs, sex, and rock and roll. It was more that she'd never had a chance to try it. Her life had moved straight from school into the trapped world where she now resided. No wonder she was restless.

She slowed down to stop at the traffic lights. This was no good, she could feel these doom laden thoughts pulling her down. Fiddling with the car radio she found some cheerful Bach. It was music that always lifted her spirits.

So she drove on to her last assignation with Dr Strutter that summer.

NINTH SESSION   June 12th 1979

For once, it was Dr Strutter who kept me waiting. Mrs Maitland looked rather flustered when I arrived and told me in hushed tones that I would have to wait as the Doctor was on an urgent call. I sat wondering what on earth that could be? An attempted suicide?

A patient gone missing? Some mother worried about a delinquent child? It left me with a stab of guilt. I had no such urgent problem.

I was finally summoned in and he appeared completely unruffled as he apologized for the delay. I told him there was no need to worry, especially as I had cancelled and changed so many appointments. He smiled and said, "Well I am thankful to say the redoubtable Mrs Maitland protects me from that side of things."

He was stroking his knees in that peculiar way of his and looked as if he was trying to make up his mind whether to say something so I waited.

After a moment he said, "I mentioned your 'Parallels Theory' to my wife."

I was intrigued. "And what was her reaction? What did she say?"

"Well you must understand she is mid-European, so she has a rather different background to you. However, she did acknowledge that there were 'coincidences' as she called them, 'parallels' as you call them, that went from generation to generation."

I was beginning to build up a picture here, two teenage sons, a mid-European wife and a dog called Gustav.

"So, did these 'coincidences' worry your wife? Did she feel as trapped by them as I do?

He shook his head and smiled. "On the contrary, she found them rather comforting, just because of their continuity."

I sat silent for a moment working this out. "I do see that if the experiences are good ones it could be comforting, but mine in general are not." I added gloomily. "I suppose that makes me neurotic."

He frowned and looked almost annoyed. "No, no, not at all. I think it only emphasizes the fact that the occurrence of the parallel events is not the worry in itself. It is the way in which we deal with them."

That made me even more depressed. "Obviously I'm not dealing with them very well."

He suddenly looked concerned. "That is not true at all. Just the way you are telling me about these parallels is positive in itself, quite apart from the great talent you have in recalling them so vividly."

His expression was now half kind and half amused. "Why don't you tell me the second half of the last parallel?" He wiped his glasses on his tie. "I presume it must be a similar dinner party?"

"Yes it is, one from my childhood." I paused. "Do you mind if I smoke? It helps me to concentrate."

It was a pathetic excuse. But I knew I needed one before going into this final narrative.

Once lit up, I gathered my thoughts and began.

"It took place during the summer holidays in 1960, when I was fifteen. I only mention my age to make it easier for you to understand my reactions."

He gave a curt nod as if he wanted me to get on with it. So I did.

"I was home for a week, before going to spend the rest of the holidays with my cousins."

He leant forward, "Were those the same cousins who persecuted you in one of the earlier parallels?"

I smiled, "Yes, but it became easier as I grew up and I sometimes even enjoyed their company, particularly David, who was by then up at Cambridge. He was languid and very charming and his world seemed endlessly glamorous to me.

But I digress. By the time I was fifteen, even to spend a week in the Oxford house, was a terrible ordeal. Luckily I was away most of the year at school, but it was difficult not to notice the crumbling fabric of my parent's relationship. There was no affection left. They lived almost separate lives and on the few occasions they did meet they were barely civil to each other. My mother, luckily, had achieved enough success with her book illustrations to make her greatly in demand and she rarely emerged from her studio. Bernard too, was busy with his books and his lectures. However in the last couple of years there had been another problem to contend with. Bernard's drinking. This was like a great black cloud that hung over the house. He tended to have several days on the drink and then, after these bouts, he would go back to normal. Just as we would be getting used to the normality he would go off on another 'bender', as Dolly would call them. During these benders, life became impossible for those who had to live with him. He would be unpredictable, unpleasant and nearly always violent in some way. It wasn't physical violence towards my mother, but he would break things, such as china, furniture, or whatever came to hand. Audrey did her best to remove any bottles she found, but Bernard had his own cunning hiding places and Oxford is well equipped with wine merchants and he purchased whatever he wanted. It was a losing battle, but we did try desperately to save him from disgracing himself in public. Thankfully most of his drinking was done in private, but there was the odd occasion when it wasn't.

Dolly later told me that it was due to a drunken scene that he was asked to leave the school. This dismissal sobered him up for a while but inevitably it all started again.

There was a definite pattern to these drinking bouts. They were nearly always triggered off by some chance remark, usually quite trivial and often something he had misheard. To me it seemed he was almost waiting for an excuse. On one occasion my mother made a chance remark about an article in the paper about Sir Stafford Cripps, one of Bernard's great heroes. Although my mother assured Bernard she was only pointing out the article, he immediately flew into a rage, 'You implied you agreed with the bloody fool who wrote it. You don't know the first thing about him. He's the only decent politician we have. Bloody fools the whole lot of you.' On and on it went and we were powerless to stop it. The whisky would be poured and he'd sway around, getting more and more aggressive with his shouting, bantering, sneering, until finally he would take the bottles to his study. There he would remain, and after some violent throwing and kicking of things, he would start muttering to himself."

Dr Strutter's eyebrows went up. "Muttering?"

"Yes. It would go on for hours. Always the same sort of speech patterns, over and over again, things like, 'they don't realize who I am… when I was fighting the fascists in Spain….they forget about the hunger marches…' on it went for hours. It was like a huge anger at the start and then he would become sorry for himself. 'I'm surrounded by fools…nobody understands me…' until finally there would be silence. Later he would emerge, pale, unshaven, and shaking. That would be it, over until the next time.

In these circumstances it was not surprising that my mother, who had few friends anyway, rarely invited anyone to the house and nothing would have persuaded me to have anyone to stay. Unfortunately Bernard liked to be sociable and would often invite people over for a drink and very occasionally for a meal. On these occasions we would all pray that it didn't coincide with one of his drinking bouts.

I found it a frightening experience to watch my father become a disgusting monster in front of me. I have since been wary of any male who drinks excessively."

Dr Strutter made no comment at this point. I thought he might ask me about George's drinking habits, but he didn't, so I continued.

"On the day in question I had returned late from the library to find my mother in a pretty worried state. I knew at once from her expression what had happened. She'd told me at breakfast that we had people coming to dinner. Now she informed me that Bernard had been drinking heavily most of the day and there were still a few hours to go before the guests were due to arrive. I asked what had set him off. She wasn't sure but thought it might have been a letter from his publishers which had angered him. I then nervously inquired where he was now. Apparently he'd gone out and my mother angrily said she hoped he didn't come back. For a while it seemed her prayers might have been answered. The evening started without him. Even so, it was rather embarrassing as I hardly knew any of the people he'd invited and Audrey was fluttering around like a nervous bird and kept disappearing into the kitchen leaving me to cope on my own.

The one man I vaguely knew was called Howard. He'd been on the Council with Bernard. I handed him a sherry, saying feebly that Bernard had been delayed at work. He smiled in an ingratiating way and said in a smarmy voice, 'It must be wonderful for you Celia to have such fascinating parents.' I nodded politely and he continued, 'I mean, there is your father, such a brilliant man and your mother, a genius with the paintbrush. So what does the clever daughter do eh?' I felt very embarrassed and said reluctantly, 'I like music. I play the piano.' He looked triumphant. 'You see? I knew it would be something artistic! What a talented family. So you play the piano. When are we going to see you on the concert platform eh?' I was floundering around for an answer when the door burst open and Bernard made his entrance. He staggered in with two bottles of wine under his arm. It must have been obvious to everyone the state he was in. His cardigan had stains all down it and the buttons were done up wrong, his flies were undone, his face flushed, his expression glazed, his walk unsteady and he reeked of booze.

'There you all are' he boomed. 'Sorry to be late. Getting in a spot of the old vino.

Can't do without the old vino can we.' He lurched towards Howard. 'You'll like this one Howard. It'll remind you of those Council lunches. Remember those Council lunches Howard? You used to get well oiled.' He gave a roar of laughter and stood swaying, trying hard to focus on Howard whose face had gone a strange shade of purple. Bernard beamed benevolently at each of the guests and then launched himself towards the drinks table. Audrey intercepted him and rescued a bottle of wine which was about to fall. 'We have wine on the table Bernard.' And she turned to the guests, 'I think now Bernard's here we'll go through.' Bernard clutched at the drinks table to steady himself.

'Right you are old dear. Anything you say.' With difficulty he gathered the remaining bottles and carried them into the dining room banging them on the table. Everyone shuffled to the nearest place and sat down. Bernard started to poke at the food.

'What is this muck?' My mother told him it was avocado salad. 'Rabbit's food' he said rudely. 'Anyone would think we were a lot of rabbits. Don't you agree Margery?'

He addressed himself to a starchy woman sitting on his right who said stiffly, 'Personally Bernard, I find avocado salad quite delicious.' He turned on her, 'Then you're another bloody rabbit aren't you'. 'Bernard!' my mother's reproach was sharp. He waved an airy hand and we ate on in silence. The moment the eating stopped, my mother asked me to collect the plates and disappeared to the kitchen. Bernard pushed his plate away uneaten and staggered to his feet. 'You're going to enjoy this claret Howard.' After several attempts he managed to uncork it and swayed round the table aiming it at people's glasses. 'Oops. Sorry my dear. I'll come back in a minute and mop up the spillages.' He went on round the table. It was a nightmare to watch. No-one spoke.

We were all waiting for a major accident. 'You'll enjoy this one Howard.' 'So you keep saying Bernard.' Howard's voice would have cut through ice, but

Barnard didn't notice. Audrey meanwhile had brought in the second course. At last Bernard sat down and sniffed at the food in front of him. 'French muck,' he said. 'Why can't we have plain English food? Beef and two veg. That's what I like. English food.' Someone timidly ventured, 'You like French wine.' Bernard exploded. 'Of course I like French wine. Are you suggesting I give you English wine?' What sort of host do you take me for?' Audrey said, 'I thought you'd like this Bernard. You usually like Mrs Baker's food.' He poked at the plate and said crossly, 'She doesn't usually give me French muck.' There was another silence and then someone turned to me. 'You go to boarding school don't you Celia? How are you enjoying yourself?' Before I could answer, Bernard shouted, 'Enjoy herself? She's not meant to enjoy herself. I'm not paying all those fees so that she can enjoy herself. She's there to be educated.' He looked around and said gloomily, 'Although a fat chance our children have of getting a decent education these days. The whole system's gone to pot.' Nobody felt brave enough to contradict him. Instead Howard said, 'You ought to be proud of Celia Bernard. I hear she's going to be a pianist. I only wish I had a daughter.' Bernard snorted scornfully, 'Daughters! What use are daughters? My secretary's more use to me than my daughter.' He slopped a lot more wine into his glass and said in a maudlin way. 'She's wonderful to me my secretary. Wonderful'. There was more than one person in the room who suspected the nature of Bernard's relationship with his secretary. I stared at my plate. There was a shocked silence, broken by Bernard roaring with laughter. 'Have you heard the latest about old Professor Wilson?' My heart sank. I knew all about Professor Wilson. Indeed, Bernard had talked about little else all week. 'Poor old bugger. Really caught with his trousers down this time! Might as well have been at in the middle of the Quad!' And he gave another roar of laughter. 'Bernard!' Once again my mother's voice was sharp, but failed to make any impression.

The meal dragged on. It seemed an eternity. I didn't dare catch anyone's eye.

Bernard continued with his unsavory monologue, sometimes losing track of his own stories, saying, 'Where was I?' and when nobody sprang to his help, he would continue, embellishing them with 'bloody this and bloody that.' If anyone tried to speak he just shouted them down. Someone left the room saying, 'I'm sorry Audrey, I can't take any more of this.' My mother followed, turning back to say, 'Celia, you make the coffee?'

Bernard stood up and swayed round the table with more wine. Most people put their hands over their glasses. It made no difference, he poured just the same. As I left to make the coffee I heard Bernard saying, 'Where's everyone going? Why's everyone leaving? We haven't finished the wine.' By the time the coffee was made, the guests were by the front door. I could hear Audrey's apologies. 'I'm so sorry. He's been overdoing it lately. He's very overtired.' There were murmurs of 'Quite, quite. We understand. Lovely meal Audrey. Thank you so much. Good night. Good night.'

I walked back into the dining room. Bernard was slumped in his chair. Audrey walked past me and stood in front of him. She was white and shaking and she shouted,

'How could you Bernard? How could you?'

I could take no more. Without waiting to hear Bernard's reply, I ran out of the house and fled over to Dolly's. Here I was met with a peaceful scene. She and Tinker were sitting by the fire, listening to music. Tinker was doing the crossword, Dolly was sewing.

'Oh Dolly' I wailed, and poured out an account of the evening's events. When I had finished Dolly looked at Tinker and said, 'What did I tell you? It had to happen sooner or later.' She turned back to me. 'Who was at the dinner? I told her there was no-one I really knew, except someone called Howard who used to be on the Council. Dolly groaned. 'Oh Lord. It will all be over Oxford in the morning. He has an awful wife called Margery.' I nodded. 'Yes, she was there as well. Actually Bernard was terribly rude to her and she left the room.' Dolly made a hopeless gesture, 'Well that's it. She's the biggest gossip in town, and malicious. This means that Bernard will definitely have to go to Waverley Hall.' I knew that Waverley Hall was a sort of drying out place for alcoholics. Several of Bernard's academic chums had already paid visits to the place.

Dolly suddenly looked worried. 'How's Audrey? Is she all right? I shook my head. 'No. She was terribly upset and angry. Well, hysterical really. It was awful. I think they were about to have an almighty row when I left.' Dolly said, 'Oh duck. How dreadful. Do you want to stay the night?' Reluctantly I decided against it. 'Thank you, but I'd better get back. There's all the clearing up to do. And I'm worried about Audrey.' Tinker gave me a hug and in his stuttering way said that I should come back later if I wanted to. It was some comfort.

On reaching our kitchen it was immediately obvious that nothing had been touched. So I went into the dining room. Bernard had gone, but my mother was still there. It took me some moments to work out what was happening. She was pacing up and down muttering to herself. She had a bottle of whisky in one hand and a paper knife in the other. On seeing me she put the bottle to her mouth and took several large gulps. Not surprisingly she was reeling. Audrey never touched spirits, well, she hardly drank at all. Now here she was with at least half a bottle consumed. With difficulty she managed to say in a voice that was heavily slurred, 'Tell your father I wish to see him. I'll show him! I'll show him what it is like when people are drunk!' She swayed so violently I thought she was going to fall. In complete panic I ran to the study and for the first time in my life I didn't knock. Bernard was asleep in his chair. Hysterical with fear I started to shake him. 'Wake up Bernard. Wake up. It's Audrey! Wake up!

Something in my voice must have penetrated his fuddled brain. He opened his eyes and said, 'Wassa matter?' I shook him again and shouted at the top of my voice, 'It's Audrey. You must come quickly.' I pulled him to his feet and he staggered after me into the dining room. As soon as she saw him, Audrey lunged at him with the paper knife. It missed Bernard but threw her off balance and she fell to her knees shouting, 'I'll show you what it's like to be drunk. I'll show you. I'll show you.' She was crying, swaying around on her knees, looking like a madwoman. I started to cry.

Bernard's voice cut through my fear. He was suddenly completely sober and calm as he barked out stern orders. 'Take one side of your mother Celia. We must get her upstairs.'

He took the bottle out of her hand. 'How much of this has she drunk?' I told him I thought she had drunk nearly the whole bottle.' He nodded grimly, 'She'll be very sick then. Help me up the stairs with her.'

How we reached her bedroom I will never know. She was a dead weight and had turned a nasty greyish-green colour. Bernard said sharply, 'Fetch me a basin and some wet towels.' I did as I was told.

When I returned she hadn't moved. I sobbed, 'She's dead isn't she?' I think he did his best to calm me but he did look worried. 'No, no. She'll be all right. You go to bed. I'll stay with her.'

I lay in bed, shivering with shock, unable to sleep. I hated my life, my parents, the scenes, the drinking. The tears rolled down my cheeks until I eventually slept through sheer exhaustion.

Next morning Bernard told me that my mother would recover, but that she had severe alcoholic poisoning and was to remain in bed for several days.

When I went to say goodbye to her I was really shocked by her appearance. She was deathly pale, her hair tangled and untidy and her eyes were ringed with black. But I think it was her expression that shocked me most of all. It was blank and despairing. I sat on the bed and said awkwardly, 'I'm sure I shouldn't be leaving you like this Audrey. I could easily stay here a bit longer, until you are feeling better.' Her voice was surprisingly firm. 'Nonsense Celia, you can do no good by staying here. You go and have a nice time with your cousins. I insist.'

I wanted to say something to comfort her but couldn't find the words. At last I blurted out. 'I am so sorry Audrey. About everything I mean.'

She gave a wan smile. 'It's all right you know. Bernard's had a fright. He will behave himself for a while.' For the first time she didn't even try to make excuses for him.

'Life will go on,' she said sadly and turned her face to the wall. 'Life will go on,' she repeated and I could tell she was crying.

At that moment I knew with horrible certainty that she didn't care if her life went on or not. She had finally given up."

I looked down and realized I had been twisting a handkerchief in my lap. I blew my nose and said as briskly as I could manage, "So there you have it. You see? She wasn't suicidal either, but she did have the same feelings of despair."

I shrugged. "What the hell. She was right. Life does go on."

Dr Strutter stroked the knees of his trousers and then put his hands together under his chin and regarded me thoughtfully.

"So, if that was the last parallel you are going to tell me, what are your feelings about them now?"

I was exhausted and couldn't really think lucidly. "I don't really know. I feel as if I am living in some kind of limbo, waiting for the next parallel to happen I suppose."

He stood up and smiled at me, "I think while you're waiting for that to happen, it would be helpful to examine those parallels more closely. We can pick it up after the summer holidays if that would be good for you?."

I was relieved he wanted to continue to see me and just hoped fervently that George wouldn't be difficult.

I also stood up. "I'd like that, but I am going to be away for almost the entire eight weeks."

He nodded. "Just ring Mrs Maitland to make the appointment when you are back."

I walked to the door, turned back and said, "Have a good summer."

He smiled. "You too."

He was at the window watching me as I climbed into the car.

I know it sounds a little ridiculous, but there was something almost sexual about this little ritual. Maybe it was partly because of this that for the first time I waved to him.

He waved back and was still there as I turned the corner into Devonshire Place.

The end of the ninth session.

INTERLUDE

It was a long hot summer, one of the hottest on record. The farmers complained about their wilting crops and holiday makers in the West Country were reduced to the use of one bucket of water a day. England's green and pleasant land became brown and parched. The cities were humid and unbearable and as the temperature soared, so tempers became frayed. Patience and politeness were things of the past. Wimbledon came and went, with both players and spectators suffering from heat exhaustion. The Test Matches were unremarkable, except for the fact that rain for once didn't stop play. Only towards the end of August did the weather break and then it was with massive thunder storms.

For Celia, all the heat was a blessing. She had removed herself from Civolds to Norfolk for the whole of August and for once she didn't suffer the usual pangs of unbearable cold. Maddie had organized a piano room for her use and here she had plenty of time to herself. Nor did she have to worry about Natasha, who was surrounded by children of her own age and happily re-united with Livvy, of whose company she never seemed to tire. To add to all this, George had remained in Civolds, ostensibly to supervise the new buildings on the science block. He also explained to Celia that the last place he wanted to be was in the crumbling ruins of what had once been an elegant family home. However Celia suspected the real reason for him remaining at Civolds was to be near his latest female attachment, a fact that didn't worry her in the slightest. She was relieved to have four weeks away from him.

A few days before they were due to leave Norfolk, the weather changed. The blue skies turned to grey and the heat, almost overnight, disappeared.

The British summer returned to normal. Celia's buoyant mood gradually evaporated during their return drive. The car, unlike the weather, was over-heating and they had to stop every twenty miles to let the engine cool down. In spite of Natasha's endless cheerful chatter she felt exhausted and stressed by the time they arrived at the house.

As she turned into the drive the familiar feelings of gloom swept over her. George showed little enthusiasm at their arrival back and as Natasha left almost immediately to see one of her friends, Celia and George were let to share a dismal meal together. It was as if she hadn't been away at all. Conversation was stilted. He looked bored if she tried to tell him about Norfolk and hostile when she asked him about his summer. In the end she pleaded exhaustion and made her escape.

Once in her room she took out the black book from the drawer and re-read the accounts of her sessions with Dr Strutter. It was actually a surprisingly good read and because she had put in the dialogue, it leapt off the page. What a huge amount she had covered in only nine sessions. But what was there left to say? No amount of comment or advice from Dr Strutter could make any difference to her life. She snapped the book shut and put it away. She was in limbo land and had to put up with it, just like poor Audrey.

She kicked off her shoes and lay on the bed. Bloody Bernard and bloody George.

There was no escape from either, for her or her mother. They just had to accept it.

They were caught in the parallel lines of life. Fat chance of a 'breakaway'. She wished she'd never heard the bloody song.

During the following few days she busied herself getting Natasha ready for school.

Between her and George there was a civil politeness nothing more. Occasionally, when there was a slightly sharper exchange Celia caught Natasha giving her a critical look, but decided not to pursue this further. She really didn't want to discuss with her daughter, her relationship with George. Not yet anyway. When Natasha was older she might be able to understand all the complexities.

Term began and soon after George announced he would be bringing back a couple of new masters for supper. Nothing unusual about that, he made a habit of welcoming new members of staff. However this was Sarah Lodden's madrigal night, which would make her a little late back. When she informed him of this, he looked annoyed and remarked sarcastically he was sure they would manage until she was able to join them.

To avoid further sarcasm she made her best effort to be back as early as she could.

In spite of this, George was already with the masters having drinks when she arrived. Flustered from rushing she didn't really take in the name of the first master, but when she shook the hand of the second, she felt the strangest sensation. It was if she had suddenly been transported to another existence. It wasn't so much that time stood still. It was if it didn't exist at all. As if from a distance she heard George say, "Celia, this is Euan Mackay who has joined the English department. Apparently he knows a cousin of yours." She looked at the man shaking her hand. He was a stranger and yet it seemed there was instant recognition between them.

After what seemed a long time, but was actually only a moment, he let go of her hand. She tried to keep her voice calm. "So which cousin is it that you know?"

George at once became bored and walked away leaving them together.

Euan Mackay spoke with a slight Scottish accent. He explained he had been at Cambridge with Wal and although a good deal younger they had over-lapped because Wal had done his National Service. Celia started to reply and found her words coming out in a rush. "Luke, Wal's younger brother, also missed National Service. I think Wal must have been in the very last batch. Did he tell you that he and Luke persecuted me quite dreadfully when we were children? They were truly horrible to me. Actually I haven't seen either of them for some time but I hear Wal is very successful."

She stopped, realizing she was talking a lot of waffle and gave an embar-rassed laugh.

"Anyway, I am quite sure Wal didn't have anything good to say about me."

Euan Mackay smiled. "On the contrary, he told me you were glamorous. I told him I was coming here and he said, 'You will meet my glamorous cousin Celia.' Those were his exact words."

Celia wrinkled her nose in surprise. "Good heavens you do amaze me."

And to cover any further embarrassment she asked, "Do you see Wal often?"

He nodded. "Quite often. I am godfather to one of his children."

Celia's eyes widened, "How extraordinary. I hesitate to use the cliché, but it really is a small world." She broke off. What on earth had made her say something so crass and stupid? Luckily George came round at that moment and filled up their glasses with champagne. After he left, Euan looked down at his and remarked dryly, "This is all very lavish." Celia gave a laugh, "Oh it's only the best with George," and there was a hint of sarcasm in her voice. Euan gave her a strange look.

She quickly asked, "Do you know my cousin Luke as well?"

He replied that he'd only met him once or twice but knew that he had the reputation of being rather brilliant. Celia laughed. "They do tell me so. He just seems slightly mad to me. Euan again smiled. "Eccentric perhaps." She looked straight at him for the first time. "Are you Scots?" He threw back his head and laughed. "With my name and accent that's very percep- tive of you." Celia also laughed. "I'm sorry. Of course you are. I don't know Scotland very well. Which part do you come from?" He told her he was from a little village on the West Coast just north of Oban. He added that his father had been the minister and that his mother had run the village school.

So it went on, just trivial, idle chatter, but Celia felt overwhelmed by him. She couldn't think straight and her usual cool, sophisticated manner, that had taken her so long to cultivate, now deserted her. She tried to play her prac- ticed role of headmaster's wife, but found it impossible. Tonight she felt as if there were only two people in the room, Euan Mackay and herself.

After the masters had departed George said, "So what did you make of Euan Mackay? I noticed you talking to him quite a lot." "He seems very pleasant." Celia ventured cautiously. As usual George didn't listen to her but continued, "He has a pretty good track record, in spite of being a grammar school product." That was typical of George and Celia frowned with annoy- ance. He was always talking of people as 'products'. It was 'public school product' or 'state school product' and he usually didn't have much time for the latter. If George noticed her irritation he didn't show it but went on, "He had scholarships all the way I believe, a first at Cambridge and a rugby blue as well."

"He sounds too good to be true." Celia remarked with mild sarcasm, but this was lost on George who was by now in full flow. "I'm told Mackay is a writer too, scripts for television. I've suggested he write a new school play for us." He poured himself another whisky, casually adding, "I told him you would do the music for it."

Celia's voice rose in panic. "George, I couldn't possibly do that. I'm not a composer."

George slammed down the decanter. "Nonsense. I'm always hearing you fiddling around with tunes on the piano."

"But, that's quite different. And I don't write them down."

Annoyed by this response George said, "Well, I'm sure you can manage a few tunes. Nothing complicated. Mackay seemed keen on the idea."

He started to leave the room and then turned back, "Did you notice the way the man bolted his food. I know dinner was late, but he behaved as if he was half starved."

Celia smiled and said as a joke, "I expect he lived on a sparse diet when he was young."

George missed the humour and said sharply, "Do you mean he came from the slums?"

"No" she replied with a certain impatience, "not the slums. But I imagine he was brought up in somewhat Spartan circumstances. He's a minister's son, from a small village in Scotland." George seemed strangely relieved by this. "He's certainly quite presentable. Good looking fellow. That should send a flutter around the female staff."

With which Parthian shot he departed.

Celia thought about this. Was he good looking? She hadn't really noticed what he looked like and now tried to recall something about Euan's face. His eyes were the only thing she really remembered because they were a steely grey blue. She did recall his hands. They were finely shaped and strong. And his touch, which had given her that strange lurching feeling in her loins. She shivered. It was ridiculous. She had probably imagined the whole thing.

The next day, to clear her head, she decided on a walk.

About three miles from the school there was a steep hill and it had become a habit with her to climb to the top and then sit under a great oak tree to admire the 'coloured counties' stretching out in front of her. She was out of breath as she neared the top and slowed down. At this moment she caught sight of Euan Mackay, sitting under the tree.

"Hello" he said as she approached, and the same feelings that had overwhelmed her the night before hit her with a force that was startling.

"Hello" she panted, hoping she just sounded as if she was out of breath.

"Come and sit down. There's an amazing view from here."

She walked the last few yards to join him. "I know. As a matter of fact this is my favourite spot and I look on this tree as my property. I visit it as often as I can."

She sat down beside him and saw that he was smiling, "That's a coincidence. I spent a holiday near here once and discovered this place. Perhaps we could share it during the term?" This made her laugh. "Of course."

They remained silent for quite a while, just listening to the birdsong and watching the September sun make its watery way through the Autumn mist. With George any silence seemed threatening and hostile, but not with Euan.

Suddenly he turned to her. "George tells me you are a musician."

Celia felt a flash of annoyance.

"I wouldn't say that, I just play the piano." "But you compose?" Euan asked.

The panic started to rise again. Damn bloody George. She said rather feebly,

"I wouldn't call it composing, I just dabble." Euan nodded. "Good then you can dabble with some music for the school play I'm putting together. It will need a few numbers." Celia mumbled that she wasn't sure but Euan brushed her fears aside telling her it would be fine, so against her better judgment she agreed.

Another silence ensued which she finally broke by asking, "Have you known George long?" He chewed on a piece of grass. "Not really. I met him about six months ago, at a party..." Then he broke off and from his expression Celia realized that George must have been with one of his women at this party and Euan wanted to spare her that.

The sun went in and she shivered. He leapt up. Celia was to get used to these sudden, impulsive movements over the coming months, but at the time it just struck her how different he was from the cold and calculating George. He threw the blade of grass away and pulled her to feet. As she stood opposite him he held on to her hand in a fierce, strong grip and in that moment she knew, with absolute certainty, her life would never be the same again.

After that, things progressed pretty rapidly. It took three weeks for Celia to admit to herself that she had fallen in love with Euan Mackay and once she accepted this fact she gave herself over to it entirely and was amazed by the strength of these sudden emotions. It could not be denied. She had fallen totally, absolutely and hopelessly in love. Euan now became an obsession. She could think of nothing and nobody else. Her nights were spent wondering what sex with him would feel like, and these thoughts, although titillating made her a little nervous. There was no doubt in her mind that it would happen, but wouldn't Euan find her hopelessly inexperienced? She remembered with horror the demands George had made of her, demands which she had refused, finding them totally repugnant. In the end their love-making, if you could call it that, had been brutally swift and had always left her with feelings of hopeless inadequacy.

Since sleeping alone, any carnal thoughts she'd had were rare and quickly suppressed. Of course she had read novels and seen films, both full of erotic scenes, but although enjoyable, she had felt quite detached from it. That is until now. Now she thought of little else.

Another thought disturbed her. What was she to do about Dr Strutter? The very idea of telling him about this latest development filled her with alarm. He would almost certainly dismiss it as an infatuation or a schoolgirl crush. There was simply no point in putting herself through that sort of humiliation. After dithering for a couple of weeks she finally rang Mrs Maitland and told her it would not be possible to visit Dr Strutter in the foreseeable future. She then told George of this decision, giving as her reason the work on the school play. He seemed genuinely pleased with the way things were working out. Sometimes Celia felt surprised that he hadn't noticed her obsession with Euan. But then George never really noticed her at all, until she did something to annoy him. So she put this worry aside. Now she lived only for the moments she spent with Euan and her life took on a dreamy, unreal quality.

A week before half-term George announced that he had to be in London for the weekend. He didn't offer an explanation, nor did Celia ask for one. However she was quick to impart the news of George's departure to Euan. He promptly asked her over for supper at the cottage, which he stayed in during term time.

They ate and they drank, but neither of them really noticed what they were eating or drinking and hardly had they finished the meal when they fell into bed and more or less stayed there until Sunday night.

At one point Euan remarked, "Having sex with you is like taking the cork out of a champagne bottle."

For Celia, it wasn't so much the explosive quality of their love-making, it was the sense of release. The power of her passion and the abandonment with which she flung herself into it, had taken her by surprise. No longer was she repelled or frightened. The inhibitions she had previously felt completely disappeared. From the moment Euan had stripped her naked and started to touch her she gave way to every feeling and sensation. For the first time in her life she was a person who could *feel*.

It was all very alien to her, but she was overwhelmingly and deliriously happy.

Euan too seemed to take a delight in driving her further and further into frenzied delights.

At first he was gentle and considerate only too aware of her damaged sexual past, but no longer. At one point he said rather wonderingly "I have never fallen in lust quite like this before." Celia didn't care whether it was lust or love. She just wanted it to go on and never stop. Dolly had certainly been right about her needing a passionate love affair.

So fast and furiously had it all happened she never anticipated any of the complications that were to follow. Naively she thought that now she was at last happy, she would remain so, and for a while this seemed to be the case, with no dark clouds on the horizon.

One lunch time, as they were lying side by side under the oak tree, Euan asked, "How long have you been so unhappy" For some reason she went on the defensive and asked him why he thought she was. Euan rolled over and gave her a long look.

"The first time I saw you I thought, 'That's a really beautiful woman, but why is she so bloody unhappy?' Aren't I right?"

Celia shrugged. "Most people would say I was in an enviable position. I'm the wife of a successful headmaster, with a lovely daughter, large house, plenty of money. I have no right to be unhappy."

Euan looked almost angry. "For God's sake Celia, you're just telling me what you *have*, not how you *feel*. Not what you *are*. Don't you see? Your whole life is a fucking charade, it's just play-acting, and the sooner you face up to that the better it will be."

He turned away, leaving her to take that in. Her first feelings were of anger and surprise that he could sound so cruel, and then, rather miserably she began to accept that what he said was probably true. For a long time she had been in denial. Euan had held the mirror up and she didn't like what she saw. She had no words but remained silent and downcast, her miserable life welling up before her. He turned back watching her in silence.

Suddenly she burst into tears and before long this turned into a howl. Once she started she couldn't stop. She howled and howled. Euan said nothing until the heaving sobs began to subside. Then he took her in his arms and dried her tears with a large handkerchief. "So practical," she said almost crossly. He smiled but his expression quickly changed. "Why don't you tell me about it? I imagine life with George is pretty good hell, but there's obviously more to your misery than that."

She tentatively started to tell him the things she had told Dr Strutter and then finally it poured out of her like a torrent; Bernard, Audrey, her childhood, Wal, Luke, Dolly, George, even her parallels theory. He laughed at those, "It sounds like bloody Dallas in Oxfordhire." Celia looked sulky, "I knew you'd mock me." Euan was immediately contrite. "Believe me, I'm not mocking you. I find the whole saga fucking unbearable."

There was silence for a while and then he stood up pulling her to her feet and he kissed her gently as if soothing away her pain. She swayed against him feeling some comfort.

"It'll be all right," he said and then gave a short laugh. "Let's face it, it couldn't be much worse!" Celia gave a wan smile, but for the first time in her life she felt a glimmer of hope about the future. If Euan said it would be all right, then it had to be.

She now sought his opinion on everything, even George. "Seriously Euan, I want to know what you think of him. I mean do you like him?"

He took a long time to answer and she instinctively knew that there was a great deal he could say about George but probably wanted to spare her feelings.

At last he said, "I don't trust him. He's too bloody calculated."

Celia persisted, "But apart from that what do you think of him?"

She knew Euan well enough already to know he didn't like this sort of cross examination, but it suddenly seemed important for her to know his opinion of George.

There was another long pause. Finally he said, "If I'm honest I have to admit in many ways I have a sort of reluctant admiration for the man. He's a good headmaster, no getting away from that. Look how he's put this old fashioned, antiquated place of education on the map."

Celia laughed, "If Civolds is so terrible, why are you here?"

Euan shrugged and said sourly, "Believe me, if I didn't need the job I wouldn't be."

She knew of his ambitions to be a writer, so let that one go.

He seemed lost in thought for a while but suddenly said, "I'll tell you what I think about George. He's bloody ambitious, ruthless too. Every move he makes is carefully thought out. If he makes a decision it has to be in his interest, even if his motives are suspect." He paused, "I think he's too canny to make a mistake, but if he does it could be a fucking disaster. He likes to live dangerously, does George, and that is always interesting."

Celia smiled to herself. She noticed that Euan always used strong language when he was worked up or annoyed about something. At first she had been a bit shocked. Apart from the occasional 'bloody' or 'damn' from Bernard and George she had been unused to anything stronger. Somehow, she thought, it was less offensive in a Scottish accent.

Euan burst through her thoughts and he sounded angry, "To answer your original question Celia, no, I don't like him. In fact I bloody hate the man. I hate what he's done to you for a start. He's using you. You're just part of his image. He treats you like a fucking possession, not a wife. Nobody has the right to use another human being like that. It's fucking prostitution. And there are other things I dislike about George. I despise his values, his arrogance and his cruelty. He's a snob and he has no integrity. I know George will always come out on top, he's a winner and the man gets away with it every time, which makes me dislike him even more."

His anger surprised her as she said sadly, "I thought I was practically on my own in my opinion of George, although my aunt, Dolly, disliked him from the start."

She noticed Euan's jaw was still clenched. He burst out again, "It's the sheer bloody hypocrisy of the man. I hate the way he say 'my wife this' and 'darling that' as if you were the most devoted couple in the world. Even if I didn't know what I do about your relationship, a great many of us know about his womanizing and his drinking."

She was startled. "His drinking? I didn't think anyone noticed that. He's very discreet about it. Not like my father." Euan gave a wry smile. "If he keeps it discreet he might be all right. But George is a flawed character. There's a weakness in him somewhere. One day one of those weaknesses will betray him." He stopped for a moment and when he spoke again it was in more measured tones. "In fact, it's you who could be the cause of George's downfall." This took her completely aback. "Me? No, no. You have that wrong. He doesn't care a jot for me." Euan frowned. "As a person, probably not, but as a possession he does. You are his prize possession. He cares about that. If you left him it would seriously dent his ego." He looked at her and said firmly, "You'll have to do it Celia. At the moment your life is a lie and you are just going along with it, the nice little headmaster's wife, with the nice little easy life. You play along with the snobbery, the middle class values, the whole fucking chicanery and to make matters worse you are bloody miserable as well." He broke off as if he didn't trust himself to speak further.

Celia stared ahead and felt shock wave go through her. It was all very well for Euan to say she should leave George, but how could she? She was trapped in this way of life and there was no way out. She had no money of her own and no way of getting a job. She was dependent on him. He'd made sure of that. And then there was Natasha to think of as well. It was that wretched 'parallel line' – like mother, like daughter.

They sat on, side by side, under the oak tree. It was a misty, autumnal day and there was a steamy, mushroomy smell of damp leaves. The gentle melancholy went well with her mood. Euan's outburst had stirred up a quagmire of emotions that she had tried hard to keep buried. Was he suggesting she should leave George to live with him? She didn't think so and in any case that seemed premature. She sighed.

No more thinking, she'd had enough of a battering for one day.

Euan heard the sigh and put his arm round her. "I'll tell you something. George is a bloody fascinating character. Wonderful novel fodder, or perhaps a play? I'd call it 'The Pack of Cards'. It would be about this man who built up his success slowly, carefully perching one card precariously on top of the other, until, whoosh… one card is removed and the whole fucking lot comes tumbling down."

Celia laughed, "Not very original." He gave her a shove. "It would all be in the writing."

That particular conversation had an unsettling effect on Celia. For the first time she became aware of the demands George made on her time and how this now threatened her relationship with Euan. Time and again she would be forced into making her apologies. "Sorry Euan, I can't see you tonight, George has asked people over." Or, "I can't be with you tomorrow, George wants me to give tea to the new boys."

Each time this happened she would be aware that Euan's face took on a shut expression. It wasn't that he was sulking exactly, or even upset. It was something deeper than that and it frightened her, conscious that she might lose him. Even when she did manage to get away she spent a good deal of time looking at her watch, in a panic that she would be late back and George would start to get suspicious.

"I honestly think George is purposely making extra demands on me," she remarked crossly one day. Euan looked a little alarmed, "Don't be bloody silly. Why should he? He doesn't suspect anything about us does he?" Celia shook her head. "I don't think anyone has noticed us, which is quite a feat in such a tight knit community."

She would never have admitted it to Euan, but part of her longed for everyone to know about them. However, it was only by keeping it a secret that the affair could continue, and the strain that caused was worth it just for that.

It was at this time, something else started to trouble Celia, something she had never experienced before. It was jealousy. The 'green-eyed monster' now moved into her life with a vengeance and began to take it over. It was like an illness, but one for which there was no cure. She only had to hear Euan's name linked with another woman and she felt the urge to scream out loud, 'You're wrong, he's mine!'

Things came to a head with a chance remark from George at breakfast.

"I've got some gossip for you." His little piggy eyes lit up with excitement. He loved gossip, especially the more malicious variety. Celia asked him wearily what it was.

"I think Helen Ainsworth has fallen for Euan Mackay. She blushes every time he comes into the staff room. Not that I think he's noticed. He's an arrogant bastard. Most grammar school types are." Celia ignored the latter remark and tried to sound as if she hadn't been hit very hard in the solar plexus. "Helen Ainsworth? I don't think I know her. What does she look like?" George said in a rather dismissive way, "Young, pretty, dark haired, with a damn good figure. I think the blighter should give it a go. I might try and engineer them together. It's always good publicity to have a school wedding."

Celia tried to control a rising sense of panic. "I don't think these contrived relationships really work in this day and age George," and added as casually as she could manage, "What does she teach?" He picked up his paper, "French, but I'm glad to say she takes a good deal of interest in all the school activities. Not like some I could mention…" and he grumbled on about masters not pulling their weight. Celia wasn't listening. Her mind was racing. If this Helen Ainsworth was so pretty surely Euan must have noticed her? He'd never said anything. Perhaps that was a bad sign. What chance did she stand against a pretty, unattached woman?

Her private hell now began. The Ainsworth jealousy became an obsession. Celia watched her every move. A sort of madness possessed her, made worse by the fact that she couldn't possibly mention it to Euan.

The situation finally came to a crisis point on the last day of the Autumn Term.

They had sat through a long Christmas concert. George had asked a selection of governors, staff, boys and their parents, back to the house afterwards. This was always a ghastly affair with non-alcoholic punch and soggy mince-pies.

It was even more of an ordeal this year because Celia happened to know that Euan had been asked to a party, being thrown by Helen Ainsworth. George had spoken about the clash of engagements with some annoyance.

The evening now became a nightmare for her. At the end of the concert the staff who were not coming over to the house came to say their goodbyes. Euan formerly shook her by the hand. Shook her by the hand! And after he had gone she had to try and behave normally, entertaining people she didn't want to be with at all, knowing that Euan was elsewhere at a party, with a very attractive woman, who by all accounts was relentlessly chasing him. It was an agony.

By the time all the guests had gone and they'd had supper, she was convinced she had lost him. Giving George the excuse that she needed some air, she walked over to Euan's cottage. It was nearly midnight, but he clearly was not back. Not daring to stay out any longer, she returned to the house and spent the night consumed with jealous imaginings.

The next day, on a cold December afternoon, she walked up to the oak tree.

Euan was already there and looked up as she approached and remarked drily,

"I thought I might see you here today."

His tone annoyed her and she burst out, "You obviously had a good time last night."

He replied calmly, "Yes I did. It was a very enjoyable party." This goaded her to say, "It must have been, judging by how late you stayed out."

She knew this would annoy him, and it did. When he spoke it was obvious he was having difficulty in controlling his temper and his Scottish accent was even more pronounced than usual. "It may not have occurred to you Celia, that what I do with my time, and with whom, is my business and my fucking business only. What we are to each other gives you no fucking rights over my time, or what I do with it. None whatsoever. Your life is still bound by George. My life is bound by nobody. So there is no point in you indulging in pathetic jealousy."

She winced. He had never been so cruel to her before, nor had she seen him so obviously angry, but she was too overwhelmed by her own feelings to stop now.

"You didn't think it would matter to me if you stayed out all night with another woman?"

His voice was now calm, but controlled. "I didn't stay out all night. Not that it's any of your business. I actually got back here about three." Before she could stop herself Celia screamed, "What the hell were you doing all that time?" His voice was icy cold. "The party went on pretty late, then I stayed on and listened to records."

"With her?"

"If you mean Helen, yes, with her."

Celia's mind began to race. Did he kiss her? He must have kissed her. And what then? A chill ran through her, but she couldn't ask him outright.

"What records did you listen to?" It was all she could think of to say. He laughed then, but it wasn't a pleasant laugh, "Oh Celia, does it really matter?"

She said nothing but the desperation in her face made him relent. "We listened to Beethoven mostly. Helen had a recording I hadn't heard and it was excellent, so as we were rather drunk we played it through several times." He added mockingly, "Hardly a crime was it? All very harmless I assure you."

Celia said nothing, feeling exhausted and somewhat ashamed.

After a few minutes he quipped, "What? No further inquisition?"

She sat down under the tree, miserable and hunched, watching her breath steam out through the chill air. No birdsong, not a sound except in the distance a tolling bell. She thought moodily 'the times are out of joint.' Euan moved a few paces away and stared across the valley lost in thought. She watched him, only aware that she loved him unbearably. The one question she had wanted to ask him, she hadn't been able to.

It tormented her to think of him spending time with another woman, let alone kissing her, or worst of all, sleeping with her. A stab of pain went through her. But he was right. She had no hold over him. There was nothing binding in their relationship. For years she had lived out a lie with George, their life based on secrecy and lies. Now all she longed for was to be with someone she loved and trusted, and stupidly she had angered him and probably blown her one chance of happiness.

The tolling bell ceased. Celia stood up and walked down the hill to join him. He made no move. She longed to touch him, but didn't dare. Miserable and frightened as last she burst out, "I'm sorry Euan. You're right. I shouldn't be jealous. But I just can't help it."

He turned round and seeing the anguish in her face he relented and took her in his arms. Neither spoke for a long time. At last he said, "You stupid bloody woman. Don't you understand? I am jealous too. I can't bear it when you are with George. It's an impossible situation. Wanting you in these circumstances is bloody frustrating. In fact, it's pretty good hell." There was another silence. Although terrified of the answer she at last stammered out, "Are you going to give me up?"

He looked at her. "How can I? You're in here aren't you?" and he put her hand on his heart. It was the nearest he had come to saying he loved her.

Celia now seriously began to think of leaving George.

Chapter 9

The Christmas holiday proved to be the nadir of Celia's existence.

Euan went up to Scotland and his departure left a void, which in no way was filled by her irritable husband and restless daughter. She missed Euan horribly and thought it quite likely George was missing someone too, as he was at his most impossible.

She had never liked Christmas, and this year it seemed even more vulgarly commercial than usual, with all the tinsel, the hype and the piped music blaring out wherever she went. It was no wonder depression soon set in.

In some desperation she rang Euan, but this didn't help either. She knew he disliked the use of the telephone and his replies were monosyllabic. Several long silences followed until finally she asked, "Are you missing me?" His voice was abrupt as he said, "of course." After a few more attempts at conversation she gave up.

Left alone with her frustration she thought crossly that he could have been a bit more forthcoming.. After all, he knew her situation and could at leave have made an effort. Sometimes Euan was a selfish bastard and she might as well accept that fact. If she opted for an existence with him it certainly wouldn't be easy, but quite honestly, she wasn't sure she could live without him now. It was the devil and the deep blue sea syndrome.

Perhaps she should weigh up the pros and cons of a life with Euan.

The pros were easy. She loved him and she was pretty certain he loved her, in his own way. He was clever, funny and he could be kind, understanding and sympathetic - and of course the sex was wonderful. The cons were more difficult. Trying to be realistic she took off the rose coloured spectacles and had to admit to herself that he was moody, and at times, downright prickly. He could also be cruel, she had already witnessed that. There was something of a chip on his shoulder, which made him despise anyone who was remotely privileged. That she found rather tiresome. There was also a sort of Puritan meanness about him which she found puzzling. For instance, he hadn't given her a Christmas present, not even a card. She was aware that he despised frivolous gestures but it would hardly have hurt him to make a small effort and he must have known it would have given her pleasure. So there was selfishness to add to the list. And then, could she trust him? She wanted to, but wasn't even sure of that. There was something about the way he had reacted over the Helen Ainsworth night. Was it all as innocent as he had made it sound?

She sighed. There was no point in wearing herself out over insoluble problems. The days ahead were going to be quite enough of a strain.

She walked down the stairs, to witness a moment of light relief, as George sat down on a bunch of holly. He yelled "What on earth do you think you're doing Celia, leaving these damned decorations lying about?" She tried to look contrite. "I'm sorry George, but I am trying to make the house look its best for the hordes of people you have invited over." George looked irritated. "Try not to exaggerate my dear. The fact that we are having some friends round is no excuse for turning the damned place into a danger zone."

Celia meekly removed the offending holly and reflected that her remark really wasn't an exaggeration. George had been throwing invitations around like confetti and she couldn't help feeling that all this frenzied entertaining was to forestall any likelihood of them being left alone together.

To make matters worse, he insisted Natasha attend all these gatherings and his daughter, usually so easy going, was now in a state of open rebellion. Things came to a head on Christmas Eve when George insisted she stayed in to listen to the Carol Service from King's. Natasha had other plans. She wanted to go down to the local farm. The children there were a fairly wild bunch but Celia thought them harmless enough. George of course disagreed. "She's nearly fourteen now. We should be choosing her companions more carefully. Those farm children are a bad influence on her." Celia thought this ridiculous and rather snobbish and pointed out to George that Natasha would be spending most of her holidays with her cousins, so the odd afternoon at the farm couldn't hurt. But George wouldn't listen, and after a great deal of shouting and argument, Natasha stayed, boot-faced and sulky.

To add insult to injury, the programme was completely ruined by George's running commentary throughout the entire service, with an endless stream of pompous remarks... "Did you know the Provost is a friend of mine?... The standard of the boys seems less good this year...A pity so many of the readers have such bad speaking voices".

On and on it went until Celia was at screaming point.

If Christmas Eve had been bad, Christmas Day plumbed even lower depths. Dolly rang first thing to cancel coming to lunch as Tinker has been taken ill in the night. This was a catastrophe for Celia as they had been the only people she had wanted to see over the holiday, and it had taken a good deal of persuasion to get George to invite them in the first place. The dismal opening of presents that followed a silent breakfast, was not helped by Natasha still sulking from the day before. Celia opened George's present and stared at it with frozen horror. For some reason he hadn't given her the usual cheque. Instead there was a scarlet silk and lace, extremely scanty, underwear set.

Her expression said it all. Natasha left the room.

After she'd gone Celia said icily, "I don't know who you bought these for George, but it certainly wasn't for me." He looked at her with an expression that made her wince,

"Oh but they were Celia. I thought it might put a little zest into your life."

He rubbed his hands together and she knew exactly what he meant. Her voice would have cut through glass. "Then you thought wrong. I suggest you either return them to the shop or find someone more suitable to give them to."

With obvious relief Natasha departed on Boxing Day to ski with her cousins. Celia was left even more isolated as the days dragged on. She went for her usual walks up to the oak tree, and although a relief to be out of the house, it only increased her pain at being without Euan. She dutifully attended all the social engagements George had arranged, and spent the rest of her time carefully avoiding him.

Then, quite unexpectedly, Wal rang, asking them both to a New Year's party. George immediately declined. Celia suspected he was bidden elsewhere as he seemed extremely keen she should go. So she did.

As she entered Wal's house, she knew with certainty that Euan was there.

A minute later he crossed the room and they stood staring at each other. She could hardly breathe. "Where have you come from?" He smiled, "Scotland," and added, "Wal rang and asked me to the party and said you'd be here, without George, so down I came."

She gasped out, "To see me?" "Of course." "You missed me?" "Of course."

"Oh Euan!" In spite of the fact she knew he didn't like demonstrative gestures in public she threw herself into his arms.

Some time later, when she was standing alone, Wal came over. He'd changed a good deal over the years and somehow seemed less frightening, but he still had his funny thin, freckled face with the prominent nose. Celia also noted with some amusement that his auburn hair now had a touch of grey and he was getting a definite paunch.

She complimented him on his house. It wasn't to her personal taste, but she couldn't help but be impressed by its opulence, with its palm trees, marble floors and black leather sofas. He certainly had all the trappings of a successful man and he hadn't stinted on the hospitality either, as the waiter yet again filled her glass with champagne.

Wal eyed her thoughtfully. "So, my beautiful cousin has fallen for Euan Mackay."

A little embarrassed she asked, "How did you know about us?" Wal smiled. "I only had a suspicion before tonight because of Euan's reaction over the telephone. But after I saw you throw yourself into his arms, well, I didn't really have to be Sherlock Holmes."

She laughed, "I suppose not." He looked at her curiously. "What does George have to say about it?" Celia shrugged. "He doesn't actually know." Wal looked startled. "Good heavens. He must either be blind, or absorbed elsewhere. Actually on second thoughts it has to be the latter. George seems to be involved with many of the wives of my clients. It must take a good solicitor to keep his name out of the papers. Rumour has it that 'Private Eye' are on to him. Does he have a secret ambition to be the most notorious schoolmaster in the country?" Celia shrugged again. "I wouldn't know. We lead very separate lives." Wal looked at her with admiration. "My God. You are the cool one. My friends always did call you the 'Ice Maiden'." She made a face, but he carried on and asked, "How serious are you and Euan?" She said, "Well I'm serious." Wal beamed. "And he seems to be too. Good. You'll have to leave George.

123

About time too, I never did like the man and Mother will be delighted. She disliked him from the start and always referred to George as 'that horrid little man.' She's never stopped blaming herself for being away and unable to stop the wedding."

Celia burst out laughing. "Don't go so fast Wal. It's early days. I have no idea what Euan wants." Wal looked at her and said earnestly, "Euan wants you, that's obvious. You're good for each other. I know about these things. It couldn't be better."

He paused, "To be honest we were a bit worried about him when Rachel left. He was in quite a mess. First it was a different woman every night and then the man became a recluse."

Celia clutched the side of a chair to steady herself. Was she in reality just someone Euan had found on the rebound? "Who's Rachel?" she asked.

Wal groaned, "Oh God. Don't tell me he hasn't told you about Rachel?" She shook her head. "She was his girlfriend at University and it lasted quite a while after they came down. It broke up suddenly a few years back. She's a doctor, in India now I believe. You should ask Euan about it. I don't believe in skeletons in the cupboard. When you've cleared the air, come and have lunch with me. I'd like to help."

He gave a smile, "Apart from anything else I owe it to you. I was terrible to you as a child." He lurched towards a waiter, had her glass refilled and then disappeared.

How very strange, she thought, to have found such a firm ally in Wal.

She didn't see him again until they said goodbye. He kissed her on both cheeks and said,

"Well Celia, if you need a good divorce lawyer, you know where to find one."

She looked anxiously at Euan to see if he was offended by this, but he was smiling.

They took a taxi to a small hotel in Soho where he'd booked a room. It was her first experience of sharing a hotel room with him and she felt a surge of nervous excitement. Euan ordered a bottle of champagne, which on top of all the champagne at the party began to make her feel quite tipsy, but it gave her the courage to ask about Rachel.

Euan drained his champagne. "Why haven't I mentioned her? Well, you never asked me about my past life. Too busy talking about your own!" Celia was indignant. "That's not true. I just didn't want you to think I was intruding or being inquisitive. You seemed to like your privacy." He smiled. "Quite true. And anyway your past is far more fascinating. You've kept me entertained for hours." She gave him a shove, "Well now's your chance to catch up. Tell me about Rachel." Euan sighed. "There's really not much to tell." Celia tried not to sound exasperated, "Well, tell me what she looked like?"

Euan roared with laughter. "How fucking typical of you to ask that question first. I'm not interested in what women look like." Celia said sulkily, "You noticed me and told me I looked beautiful." Euan smiled, "True. Difficult not to notice that."

They were silent for a moment and then he sighed again, "All right. I know I'll get no peace until I've told you something about her. Let me see…She was dark, attractive, good figure, with not much sense of humour. In fact, she really had no sense of humour at all. I met her at Cambridge and we were together after that for nearly five years. It was kind of intense at the beginning, the first major affair for both of us, but in all honesty it never really worked. She was dedicated to medicine – and to me. I was dedicated to writing – and not really to her. She was making a success of being a doctor. I was making no headway at being a writer. This produced a certain amount of tension. I finally decided to teach, until my writing took off, and this probably made me disagreeable and difficult to live with. We were in a kind of limbo until one day she suddenly announced she was leaving me and going to India. And that was more or less that." He shrugged. "She'll be very good with the natives. They need her drugs and expertise. Luckily they don't need someone to laugh with."

He lit a cigarette as Celia said, "That sounds a bit bitter to me." He handed the cigarette to her and lit one for himself. "Not really. However, it was a shock at the time. I knew the relationship had nowhere to go, but I think I was too lazy to do anything about it. Even so we had been together for nearly five years. It only took her five minutes to end it. So it remained an open wound for quite some time. It wasn't that I actually minded her going, it was the way she did it. It was partly hurt pride and partly that I knew I should have had the courage to end it myself." He blew the smoke out slowly.

"Anyway my friends presumed I was in a state of near collapse, especially Wal. He kept trying to find me replacements." Celia smiled and said she'd got the impression from Wal he was with a different woman every night. Euan gave a short laugh.

"That's typical of Wal. If I saw a lot of women it was entirely out of politeness because he kept finding them for me. What he never understood was that the break-up with Rachel was a good thing. Painful at the time, but a good thing nevertheless and Rachel's well out of it. I was frustrated with my writing and a bloody pain to live with."

Celia considered all this. "And now?" Euan finished his cigarette, "What about now?"

She ventured nervously, "Are you still too wrapped up in your own frustrations as a writer to care about anyone else?" She knew this question would change the mood of the evening, but it was something that had to be sorted out.

Euan looked at her long and hard. "What you really mean is, am I serious about you?"

She nodded and then looked away, almost not wanting to hear his answer.

He put out his cigarette and sighed. "As things are Celia, I mean while you are with George, there is little point in my being serious about you. Deep down I do care for you, more than I have for anyone else. Somehow you've managed to get under my skin."

He paused. "And of course I fancy you rotten!"

He rolled over and grabbed her roughly.

Much later he suddenly said, "Do you remember the night you were jealous over Helen Ainsworth?" She nodded, remembering it only too well. He went on, "In some ways your suspicions were justified." Noting the alarm on her face, he said quickly, "No, I didn't go to bed with her, but the point is, I could have. She made a definite pass." Celia was puzzled, "So why didn't you?" Euan put his hands behind his head and stared up at the ceiling. "Well, if I'm honest, I'd had far too much to drink and I just didn't want the fucking hassle." She tried to speak calmly. "What you're saying is that our relationship had nothing to do with your decision of not sleeping with her."

Euan frowned and said impatiently, "It's more complicated than that Celia. I've told you, I feel angry at the situation between you and George and I feel jealous too. Of course I have feelings for you but I've nowhere to take them. You are committed to someone else...."

She yelled in frustration, "But I'm not committed to George. I have no feelings for him at all. Why can't you understand that?"

He looked sadly at her, "You're committed legally Celia. You are bound to George in every way, except emotionally. And that does make a difference. It stops us from having a proper relationship."

She was silent. He was right of course and it left her feeling a sense of despair.

He took her in his arms. "Cheer up. It'll work out. We just need to find a way."

However, over the next few months it became increasingly difficult even to find a moment to be together. So they started taking risks.

One afternoon they were lying in bed in Euan's cottage, when there was a knock at the door. Euan quickly pulled on his jeans and a tee shirt and went downstairs to find it was George on the doorstep. He had come over about some changes to the timetable and when he had gone through these, he said, "I'm extremely pleased with the way the play is progressing. Everyone taking part seems to be enjoying it..." He lowered his voice, "and to be frank with you, I haven't seen my wife so happy in years. I don't know whether you knew, but she has suffered with ill health lately and this work with you has made all the difference to her. We must find something else for you both to do next term."

Celia heard Euan say dryly, "I should enjoy that very much."

After he had gone, Euan dived back into bed and they both lay there laughing helplessly.

"Really," he gasped at last, "I almost started to like the man. Can you believe it? He said I was good for you and he wants us both to do more together."

The school play was a success, mainly due to Euan's efforts. Celia knew that her music was simple and basic, but it somehow worked. George was positively effusive.

"It was a stroke of genius getting Mackay involved. You did well too Celia. It's a great bonus for the school to put on something like that. I've never seen the Governors so enthusiastic."

For the last two weeks of term Celia managed to juggle her affair with Euan and her life with George a little better, as George was busy with the demands at the school. To add to her general feeling of euphoria he suddenly announced he would be away in the States for the entire Easter holidays. Apparently a school in Boston wanted to arrange an exchange scheme with Civolds and he had been invited over to sort out the details.

"I would take you with me Celia," he said rather half-heartedly, "but I thought you would want to be with Natasha." She replied quickly, "Oh, you're right George. In fact Natasha and I have already made plans." He looked relieved. "That's all right then."

Of course no plans had been made and she asked Euan's advice. His instant reply was Scotland, and over the next few days he organized everything. "You can collect me from my mother. I'll have to stay with her a few days. Then we'll drive to Oban and go on to Iona. Everyone should see Iona once in their lifetime."

Natasha seemed happy enough with the plan and after a long drive they arrived in the small village where Euan had spent his childhood.

It was a dark and gloomy place, and his mother, Annie Mackay, was a tough, dour woman of few words. Euan seemed moody in her presence and there was no outward show of affection between them, although his mother talked more about Euan than she did of her other son Calum, who was only mentioned once, when they went round the house and a reference was made to his room. The place was sparsely furnished and Celia found it curious there were no photographs of the family anywhere to be seen. She knew his father had been the minister, but there was no reference to him either.

After lunch, and much to her relief, they set out for Oban. She had felt that Annie Mackay disapproved of her somehow. Her only show of warmth was when she talked to Natasha.

As they reached the edge of the village the sun came out from behind the clouds and suddenly the landscape was bathed in light.

Celia said, "I didn't know you had a brother?"

Euan shrugged. "I haven't seen Calum for years. He left home before I did."

"Why was that?

Euan shrugged again, "My father didn't exactly make our home life agreeable. Calum was a poor scholar and suffered even more than I did. He's now a crofter on Lewis, married and has two children." He looked at her and smiled, "Satisfied?"

She wanted to know more but could tell he wanted the subject closed.

As if reading her mind he said, "No more talk of my family please. We are on our way to the most beautiful place in the world, so don't let's spoil it with bloody family sagas!"

She gave a light laugh, "Do you know your Scottish accent is getting more pronounced by the minute?"

Euan was right about Iona. It did seem to be the most beautiful place in the world. He'd found a small guest house, halfway between the harbour and the Abbey and for a fortnight they spent their time walking, reading, listening to music, playing games, having silly conversations, and eating huge meals in front of a log fire.

Every evening they would perform the ritual of climbing three hundred feet to the highest point on the island and from there they would watch the sun slowly setting. The white sands would be streaked with the shades of the sunset. There was no sound. Even the seagulls stopped their cries. Nobody spoke until the great red disc had sunk into the western sea.

On the final evening Celia was alone with her daughter, Euan having gone for a last walk.

Natasha was sitting cross-legged on the floor, deep in a book. She looked at her and smiled. Natasha had never once questioned her relationship with Euan, even the sleeping arrangements had passed off without comment. Of course Euan had scornfully brushed aside her worries about Natasha's reaction to them sharing a room. "For God's sake Celia, we're liberated now. Didn't the sixties have any effect on you at all?"

She was about to explain that the sixties had actually passed her by, when he added, "Natasha's not stupid. She knows exactly what's going on and is perfectly fine with it."

Even so, now they were on their own, Celia felt she ought to say something.

"I do hope this holiday has been all right for you darling. I mean, perhaps we should have brought one of your friends along with us."

Natasha put down her book. "No, it's been brilliant. I wouldn't have had it any other way." She uncrossed her legs. "And Euan is great." Celia felt a great wave of relief. "You like him?" Natasha sounded impatient, "Of course I like him. He knows so many things and he's taught me backgammon and how to do crosswords. I tell you he's great." And she went back to her book.

The next day, as they were about to leave the island, there was a moment that Celia knew would be imprinted on her mind forever. They were waiting for the boat to take them back to Oban. The colours were brilliant, the sky was at its bluest and the white sand and the Abbey walls gleamed in the sunlight. Euan and Natasha played ducks and drakes at the water's edge and the gulls swooped and cried above them. Time stood still.

It was all so unbearably beautiful that unbidden, the tears started to roll down her cheeks. Euan came across and took in her mood at a glance. She stooped to collect her bag, ashamed of the tears. He bent down and handed it to her. His eyes were steady with hers and she knew he totally understood how she was feeling, without her having to say a word.

Once they were on the boat, Euan went off to check the tickets, leaving Natasha and Celia leaning against the rail, watching the shoreline of Iona disappearing from view.

Suddenly Natasha said, "Why don't you leave Father?" Celia felt a mixture of surprise and shock. "Leave him?" Natasha said firmly. "Yes, leave him. Before it's too late, like poor Grandma." "Grandma?" Celia echoed again. "Yes. Your mother!"

Natasha grinned. "She should have left grumpy old Grandfather ages ago. I suppose she wasn't attractive like you, so nobody asked her, and that's very sad. But with you it's different. You have Euan."

Celia suddenly felt faint. It was at the mention of her mother that something had struck her with such force it hit her right in the solar plexus. Of course. It was another parallel. The greatest parallel yet. She had been so completely absorbed with Euan that the significance had never struck her before. Now here was Natasha, reminding her.

Aware that her daughter was watching her she said quickly, "Wouldn't it worry you if I left your father?" "Not at all," came the prompt reply. "You and Father are hardly ever together and when you are it's perfectly obvious you don't get on. You become irritable. He becomes like a bear. I've talked to girls at school whose parents are separated. They say it's much better without all the rows and the quarrels." Celia protested at this. "George and I don't row." Natasha considered this. "Well perhaps not row exactly. But you're no good together. I mean, once a marriage is broken, it seems to me it's no good trying to pretend it isn't." She took a deep breath and frowned slightly as if concentrating on what she was going to say. "It's like when you drop a plate on the floor and it breaks in two. If you put the two halves back on the table, everyone can tell at once it's a broken plate. If you then try to stick the two halves back together, it might not look so obvious, but it still remains a broken plate. Do you see what I mean?"

Celia looked at her daughter in astonishment. "You seem to have it all worked out." Natasha shrugged. "It seems obvious to me." Celia asked, "And what in your great scheme of things happens to your father?" The reply came without hesitation. "Oh, he'd be all right. He has lots of women already and it's not as if you sleep together, so he wouldn't miss that!" She emphasized the 'that' so forcefully that in spite of her shock Celia was forced to smile. "How do you know your father has other women?"

Natasha said airily, "Danny and Livvy told me. They talk about you and Father a lot." Celia frowned, not sure she wanted to hear any more, but Natasha was in full flow. "Danny says he hears Paul and Maddie talking about it too. They say Father can't really be blamed for all his women because you and he don't have a sex life. They say that once you're in separate rooms then your marriage is on the skids."

A slight tone of bitterness crept into Celia's voice as she said sharply, "Did they ever bother to find out why we don't have a sex life? I mean, did it occur to anyone it might just have been because of all George's other women?"

Natasha said quickly, "Oh nobody blames you," and then she burst out laughing. "Danny saw Father with some blonde in Oxford. Apparently one of his mistresses is quite famous, an actress or something."

Celia remained silent for a moment. Her daughter looked at her anxiously, "I'm sorry. Have I made you angry?" Celia pulled herself together. "Not angry, no, but a bit worried." Natasha sounded impatient again, "Why worried? You are always worrying. You shouldn't worry so much." Celia said lamely, "Well I hate to think how much all this talk must affect you." Natasha dismissed this. "Oh the talk doesn't affect me. But I don't like to see you so unhappy. It seems such a waste of time for you and Father to be together, when you could be blissfully happy with someone else." And she added angrily, "I hope you're not making a sacrifice on my account, because it's quite wasted. I tell you, sometimes I feel like running away. I mean, take last Christmas for instance. It was horrible, nothing festive about it at all. I know you don't have rows but you sort of get at each other all the time, scoring points, making snide remarks. It's horrible".

Her anger subsided. "Can I go and get some ice-cream?" Bewildered, Celia nodded, but as Natasha turned to go she said, "It's not quite as simple as you think."

Natasha turned back. "Why not? It seems utterly simple to me."

Celia sighed. "Your father wouldn't let me leave. I've already asked him. He said it would be bad for you, bad for him, bad for the school. Bad all round in fact."

Natasha said hotly, "That's just plain stupid. Why don't you just leave him anyway? Just get up and go?" In spite of herself Celia laughed. "Darling life doesn't work like that, it's far more complicated. There's the financial aspect for a start!"

Natasha's voice was full of scorn, "Oh money! Well if it were me I'd leave, money or no money. And I warn you, Euan won't wait forever. With his looks he'll be snapped up by somebody else." With that she flounced off, leaving Celia a little shell-shocked. It wasn't that she minded her daughter talking to her like that. In fact she admired her. But it was the scorn in her voice that had brought back another parallel so clearly. It was that scorn she remembered most of all.

Euan walked down the deck towards her and leant on the rail. As the boat headed out for the open sea, the wind increased. She gave a shiver and he put his arm round her.

He said nothing but looked at her in that strange intense way that almost stopped her from breathing. "Happy?" he asked. She nodded, not trusting herself to speak.

That night in the Oban hotel Celia silently vowed two things.

She would return to Dr Strutter for one more session and she would definitely find a way of leaving George.

TENTH SESSION   May 4th 1980

So there I was. Back again. And there was Dr Strutter sitting opposite me in the green leather armchair. Amazing to think it was nearly a year since I had seen him. Everything was just the same, except that now it was all so very different. It wasn't that he had changed, or the room had changed. The only difference was me.

I looked across at him and caught his eye. The good doctor had been giving me long and searching looks from the moment I arrived. He obviously knew that something had happened. Ominously, as we sat in the usual silence, there was a lightning flash, followed by a loud crack of thunder, so loud it made me jump. Then the rain started lashing against the windows.

"Wonderful," Dr Strutter murmured, "this will be good for the garden. My wife has been complaining about the lack of rain."

As he was obviously not going to ask me a question, I started with a rather pathetic apology. "I am really sorry for the long gap. It was rude of me not to give you an explanation. First there was the summer holidays and then I was going to come back and see you…" I faltered, not sure how to explain about Euan, without it sounding like a silly romantic flutter.

He smoothed the knees of his trouser, removed his glasses, wiped them on the base of his tie and then put the glasses back on again. He was giving me time, but I needed more than that. I needed inspiration. I must have looked flustered because he asked in his calm way, "Did something occur during the summer holidays?"

"Not in the holidays, after that." I paused and then took the plunge. "I fell in love."

"Ah". It was a long drawn out 'ah'. That's all he said, but his face, usually so impassive, now wore a strange expression. It was difficult to read. I don't think it was shock, or disapproval, but something else. Perhaps he was worried this would be another dismal saga. At long last he broke the silence. "Why don't you tell me about it?"

I twisted the handkerchief in my lap, "I don't really know where to begin."

He gave a wry smile. "You say you have fallen in love. So you must have met someone. Can you tell me about him?" I realized he was trying to make it easy for me, so I plunged in. "His name is Euan Mackay. He came to the school as a new master last Autumn and well, after I met him, it just happened.

I know it sounds like some ghastly Mills and Boon story, but from the moment I met Euan I knew my life had changed."

I paused, hoping he'd say something, but as he made no comment there was nothing for it but to plough on. "You see, for years I had been longing for something to break the monotony of my existence and would have been quite content with even a minor ripple. But when that something actually happened, it turned out to be, well, a tidal wave."

He smiled at that but again said nothing, so I took out a cigarette and noted the ashtray on the table beside me. It was my turn to smile. "I see you've anticipated my return to the evil habit. It was inevitable really. There have been quite a few stressful moments over the past few months."

"I can imagine," he remarked dryly, "And how has your husband reacted to this?"

I had a twinge of embarrassment. "He doesn't know about it. I'm aware that sounds dreadful, but in all honesty just the very fact he hasn't noticed the change in me shows how separate our lives are."

I drew on my cigarette and blew the smoke out slowly.

"I do want to assure you that I am not here to talk about the state of my marriage. I wanted to see you again because in the middle of everything that was happening to me I realized I had found another parallel."

Dr Strutter leaned forward, interested now. "Your love affair has a parallel?"

"Yes it does, an astonishing one. I didn't actually think of it until my daughter suggested I leave George. I told her that leaving her father would be difficult, given the financial implications. She turned on me with great scorn and told me that money shouldn't come into my decision." I paused, "It was the scorn in her voice that reminded me so absolutely of the parallel. And I just thought I had to tell you about it," adding vaguely, "you know, closure and all that."

"Interesting," he murmured, almost to himself. "How very interesting."

I put out my cigarette and he looked across at me, "Would I be right in thinking it was your mother who had a love affair and that your reaction was like your daughter's?"

I nodded.

I know it was his job, but he really was rather clever.

134

"Well, I'd like to hear it, if you feel you can tell me." He settled back in his chair.

It was a long time since I had started in on a parallel and I wasn't sure where to begin.

He asked, "What year are we talking about?"

"1961. I was sixteen and if you remember I was at boarding school and on this particular occasion it was Parent's Day."

Once started, the words began to flow.

"As usual my mother was late and I was waiting on the school steps for her to arrive.

A member of staff came up to me and said rather crossly, 'Isn't your mother here yet Celia? If she's not here soon you won't have time for lunch before the speeches.'

She made it sound as if this were my fault. A few minutes later a series of explosions heralded our shabby Ford Popular making its erratic way down the school drive.

By now I was used to the smirks of people who witnessed the arrival of my mother. Today it was only the teacher who looked on, but her expression was one of mild distaste as Audrey leapt from the car looking untidy and unkempt. 'Sorry to be late,' Audrey said to me, 'the car wouldn't start.' The teacher spoke with studied politeness.

'I was just explaining to Celia, Mrs Maddington, that there isn't going to be much time for lunch before the speeches begin.'

My mother said in her breathy way, 'Oh that will be all right, I've brought a picnic.' I was shamed yet again. All the other girls had been whisked off to lavish lunches.

As we climbed into the car I asked, 'Couldn't we go to a restaurant Audrey? I think it's going to rain.' I had been looking forward to a proper meal all morning. Even a roadside café would have been better than nothing. At the thought of one of Audrey's picnics my heart sank. My mother yanked at the gears. 'No we can't go out Celia. I've brought a picnic now and you heard what the teacher said, there's not enough time before the speeches. I don't think it will rain and it's really quite warm when the sun comes out.'

I looked at the great clouds rolling across the sky and didn't share her optimism.

We parked at the top of the games fields, beneath a line of pine trees that did little to shield us from the chill winds that swept across the South Downs.

Audrey bustled about getting the picnic organized, whilst I regarded her critically. How odd she was going to look amongst all the other mothers, in her faded frock and flat, open schoolgirl sandals.

I munched silently on boiled eggs and limp lettuce and then, unable to contain myself, I burst out, 'I wish you'd dressed up a bit Audrey. Parents Day is meant to be a smart occasion. All the other mothers will look smart.' She looked puzzled, 'What do you mean smart?' I stopped struggling with the lettuce and threw it away. 'Oh I don't know. Navy blue suits and polka dot shirts, stockings and high heels. And a hat.'

She looked at me bewildered. 'I haven't got a hat. Anyway, you are a funny child to worry about such things. Do you know, I think it's one of the few times Bernard and I agreed on something? He said this school would give you middle class values. It's terrible to want to be like everyone else you know.'

I said miserably, 'Then why send me here? Can't you see how difficult it is for me to be different? The girls laugh at me. The teachers get at me. I never have the right uniform and then they're angry with me about it. All last term I was teased for wearing Wal's old pyjamas instead of a nightdress. And when I asked you for a music case, you sent me a string bag. It was useless and looked ridiculous. They laugh at me, they laugh at you, they laugh at the car, at my clothes, at your clothes...'

'My dear Celia,' my mother broke in, 'my clothes may be a bit old but they're perfectly clean and respectable. And you won't catch me in those ridiculous high heels your other mothers wear.'

I blurted out, 'Well you could at least wear stockings.' She looked baffled by this.

'Whatever for, in summer?'

I said sulkily, 'Well you ought to shave your legs then.' Audrey said crossly, 'Why? It's a terrible waste of time. Once you start you have to keep at it.'

She handed me a digestive biscuit. 'I do hope this outburst doesn't mean you are going to spend your life worrying about how people look.'

I said miserably, 'It's not just how we look. We're different in every way. During the General Election I was made to stand as the Socialist candidate in the school mock elections because one of the teachers knew about Bernard. I turned out to be the only girl in the school with Socialist parents. I only got two votes and everyone sneered at me.' She said briskly, 'Well that was very silly of them. Cheer up. A bit of suffering is very character forming.' She searched among the many paper bags. 'Look, I've brought you some chocolate.' I could see she was making an effort, so I ventured further.

'I know you don't think it's important, but I do think it could make a difference if you tried to look nice. I mean Bernard might be kinder to you if you dressed up a bit.'

I munched on my chocolate bar, feeling a little nervous at having broached such a subject. My mother gave a laugh that sounded more like a bark, 'Good heavens child, I can assure you, your father would behave no differently whatever I did. I don't think he even notices my appearance.' My words came out in a rush. 'Exactly, but I think he would if you made an effort. If you were smarter and the house was repainted and there were nice meals on the table I think…' I broke off, my new found bravery deserting me and I finished lamely, 'I just think he would be kinder to you, that's all.'

I didn't dare look at Audrey, fearing that I'd upset her. In the distance I could see the large cars churning up clouds of dust as they rolled into the car park. Parents and girls poured into the marquee. The sun suddenly came out from behind the clouds and it was almost hot. I lay back feeling miserable and guilty.

When she finally did speak Audrey's voice was different. 'Does it worry you so much? Bernard and me?' It wasn't what I had expected her to say but I tried to answer her truthfully. 'I think it does. Not for me exactly, for you really. You seem so unhappy. Bernard behaves badly and you get upset. Then because you're upset he feels guilty so he starts drinking. You get more upset because he's drinking which makes him behave even worse. So it goes on. It's as if you really dislike each other now.'

I rolled on to my stomach and chewed a long piece of grass, then suddenly burst out, 'Why don't you leave? I know I would.' Audrey said nothing so I went on almost impatiently, 'Hasn't there ever been anyone else in your life?'

The speeches were about to start, but this moment was too important to be broken. I stared across at the marquee, waiting for Audrey to say something.

She finally said, 'There was someone else. Once.'

I sat up. This was an astonishing revelation. Audrey and another man?

I stammered out, 'There was? Who?'

Her voice was soft, almost faint, 'You never met him. It all happened just after you had started at this school,' and she gave a little laugh. 'You would have approved though. For the two years I was with him I really did make an effort with my appearance.'

And she added rather sadly, 'Perhaps if I had left Bernard I might have become more the other you wanted.' I was aghast and quickly said, 'I didn't mean...I never said you weren't the mother I wanted.' She gave a wan smile. 'I know. But I do understand. You are quite right of course. I don't bother with my appearance. My work is all I care about now. And you of course.'

I considered this for a moment. 'What about Bernard? Don't you care for him at all?' She answered quickly, 'Oh I cared once, quite desperately. But now...' She broke off looking a little flustered and then went on, 'I wish you could have seen him as he was when I first met him. He was so good looking, dashing and, well, exciting. He ran away from school you know, when he was seventeen, to fight in the Spanish Civil War. Then after University came the war and he survived against all the odds. It must have been very hard for him to settle back into civilian life and somehow it's all been such a disappointment to him. He seems to live in the past now.' She sighed. 'I remember the first time I ever saw him. He was in uniform and I thought him the most beautiful creature I had ever seen. And he had enormous charm. I took him to meet my parents who adored him and urged me to marry him. So I did.'

Her voice trailed away. I said gloomily, 'I'm never going to get married.'

'Oh you will', she replied sadly. 'It's difficult not to fall into the trap once the pressure is on.'

I rolled onto my back and stared at the sky. 'Tell me about *him.*'

She looked lost for a moment, 'Oh you mean Edward. Well, what do you want to know?' I said excitedly, 'What was he like? How did you meet him?'

She peered into the distance, as if remembering. 'He was a book publisher...well, he still is I think. It was Edward who gave me my first job as a book illustrator. I can't really describe him except to say he was different from Bernard in every way.'

My curiosity was roused, 'How different?'

She smiled, 'Well to start with, he was shy, gentle and kind. Generous too. Terribly generous. I remember at our first lunch together explaining to him how expensive it would be to equip myself for this book project, telling him I was going to need different brushes, paint, paper and so forth. So he told me to buy whatever I needed and send the bill to him. I thought the firm would be paying. Only later did I find out that Edward had paid for everything.'

I was touched. 'He sounds lovely.' She nodded, 'Yes he was,' and she broke off, lost in thought. I looked across at her and was suddenly struck by something quite extraordinary. While she had been talking about Edward she had physically changed. All the hard, bitter lines had disappeared. She looked softer, gentler and, in the sunlight, even pretty. Her expression was almost happy as she went on, 'It wasn't just that he was generous. I think he really loved me as a person. He loved my work too and gave me confidence and encouragement. Somehow I could always talk to Edward, try out ideas.' She shrugged, 'I was just very happy with him.' Then she turned away and I knew instinctively she was thinking how unhappy she was now, with Bernard. I wanted to say something comforting. 'Dolly says she's convinced Bernard really loved you when you were first married.' She looked back at me. 'Yes, I think he probably did, in his way.' She sighed. 'I think he fell in love with the idea of me. I was the Bohemian daughter of landed gentry, a bit of a rebel'. A smile lit up her face, 'Your grandfather was apoplectic when I decided to go to Art School. He kept muttering on about Augustus John.'

I laughed at that as she went on, 'And then I refused to become a debutante. So they were positively relieved when Bernard proposed. It was sad really. I think he became tired of me quite early on and now there's only guilt. Guilt and habit. It's a powerful combination and difficult to break.'

There was a moments silence and a single magpie flew down in front of us, but even he wasn't tempted by the remains of the drab picnic. I turned back to my mother. 'Would Edward have married you?' She twisted a handkerchief in her lap. 'Yes. If I'd been free. In any case he wanted me to go and live with him in Italy. He had a house near Florence. It was so beautiful...' Her voice trailed away.

Suddenly something clicked. I said, 'Of course, there was a time when you went to Florence a great deal. You sent me postcards. You'd gone there to work.'

She said shyly, 'Well really to be with Edward.' I shook my head. 'I never realized. You brought me back some beautifully bound music. It was the best present I ever had.' Audrey gave a soft laugh. 'It was Edward chose that. It's ironic really. He always took a great interest in you. He'd have made a wonderful step-father.' She sighed. 'Looking back on it I suppose it might have been better all round if I'd left Bernard. But at the time...' She stopped and started to pack up the picnic. 'Anyway, too late now. It's rather pointless to look back.'

She looked up. 'Celia, how dreadful, we've missed the speeches. Now you'll be in even more trouble.' I spoke impatiently, 'Oh don't worry about the speeches. You must tell me why you didn't leave.' Audrey stared again into the middle distance and it was some time before she spoke. 'I did try. We were very much in love. It all seemed so simple when we were together, Edward and I. I should have just stayed out in Italy, but then I made the mistake of coming back. I wanted to try and sort things out in a civilized way.' A note of bitterness crept into her voice, 'I had reckoned without Bernard's reaction. For all his mocking, he is more steeped in middle-class morality than all of us put together. He brought the whole weight of the family behind him, my parents, Mark, Judy, even Dolly. They all said how wrong it would be for me, for Bernard, for his career, for you. I couldn't fight them all, I just couldn't. In the end I was so exhausted I just gave in. I was never very strong.' She smoothed out the twisted handkerchief and her eyes were filled with tears. I felt a terrible helplessness. There were many things I wanted to say, but in the end all I said was, 'I'm so sorry Audrey, I had no idea.'

She wiped her eyes. 'At the time it all seemed impossibly complicated, what with the lawyers, the dividing up of the house and possessions, most of all the fight over you. I just couldn't face it.' She tucked her handkerchief up her sleeve. 'I can see now how cowardly it was, but then...' I was both impatient and scornful. 'Why didn't Edward just come and collect you?' Audrey laughed. 'Silly child. It doesn't happen like that.'

I wasn't convinced but asked, 'What happened to Edward?'

There was a long pause and then she said with a sigh, 'He was very patient, for a long time. But finally he must have known it was hopeless. During that time he wrote me the most wonderful letters. I read them, often.' She added sadly, 'They are my most treasured possession.'

A silence fell. I listened to the wind in the pine trees. Her tragedy overwhelmed me.

Audrey stood up and said briskly, 'Eventually the letters stopped. I ceased to care what I looked like. The whole episode was over. I'd lost him. I heard later he married. An Italian girl. I hope she made him a good wife. I hope he is happy.'

She put the picnic basket into the car and then we lay in the gentle sunlight for quite a while. Neither of us spoke, but at that moment I felt a love for my mother which I had never experienced before, or since. In the years since that conversation took place, her relationship with Bernard has broken down completely and I have had to watch it all from the sidelines. So now I feel nothing for her but impatience and irritation, but at the time her unhappiness had a profound effect on me.

Anyway, I was just beginning to wonder if she had fallen asleep when she suddenly asked, 'Do they tease you a lot at this school?' I nodded, reflecting it wasn't so much teasing as bullying, but she went on, 'I'm so sorry. We are to blame for having sent you here, but at the time I thought you'd be happier away from home.' I said, 'So did I," and then saw the worried expression on her face. 'Don't worry. I'm probably over the worst by now.' She sat up and gave me an unexpected hug. 'I do hope so Celia. I can't bear to think of you suffering as well.'

I turned away from her, only because I suddenly felt like crying. Not for me, but for her. For her lost life. Her lost chance."

I broke off.

I didn't dare look at Dr Strutter for fear I might break down. The telling of that had been more difficult than I had anticipated, so I dived into my bag for a cigarette.

He leaned forward. "So that is the parallel then?"

I lit up and nodded. "Well yes. Since the similar conversation with Natasha I have thought of little else. There it was. Bernard, Edward, Audrey. George, Euan, me."

He considered this before saying slowly, "To make it an exact parallel it would mean you were going to stay with your husband."

I answered him with some impatience. "That's just it. Don't you see? This is my chance to break away, to step out of the parallels. I just have to find a way of leaving George. I know it will be difficult. In fact I will be under exactly the same pressures as Audrey, but I am determined to go ahead."

I waited for his reaction to this but instead he suddenly changed tack.

"Do you see your mother now?"

I nodded, "Yes, I went over a few months ago. I ought to go more often but I find the visits terribly depressing. She's having an awful time with Bernard and always appears exhausted. Last time, out of sheer irritation, I asked her again why she didn't leave him. She looked at me in a strange way and said, 'There's no point now.' The worst thing is that I just end up feeling angry with her. She won't do anything to help herself and I can't do anything to help her either. I don't want Natasha to feel that way about me."

Dr Strutter stroked his knees, lost in thought. I looked at the clock. Officially we had another ten minutes to go. A thought came into my head which made me smile.

He looked at me curiously, so I explained. "I've been having a curious dream lately and I thought if I told it to you I'd be more like a normal patient."

He remarked drily, 'There's no such thing as a normal patient, but I would be interested to hear this dream."

I looked again at the clock. "It won't take long as I can only remember bits of it. I think it always starts when I am in a car, with two companions. I can't really remember who these companions are, but we are obviously going on a holiday of some sort as we have a lot of luggage. We climb up a steep hill and reach a village. As we enter this village there is rubbish every-where, dustbins and those black bin bags, all over the road, which makes it very difficult to drive. People stand in their doorways watching, as we dodge around trying to avoid the obstacles. They aren't exactly hostile, but they aren't exactly helpful either. They just stare at us. Eventually we come up against a barricade of dustbins and there is no way round. So we clam-ber out, pull the dustbins to one side and go on our way. The next thing I remember is coming to this fork in the road. At the junction we make a turn and a lot of smart limousines join us. Then we come to a road block and a sign pointing back to the village saying, 'Diversion.' So we turn the car round and start to go back. Now we appear to be the only car and a feeling of fear begins to creep over me. Although we have kept to the same route, the scenery on the return journey is completely different. Everything has changed. All the landmarks have disappeared. Suddenly we come to a narrow steel bridge that sways and creaks in the wind. There are gaps where you can see the water below."

I looked at Dr Strutter. "I am very bad at heights so by now I am extremely frightened. I cry out to my companions that we have gone wrong, but they laugh at me and say of course it is the right way because there is no other way back to the village. So I start to cross. I just remember the terror, the swaying bridge and the water below.

And then I wake up."

I glanced across at Dr Strutter. He was sitting back in his chair with his eyes tight shut.

How embarrassing. I have sent him to sleep. For what seemed like an age, I just sat there watching him. Then he murmured, "Interesting."

He opened his eyes so abruptly his glasses almost fell off his nose. He stood up.

"I think next week we might discuss that dream. Yes?"

This made me laugh. "Don't tell me you are going to start behaving like a proper analyst at last?"

He smiled but ignored this remark and merely said, "We could discuss the parallels, in relation to the dream, at the same time."

I hesitated, "I really only came back to tell you the final parallel, but if you think further discussion would be helpful, I am happy to do it."

He nodded. "Good, good.

As I left I wondered if he would be at the window, as he had always been in the past.

I reached the bottom of the steps and looked up. And there he was.

The end of the tenth session.

Chapter 10

The following Saturday was to be the day of George's father's wedding. The invitation had arrived on the breakfast table three weeks previously and had caused George to choke on his toast. "That damn fool of a father!" he shouted, scattering his letters over the kitchen table. Celia said automatically, "You mean Bernard?" This was because over the years George's relationship with her father had gone into a definite decline, not because of something Bernard had done, just that George had no further use for him, and as always with George, if you were no longer useful, then you were discarded.

However, on this occasion, it wasn't Bernard that had upset him, but his own father, Malcolm. "I cannot believe the old fool could be so stupid," he muttered angrily and seemed so upset Celia asked him what had happened. George threw the wedding invitation across the table. "He's getting married again. Can you believe it? At his age!" Celia looked at the invitation and smiled. "I don't see what's so awful about that, apart from the fact that the woman's name appears to be Cindy." George shouted at her, "You don't see what's so awful? My dear girl, it's a disaster. Here's a letter from Paul that came with the invitation, explaining, quite calmly, if you please, that this Cindy is a girl from the village who works in the local store!" Celia tried not to laugh. "I don't think that matters George. Your father was probably lonely, stuck abroad after what's-her-name died. He's come back to England, found this local girl Cindy, and this means he can settle down near Paul and Maddie." George's anger did not abate. "My father happens to have been knighted for his services to charity. The gutter press will have a field day with this. I can just see the headlines, "Tycoon's Fourth Wife is a Checkout Girl!" This time she did laugh and George looked furiously at her. "I really don't know what you find so amusing Celia. My father is about to be the laughing stock of the county and all you can do is laugh." He added gloomily, "Probably what remains of the family money will now be frittered away as well."

Celia became suitably contrite. "I'm sorry George, but I really don't think you should worry. I am sure a quiet wedding in Norfolk isn't going to hit the National Press."

George looked unconvinced. "It beats me why the girl should want to marry the old fool anyway." "Oh I think that's quite easy to understand," Celia replied. "Your father may be getting on, but he's been knighted, which means she will be a lady, added to which he has a lot of money and a great deal of charm. I'm fond of him myself."

This was too much for George and he snatched up the invitation and left the room.

Later that afternoon, as they sat under the oak tree, Celia imparted this latest information to Euan. He was immediately intrigued, "What's George's father like?" Celia thought for a moment because she had only met Malcolm a few times. "Well, he's totally unlike George. He's round and jolly and likes to present himself as a bit of a buffoon. He's generous too, and fun." Euan's eyebrows went up. "How on earth did they manage to spawn such a son?" Celia said wryly. "I gather George takes after his mother. However I think that Malcolm, underneath that roguish exterior, has a shrewdness that George neglects to notice. He's far too busy despising him, which he really shouldn't. Malcolm started from nothing and became a multi-millionaire. He was obviously a clever business man and sold his drinks company at just the right time. He then took retirement early and has had a lot of fun spending his money ever since."

She paused. "To give him his due, he did give a lot to charity work. I think that's how he got his knighthood. Apart from that, he spent his money on the estate, and there have since been the cars, the yachts and the women. This will be his fourth wife!"

Euan whistled, "Phew! That can't please George. He is such a bloody hypocrite. It's fine for him to have as many mistresses as he likes, but when it comes to marriage he becomes super-critical." Celia shook her head, "I don't think George's main worry is about the marriages. He is outraged that this latest wife is a checkout girl at the local supermarket. That, and the fact that it will mean another dent in the family fortune." Euan frowned. "Surely that shouldn't worry George. He always seems to have plenty of money to me." She nodded. "Oh he has. When Paul got the Estate, a very large sum was settled on George, so he really has nothing to grumble about, although I suspect he'd like to have been lord of the manor."

They were silent for a while, then Euan asked, "Tell me about George's mother."

Celia shrugged. "I never knew her, she died just before George and I met, but he was absolutely devoted to her. From what I have gleaned, she appears to have been a strict, humourless old lady, with absolutely no sense of fun. She glares out of the family photographs with a terrifying expression of disapproval. By all accounts she doted on George and thought him the perfect son. He has never forgiven his father for leaving her, which happened almost immediately after they bought the estate in Norfolk. Of course Eileen was very well provided for and spent the rest of her life filling the house with lavish furnishings and priceless antiques." Celia gave a laugh, "Most of these are now being ruined or broken by Paul and his family." She sighed. "It will give George another reason to moan about at the wedding."

Euan suddenly said angrily, "Then don't go to the fucking wedding."

She was startled at this outburst. "I have to Euan. I can't let Natasha bear the brunt of George's rage on her own and he insists she comes with us. Anyway, why should you mind about it?"

Euan kicked angrily at a bit of turf. "Because I hate this family bit, watching you get dragged in. It's just George manipulating you again and you're too weak to make a stand."

Celia felt irritated and said huffily, "Well I've told you the reason why I have to go. If you can't understand that, too bad, but this definitely isn't the moment to make a stand."

They changed the subject then, but she remained baffled by his reaction.

When the day arrived, Celia's dread of the occasion appeared justified. She had taken the precaution of ringing Maddie to find out what sort of wedding it was going to be, and had been told it was definitely informal. She passed this information on to George, but to her horror, he arrived downstairs in morning dress, complete with a top hat. A look of horror crept over her face. How could he be so idiotic? She told him again that it was informal, to which he replied icily that as they had been sent a *formal* invitation he was merely doing the right thing. He then went on to tackle Natasha about wearing a hat. There were tears and tantrums until Celia suggested a compromise and the hat was not worn but taken with them in the car. They both sulked for the entire journey and Celia gave up all attempts at conversation.

It was a grey, cloudy day, about as gloomy as the atmosphere. Celia stared out of the window and thought of her odd conversation with Euan the day before. Oh God! Why did everyone have to be so bloody difficult!

In spite of the heavy traffic, which had George cursing and swearing, they arrived at the house, just as the happy couple returned from the Registry Office. Malcolm was looking rather splendid in brocade waistcoat, cravat and bright yellow trousers. He greeted them warmly and made the introductions. Celia looked at the bride and inwardly chuckled. She was just as she'd imagined, in her thirties, bosomy and blonde, decked in a low-cut satin dress, donned by a floppy straw hat perched at rather a jaunty angle.

For once George was rendered speechless, so Celia said offered her congratulations. Malcolm looked pleased. "Come on everyone, let's get inside. You too wench!" and he slapped Cindy on the backside, causing her to shriek with laughter. George looked in deep pain and hissed through his teeth, "He's only doing this to annoy me. I'm just thankful my poor mother is dead and doesn't have to go through this indignity."

Malcolm came over with the champagne. "Why on earth are you togged up like a penguin George? This isn't one of your society weddings you know."

George ignored this and sipped his champagne as if at a wine tasting and declared it excellent. Malcolm looked amused, "Of course it is, only the best." He nodded in the direction of Cindy. "What do you think of 'it'?" George was still looking down at the champagne and replied. "It's very good. What vintage?" Malcolm bellowed back, "What vintage? What vintage? Dammit boy, I'm referring to my new wife." George said huffily, "I'm sorry father, but you did refer to her as 'it'. This brought a roar of laughter from Malcolm. "Of course I did. I always refer to women as 'it', otherwise they get above themselves. Don't you agree Celia? Once you give women status, you get all that feminist rot, throwing away their bras and knicks!" Celia smiled, "Only their bras I think Malcolm." He handed her a glass. "It's a lot of damned nonsense if you ask me. Cindy's frontage would collapse if she threw hers away. She's built like a flying buttress." George glared, but Malcolm ignored this and continued, "We have the whole village here, everyone from the estate, even Ron the Poacher. He gave me one of our own pheasants as a wedding present!" Everyone laughed except George.

Two hours later, the party was getting lively. George, looking pale, was still trying to suppress his feeling of outrage and spent most of his time removing the few remaining precious objects into positions of safety. Just as he was beginning to agitate about leaving, Malcolm decided to make a speech. Mercifully it was short. There were three loud cheers, the cake was cut and toasts were made.

"Now we can definitely leave." George hissed at Celia, but his father overheard him.

"You can't leave yet. The fun's only just beginning. There's a disco in the barn. Natasha will enjoy that." George was about to object, but before he could say anything, Livvy led Natasha away. He told Celia they would give it half an hour and he went off to the library to escape the noise. Celia made her way to the kitchen and sat having a cup of tea with Maddie. About fifteen minutes went by when Natasha and Livvy appeared. Natasha was looking disheveled and upset. Livvy explained, "It was Billy Oakley Mum. He's terribly drunk. I don't think he knew what he was doing."

Celia's mind began to race with horrible imaginings.

"What happened?" she asked Livvy sharply. Livvy looked uncomfortable. "Everyone was dancing and then Billy got hold of Natasha and wouldn't let her go. He was kissing her, you know properly. Ugh. It was horrible. They don't know what they're doing Mum, Billy and his crowd. Honestly, I think it's getting out of hand."

Maddie, calm as ever, said, "Come on Livvy. We'd better fetch your father to sort it out and send them home."

After they left, Natasha sat down, not her usual ebullient self, and her voice was shaky.

"I'm so sorry, I did try to please Grandpa and mix. I didn't want to look snooty. They kept saying 'little lady this' and 'little lady that'. And then this boy Billy put his arm around me so tightly I couldn't get away and he said, 'how about a kiss from the little lady then?" She looked close to tears. "He smelled horrible and there was beer all down his chin and shirt. And he kissed me on the lips. It took forever and it was horrible and it hurt." She felt her lips. "I thought I was going to be sick. The more I wriggled, the more he held on to me, until at last someone pulled him off and Livvy brought me in here."

Celia fetched a wet cloth, gently wiped her face and said crossly, "I'm afraid they have all had far too much to drink." That didn't seem to comfort Natasha, who burst out, "They'll think I'm a snob and I'm not!" Celia looked grim. "Of course you're not. Anyway, I don't expect they're going to remember any of this in the morning. It was stupid of Malcolm really, to make so much alcohol available." Natasha sat hunched and miserable. Celia took her hand. "Darling it wasn't your fault. I know it's made you feel horrid but it's all over now and it meant nothing." Natasha snatched her hand away. "How can you say that? You didn't have beastly Billy slobbering all over you. How could you know what it felt like?"

At that moment something struck Celia with such force that she felt almost faint.

She looked at Natasha, "Actually, something quite similar, did happen to me when I was about your age. It was with an older man, but the same sort of nasty experience."

Natasha didn't look up, so she said briskly, "Looking back on it now, I promise you, it just seems like part of growing up. One of the less pleasant moments that's all."

Celia hesitated, "If I were you darling, I wouldn't mention this to your father. It would only make him even angrier with poor old Malcolm." She thought grimly of the drive home. Natasha nodded and suddenly looked worn out. Celia went to look for George who was already on his way to find her. "Right Celia. No argument. We are leaving now." After the briefest of farewells they climbed into the car. Natasha immediately fell asleep, leaving Celia to listen to George's furious mutterings the whole way home.

The next day Celia drove Natasha back to school. The Billy incident wasn't mentioned at all and she was relieved that her daughter seemed back to her usual cheerful self.

Not so Celia. Her night had been haunted by memories of yet another parallel and now she couldn't stop thinking about it. Why did these damned parallels have to keep on happening to her? Was there to be no escape from them?

She didn't see Euan for another couple of days, but finally managed to make an assignation to meet him at the oak tree.

"So," he asked as she joined him, "how was the wedding?"

Celia, out of breath, said rather huffily, "I thought you didn't want to hear about that."

He shrugged. "I don't particularly, but you are looking stressed, so something has obviously upset you."

Celia hesitated. "You're going to mock me if I tell you." He smiled. "No I won't. I promise. Come on, let's have it." She took a deep breath, "Well, something occurred at the wedding that reminded me of another parallel." He threw back his head and laughed. "Not more bloody Dallas in Oxfordshire?" She looked sulky. "Norfolk actually, and I knew you'd mock me." He gave her a long look. "I'm sorry. Why don't you tell me what happened?" She sat down and leant against the trunk of the tree. "All right, but no more mocking." He smiled and sat down beside her. "No more mocking. You can go ahead."

Celia took a deep breath. "Well, the actual incident was rather trivial. One of the local lads made a pass at Natasha." Euan's eyebrows went up, "How serious a pass?" "Enough to upset her. This boy gave her a rather brutal kiss and it left her bruised and very shaken."

He was silent for a moment. "And this reminded you of something that happened to you?" She nodded. "Also at a wedding?" She nodded again. He looked at his watch.

"Why don't you tell me? I've time. I'm not on again until three." He gave her an ironic smile. "Just imagine I'm Dr Strutter." Celia laughed. "That would be impossible, but I'll do my best." She collected her thoughts and then started in.

"This incident, the parallel with Natasha's, occurred at Dolly and Tinker's wedding. Dolly's first husband was killed in the war and the announcement that she was getting married again came as something of a shock. We'd all got used to Dolly being on her own, and there she was, suddenly behaving like a starry-eyed teenager. My father was predictably scathing. He thought her far too set in her ways and was worried by the age difference.' "Age difference?" queried Euan. "Yes. Tinker is ten years younger, although to look at them you'd never know. I think Tinker was born looking old."

"So what did you mother say about this marriage?" Celia thought about this. "I think she was sympathetic and pointed out that Dolly had probably been lonely since the war bringing up the boys on her own. This made my father even more scornful, saying rudely he was surprised she had got married the first time as she was certainly no oil painting. I felt I had to pitch in here and told him I thought Dolly was very interesting to look at and Audrey added, 'Yes, rather like Dora Carrington.' Of course my father exploded at that, pointing out what an unfortunate end that lady had come to."

Euan smiled and she said, "Did you ever meet Tinker?" He shook his head. "No, Dolly came up to Cambridge once, but not with him. Presumably Tinker is not his real name." Celia shook her head. "No, his real name is Timothy Linklater, but everyone calls him Tinker. He's pretty odd to look at, rather like an owl, with a flat funny face and huge round glasses and a mop of grey hair which sticks out in tufts. When he's about to say something of great import, he takes off his glasses to reveal large pale blue eyes that seem to blink a good deal. He's a really lovely man." Euan asked, "And what does this Tinker do?" "He's a distinguished bookbinder and works all over the world. Apparently he's one of the greatest authorities on fifteenth century manuscripts, but apart from that, he seems to have a fund of knowledge on almost any subject you can name. Not long after he arrived on the scene, Bernard's feelings for him went into a complete reversal. Tinker tactfully took an interest in Bernard's work and after that scarcely a day went by without him being summoned to my father's study to give his advice. By the time the wedding day arrived, my father was quite reconciled to the marriage and took advantage of the reception to invite many of his own friends."

Euan looked at her. Her face, usually so pale, was flushed and animated.

"You really do enjoy recalling all this don't you? In fact, you become a different person. Perhaps you should write it all down." Celia turned away, suddenly embarrassed and reluctantly admitted, "I do write it down, after my sessions with Dr Strutter. I'd let you read it, but I'm not sure you wouldn't be bored." Euan sounded tetchy. "Of course I wouldn't be bored. It's fascinating stuff. But get back to the wedding"

Celia stared out at the view and suddenly wished she hadn't embarked on it. She'd never spoken of this to anybody and knew it would be difficult.

Euan looked at her impatiently. "Get on with it woman. I've only got till three."

Celia pulled herself together. "Well, one of the guests Bernard had invited was a Commander Robert Langley, who was a governor of Bernard's school. I'd only met him once or twice, but I knew he'd lost an arm during the war. On the day of the wedding my father took me to one side and said, "I want you to be particularly attentive to Bob Langley Celia. Poor old Bob, he's had a wretched time of it. He lost his wife a month or two back after a long illness, and of course you know he had his arm blown off during the war. He's fond of children, never had any of his own. So make a special effort there's a good girl.' I agreed and was determined to try, not just for my father's sake, but because for once I was feeling quite happy myself. Dolly's wedding took place on a beautiful April day. I had been bought a new dress, a rare treat. It was long, lacey and had a Regency high waist and low cut bodice. I was aware I looked pretty in it as several people commented on this."

Celia was now talking quite fast, staring straight ahead of her and not looking at Euan at all. "The wedding was over and the reception in Worcester College Gardens was in full swing, when Commander Langley came over.

Euan groaned. "Oh God. I can guess where this is going. You're a bloody rape victim as well as everything else." Celia took no notice of this interruption but went straight on.

"He suggested we took a walk round the gardens, and remembering my father's instructions, I agreed to go. I made every effort to be as charming as possible and kept smiling at him. He seemed content to let me chatter on. We had walked some distance, in fact out of the view of the other guests, when he suddenly pushed me back against the trunk of a great cedar tree. His breath was coming out in gasps, he was very flushed and was staring at me in an odd way. You have to remember I was only twelve and far too naïve to be aware of the danger signals. He panted that it was kind of me to be so nice to an old man like him. Although embarrassed and uncomfortable I tried to reassure him, saying he wasn't so very old. That seemed to please him because he pushed harder against me. I was starting to panic and tried to break free but his one arm held me in a vice." Celia shrugged, "You can imagine what happened. As he rubbed up against me I kept saying, 'Please Commander Langley, please let go, you're hurting me.' His body now pinned me to the tree and with his free hand he started fiddling with his flies. Then he thrust his hand down my bodice." She broke off. "Of course, if I hadn't been such an innocent I would have known perfectly well what he was doing. At the time all I knew was that it was wrong. With all the force I could muster I finally pushed him off me. I think he overbalanced and fell, but I didn't wait to find out. I ran back to the party and went into the bathroom. The day was ruined. I sat there for some time feeling sick, unhappy and bewildered." She paused and looked at Euan, but he made no comment. "As we were leaving Bernard said, 'Old Bob Langley has taken quite a fancy to you Celia. He's asked you to tea with him on Sunday.' Of course I was horrified and shouted, 'I can't. I won't go and see him. I don't like him.' This made my father very annoyed. 'My dear girl, why ever not? He's a lonely man and wants some company. I think it's extremely kind of him to bother with a slip of a girl like you.' I tried to keep the hysteria out of my voice and almost in tears I said, 'I tell you I won't. Nothing you do will persuade me to go.' Bernard started to get angry, but for once my mother came to my rescue and said quite sharply, 'She's overtired Bernard. It's been a long day. Leave it for now.' Later that evening I overheard the two of them talking. Audrey said, 'Truly Bernard, I don't think the child is being difficult. Something really upset her. Perhaps you didn't notice that she was looking very pretty today. Bob probably made a pass at her. It would explain her reaction.' My father couldn't agree to that. 'My dear Audrey, the man's old enough to be her grandfather. Besides, he only has one arm.'

To which Audrey replied sharply, 'I don't think that need necessarily be a handicap.'

Bernard snorted, 'Well if you ask me it's just Celia being her usual difficult self.'

That seemed to end the conversation and the matter was dropped."

Euan burst out, "My God Celia, don't let me anywhere near your father. I think I might do something lethal to the bastard." He took out a cigarette and lit up. "You didn't go to tea with him did you?" She shook her head. "No thank God. A week later I was back at school and out of danger."

Taking the packet of cigarettes from him she lit one for herself. They smoked in silence for a while. Then Celia threw away her cigarette butt and turned to him. "You do see the similarity in the story don't you?" Euan put his head on one side and considered this. "Well sort of. But your experience was far more damaging than Natasha's. It was almost as bad as being raped. Didn't you to talk to anyone about it?"

Celia shook he head. "No. I think I was far too embarrassed and ashamed. Actually, this is the first time I have told anybody."

They were silent again. Euan looked at his watch. "I must be getting back."

He pulled her to her feet and they started the walk home. They had nearly reached the school when Euan gave a sudden laugh. She looked at him questioningly and he said,

"I was thinking about your appalling sex life. It would be funny if it weren't so tragic, first a one-armed pervert and then George. No wonder you jumped on me!"

Celia gave him a shove. "Actually Euan, you jumped on me first I think." He held his hands up. "Quite right. I fell totally in lust from the first moment I saw you."

They'd reached the gates. "See you," he said, pecked her on the cheek and marched briskly off towards the school.

As always the abruptness of his departure left her feeling unsettled and unsure.

She walked slowly towards the house and decided it might be better not to tell Euan any more parallels in the future. It was therefore something of a surprise, when a few days later he asked her if he could borrow the black book to read. So she gave it to him.

Chapter 11

The next week drifted slowly by. Celia felt almost in limbo, but knew that something had to happen sooner or later, if only to break the feeling of deadlock.

Then one morning, she looked across at George and felt a stab of alarm. He was sitting opposite her and moodily stabbing at a sausage, in a way that was compelling her to take notice.

"Is something wrong George?" she asked, with studied patience. He stabbed again with his fork, missed and the piece of sausage flew across the table. Looking at her for the first time that morning, he seemed unable to hold back his irritation any longer.

"Why should there be anything wrong?" he said in sarcastic tone. "Everything is as rosy as it could possibly be. I have a wife with worse mood swings than Vivian Leigh, who thinks it unnecessary to communicate, who refuses all physical contact, and then, just as I was beginning to think things couldn't get any worse, she takes herself back to her expensive shrink, with not so much as an explanation."

He gave up his efforts with the sausages and noisily flung his fork onto the plate.

Celia folded her newspaper and considered this for a moment. There was obviously more to his irritation than merely her return to Dr Strutter. Knowing George as she did, she suspected the problem was with a woman. Perhaps he had been left? Perhaps he was involved in a divorce? She didn't know and she really didn't care. The only difference it made to her was how it affected the timing of her leaving him. She tried to appear unruffled. "Apart from my returning to Dr Sttutter, is there anything else that's particularly bothering you? You seem a little on edge."

He poured himself some more coffee. "Isn't it a little late for you to be taking an interest my affairs?" His tone was sarcastic and Celia thought grimly that perhaps 'affairs' wasn't his best choice of word in the circumstances. She said patiently, "I can't really help you George if I don't know what the trouble is." Her calm tones only increased his aggravation. "Very well, I shall return at lunchtime and unburden myself of all my troubles. It will make a nice change." Celia drew in her breath sharply. "I can't manage this afternoon George. I have my appointment with Dr Strutter." He snarled, "Well cancel it." She replied firmly, "I can't do that. Not at such short notice. Can't we talk tonight? I'll be back by six." He said shortly, "I'm out tonight." She tried to curb her impatience. "Well, some other time then. Wednesday afternoons are the only time when I am not available." Her voice was resigned but firm. He suddenly burst out, "What's so important about this Dr Strutter? He seems to have some Svengali hold over you. Anyone would think you were having an affair with him." Before she could stop herself Celia said sharply, "Don't judge everyone else by your own standards George."

She felt guilty about this afterwards but at least it did have the effect of bringing the unpleasant conversation to an end.

Halfway through the morning she decided to wander over to Euan's cottage before setting out for London. In the last week she'd had to cancel several assignations with him and was feeling a little guilty about it. On top of which, the last time they had spoken his behavior had been a bit offhand and odd.

As she peered through the window she would see him pacing up and down in what looked like a fevered and Byronic state. What on earth was the matter with everybody?

She knocked at the door. Euan flung it open and looked at her wildly, almost as if he didn't recognize her at all. "You look terrible," she said, going into the living room.

The floor was littered with screwed up paper and there were a lot of coffee cups, half drunk. "I haven't slept," he said abruptly, flopping down on the sofa. She sat down beside him and murmured, "Well hello Celia. It's lovely to see you." He pecked her on the cheek. "Hello Celia, it's lovely to see you." She eyed him thoughtfully. "So, what's up?" He stood up again, "What do you mean, 'what's up'? Why should anything be up? I just haven't fucking slept, that's all." She began to feel alarmed. "Well why the sudden attack of insomnia?" He stood up. "I'll make some coffee." She followed him into the kitchen and he made the coffee in silence. As he passed her the mug he said,

"I think we need to talk. Let's go out to lunch. I'm free this afternoon as my class is off on a field trip." She hesitated. She didn't really want to cancel her appointment with Dr Strutter, but some instinct told her this conversation with Euan was important.

"All right. I'll make some calls and meet you back here at one."

It was one of those hazy sunshine days, not too hot, but with a gentle breeze. They went to a pub she knew, down by the river and while Euan organized the drinks, Celia watched the calm scene before her. Boats were quietly passing and re-passing and it struck her as odd that she should be feeling such a sense of turmoil amidst all this tranquility. Euan walked towards her with a grim expression on his face.. His mood was strangely unpredictable. She didn't trust it and suddenly she felt nervous.

"Nice place," he said as he sat down. She nodded and they drank in silence for a while until she asked, "What is it you need to talk about?"

He lit a cigarette and offered her one. She took it hoping it would calm her. It didn't. "We have to talk about us." She felt a rising panic and her voice was nervous, "About us?" He sounded almost angry, "Yes, us. Our fucking situation, or whatever you want to call it." She took a deep breath. "What about it?"

He hesitated and then plunged in. "It's a mess and a muddle Celia and you know it. We can't let it continue. It's driving me bloody nuts." Her eyes widened and a look of fear crossed her face. He saw that and his tones became calmer. "You don't have to look like Bambi's mother! It's not you." He emphasized the last word. "It's the situation. I just don't think I can take much more." He gulped down his beer. Celia tried to keep her voice steady, "What can't you take exactly?" He slammed down the glass and spoke wildly, "I can't take George, your marriage, your whole way of life. I don't fit into any of it. It's totally alien to me. The constant demands on your time, the school, the weddings, Natasha, the relations, in fact the whole fucking set up."

He stubbed out his cigarette angrily. "I should never have got myself into such a situation. I always swore I would avoid complicated affairs. I despised my friends who became involved with married women and now look at me? I can't think. I can't write. It's like being on the edge of a precipice waiting to fall over."

Celia stared at the boats. How seductively idyllic it all looked. Yet here she was, having the conversation she had most dreaded since falling in love with Euan.

"Do you want to give me up?" she asked at last, not daring to look at him.

"No I don't." He gave a mirthless laugh. "That's just the trouble. If I could there wouldn't be a fucking problem. But I don't seem able to."

Her relief was so great she wanted to hug him, but instead she took a long drink and waited for him to continue. "One thing is certain, I have to leave the school and find another job." This caused her to panic. Of course she had always known it would happen, but even so, she found the thought of his leaving unbearable.

"Will you find another job teaching?" she asked, trying to keep her voice calm.

"I hope not. I have a few contacts in television. Wal is setting up a meeting with some television mogul which sounds quite promising. Teaching was only ever a stop-gap. I now want to get on with my writing. It'll mean taking a few risks but it's something I know I have to do." Celia finished her drink, put down the glass and said quietly, "So where does that leave us?" He was silent for a while, staring moodily at the river. Then he looked at her and slowly shook his head. "There is no us Celia. You must know that. There can't be any 'us' until you leave George"

She turned away from him, worried that she might break down and cry. He had put it fairly brutally, but he was right of course. She knew she had to leave George. But how? She could only see a huge mountain of difficulties in front of her. Euan went on, "Once you are free we can start again, right?" "Right," she echoed, without much conviction.

He screwed up his cigarette packet and chucked it at the litter bin. It missed. He walked over, picked it up and threw it in the bin and then walked down to the river bank. He knew that his ultimatum had given her a shock, but somehow he had to galvanize her into action. George would make it as difficult as he possibly could and her life would be pretty wretched for a while, but she had to break free of him.

Walking back to their table he sat down and took her hand in his, speaking as gently as he could, although determined to remain firm. "Celia, there is one more thing that I must make you understand. I can in no way be involved in the process of you leaving George. Do you understand that? In no way whatsoever."

She looked surprised, "But you are involved Euan. Of course you are involved."

He shook his head. "No. No I am not Celia and it will only complicate things if you involve me. The fact is, you should have left George years ago, long before I arrived on the scene. For your own sanity, you have to get right away from him and get a life of your own." She took her hand away and said stiffly, "It sounds as if you are taking the coward's part to me." Euan shrugged. "Maybe it does sound like that, but think about it. You have plenty of reasons for leaving George and Wal can certainly supply you with any amount. If George knows about us, he will get very unpleasant and I think will treat you very badly indeed, and I don't just mean financially. At the moment you have the moral high-ground. You mustn't lose that. It's bad enough you not having sex with him, if he thought you were having sex with someone else, things could turn very ugly."

He turned her face towards him and spoke with more urgency. "You must understand this Celia. He could even fight you over Natasha. Think about it." She sat in shock as Euan said again, "Do you understand what I have been saying?" A nod was all she could manage. Deep down she felt she was being blackmailed, but she also knew a lot of what he said made sense.

There was a long silence. Finally she asked, "When will you leave?" He told her at the end of term and that he would give in his notice the following week. She thought bitterly that he had everything worked out. There were no problems ahead for him.

He took her in his arms. "It'll be all right. You'll see. Just break free from George."

She hardly saw Euan over the next two weeks and to add to her anxiety George began to behave even more unpredictably that usual. It was almost as if he was trying to pick a quarrel with her, even on the slightest pretext.

The day following her conversation with Euan, he asked her irritably, "How much longer are you going to need this damn shrink?"

She felt a pang of guilt for not admitting she had missed the session, but quite frankly didn't see the point of putting herself through the interrogation that would inevitably follow. As it was, the questions were continual. "Who was that on the telephone Celia?" "Where are you off to?" "How long will you be?" "Is it another of your headaches?" She couldn't fathom it out at all, but it left her at screaming point. If she and George had been in a normal relation-ship she might have been able to find out the cause. As it was, she just had to endure it and hope it would pass. But it didn't. Things actually became worse. On some evenings he would follow her around the house, doing his best to provoke her. She tried to escape by playing the piano, but he would come into the room saying, "That goddam piano. La-di-da. La-di-da. I'm sick of it." So she stopped playing. Then he'd say, "Oh don't mind me. You carry on playing. After all, that's all you're good for. No bed. No conversation."

Finally one evening she put down the piano lid, turned on the swivel stool and said calmly, "All right then George, let's have a conversation. What do you want to talk about?" He gave a mirthless laugh. "Huh! Talk! You talk to me? You must be joking. You gave up talking to me years ago, along with everything else."

She walked to the sofa and sat down. "Well, let's start now. Why don't you tell me about your time in Boston?" George looked at her sharply. "Why do you want to hear about Boston? Are you checking up on me?" Celia answered wearily, "No George."

He mimicked her then. "No George. No George. Do you ever listen to yourself? You are the most boring person I have ever met. God knows why I put up with you."

She looked at him curiously. "Then why do you?" He immediately snarled back, "Because you are my wife. Remember?"

Something inside Celia snapped. She knew it was wrong timing and she knew she should have waited, but as she looked at his mean, angry face with the narrow piggy eyes, she could contain herself no longer. "Yes, I do remem-ber," she said quietly. "And do you know George? I don't want to be your wife any longer."

If she had wanted to give him a shock she had certainly exceeded. His florid face had turned a shade paler. "What was that you said?"

She repeated, "I don't want to be your wife any more George. I want a divorce."

He went to the drinks trolley and poured himself a large drink before saying sharply, "Well you won't get one. Don't you ever listen to me woman? I've told you before. I won't give you a divorce. And that's the end of it."

"But why?" Celia almost shouted in her exasperation. "I'm not happy. You're not happy. Our marriage is over. Finished. I doubt it ever started. Anyway, I want to leave because I don't think I can carry on with this farce a moment longer."

George's voice became icy cold. "Listen to me my girl and listen very carefully." His eyes narrowed and the veins stuck out on his forehead as he said, "I haven't put up with your moans and neurotic behavior all these years to have you walk out on me now. Understand this. You are my wife and that is how things are going to stay."

He shouted the last words, knocked his drink back in one, and then poured himself another. Celia began to feel frightened. She'd never seen him this angry before. In his present mood there was no knowing what he might do.

George spoke again trying hard to contain his temper, "You actually owe it to me to remain here Celia. If you can't fulfill your duties as my wife in the physical sense, at least you can support me publicly."

Was that it? He didn't want to lose face and the public humiliation of being left?

She looked at him and realized it was more than that. There had to be sexual frustration in there as well. He'd obviously had to give up his latest mistress, which made her rejection of him all the harder to bear. However his attitude seemed to her positively Victorian. She was his possession, so he wasn't going to give her up.

George was waiting for her to say something, but as she didn't, he continued,

"I suggest you stop feeling sorry for yourself and do something useful instead of mooching around all day. Good God! I thought when I got you away from those dreadful parents I was doing you a favour. And now look how I am repaid."

He took a long drink. "Lord knows, I've tried everything, even down to paying for that damn shrink. Well from now on I don't mind what the hell you do with your life, as long as you forget this nonsense about a divorce. That will not happen. It would be bad for me, bad for the school and, if you knew it, bad for you as well. So you can put the whole idea out of your head. Do you understand?"

He turned back to the drinks trolley and she could see he was now shaking with rage.

Celia suddenly felt a determination she had never experienced before.

"Very well George," she said firmly, "if you won't give me a divorce I shall just leave."

He turned round, threw back his head and roared with laughter.

"Now I've heard everything. You? Leave? You? Manage on your own? Where would you get a job? And don't imagine your parents will take you back. They couldn't wait to get you off their hands. And how do you think you are going to support yourself Celia? Tell me that, because you won't get a penny from me!"

Now if Celia had been thinking straight she would have bided her time, taken Euan's advice and gone to see Wal first. There were plenty of grounds for divorcing George and for getting a generous settlement afterwards. George knew this too, and this panic probably accounted for his anger. But Celia wasn't thinking straight. She only knew that for once she'd summoned up enough courage to broach the subject and having done so, she couldn't give up now.

George, was still on the attack, trying to bully her into submission and now changed tack, "What about Natasha? Had you thought about her? Because if you walk out on me I will make very sure she stays with me."

Celia, shocked by this, was unable to answer and George leant back, pleased with himself, knowing that last attack had gone home.

Is this what Euan had meant? Why, oh why, hadn't she listened to him and waited?

Instead she said, "I know you are going to make it difficult for me George but I still want to leave."

He was watching her and suddenly his expression changed. It was if something had clicked in his mind. In one move he slammed down his drink and crossed the room towards her. She shrank back on the sofa but he grabbed her by the wrist and hauled her to her feet. "My God!" he shouted, "There's someone else, isn't there? Trusting fool that I am. You've got a lover haven't you? You sly little bitch!"

Celia felt the colour rise in her face. She couldn't control it, although she knew it would give her away. George didn't take his eyes off her. "Well, well, well. All the time I was thinking you a paragon of virtue, you were behaving like a slut behind my back."

She struggled to break free. "Don't be ridiculous George. Let go of me please George." He held on. "Not until you tell me the name of your lover," and then he hit her hard across the face. She reeled back with the shock. He hit her again. "Tell me his name." His hand was raised to hit her a third time and almost without realizing it she whispered, "Euan. Euan Mackay."

He threw her back on the sofa and without another word walked out of the house.

Celia heard the door slam and then rushed to the telephone.

"Euan? Something awful has happened. George knows about us. He's in a terrible rage and is on his way over to see you now. I'm so sorry. So sorry."

Trembling and unable to say any more, she put down the receiver and went upstairs to her room. There were two nasty red marks on either cheek-bone just below the eyes. She found some Arnica ointment and dabbed it gingerly on the damaged areas. Then she locked her bedroom door and fell back on the bed, exhausted.

An hour later she heard George come in. He walked past her room and tried the door.

Finding it locked he called out her name a couple of times. Then to her great relief, he went off to his own room and she fell into an uneasy sleep.

She arrived at breakfast late the next morning. George had already gone, but there was a note on the table which read, 'Celia, I shall be back about 6.30. Please be here. There is a great deal we need to discuss. George.'

At lunch time she put on dark glasses to hide the bruises and swelling on her face and walked up to the oak tree, knowing Euan would be there. Ironically it struck her for the first time how really good-looking he was, as he stood waiting for her, moody and angry. She managed to say in a shaky voice, "I'm so sorry Euan. Was it awful?"

His voice was clipped. "Yes it was." She felt close to tears and said miserably, "I know you are angry with me." Again the cold, clipped voice. "Yes I am."

The tears started to roll down her cheeks, she just couldn't stop them. "I'm sorry. He hit me. I didn't mean to tell him. I just never thought he'd be violent."

Euan turned round and for the first time looked at her. He removed the glasses and gently touched her bruised face. His jaw was clenched as he said angrily, "The fucking bastard. Are you badly hurt?" Celia shook her head, "More frightened that hurt. He kept goading me, so finally I said I wanted to leave him and he lost his temper. I never thought he'd hit me." Euan spoke through clenched teeth. "I did try and warn you how he would react. You should have waited until after I'd gone."

Celia hung her head. "I know. I was going to, but I can't tell you what he's been like." She looked at him, her eyes full of tears. "I've messed up and you've every right to be angry..." She broke off as Euan said wearily, "Well of course I'm angry Celia. It put me in a false position and, worst of all, it has now weakened yours. You must have made it sound as if the only reason you were leaving him, was because of me. That has given George plenty of ammunition against you."

Celia shook her head. That wasn't how it had happened, and she was about to say so, when he went on, "If you came to me now Celia, as you are, neither of us would ever feel free. George would certainly see to that. There is far too much baggage, and now, because of last night there are financial implications. You have to sort all this out first. Until you have, we can't start to think about our relationship."

Celia burst out, "You don't understand. He said he wouldn't let me see Natasha!"

Euan sighed and said a little impatiently, "I did try and warn you," and he added, "George is just a bully. That could never happen. Wal would see to that."

The tears were now pouring down her face as she said wildly, "You probably don't love me anymore." He looked at her steadily and his voice was calm. "I do love you Celia. It's the only reason I haven't packed my bags and left! But I know you have to free yourself from one life, before embarking on another. It's our only chance." He paused. "Quite apart from me, your marriage is a fucking awful mess. Get out of it and find out who Celia Maddington really is." He handed her a handkerchief and she said crossly, "You keep doing that." He smiled and lay back on the grass while she mopped herself up. She lay beside him and looked up at the sky. He sounded serious when he next spoke, "You're going to need help in dealing with George. I've told you. Go and see Wal. He will know how to sort things out for you."

She nodded but didn't feel convinced. Her head was beginning to ache and her bruises were throbbing badly. A single bird hovered above her and she thought 'that's how it will be with me. I am going to be totally alone. I know Euan won't wait for me.'

As if reading her mind he said, "There is no rush sweetheart. We have all the time in the world." He had never used an endearment before, and it was somehow strangely comforting, even if it was still difficult to make sense of it all.

Euan suddenly laughed. "Poor old George. He was being terribly pompous, telling me how I would have to leave at the end of term. It came as a shock when I told him I'd already handed in my notice."

Celia gave a wan smile. She couldn't help feeling that Euan would be all right whatever happened, whereas she had a mountain of insurmountable problems ahead of her.

Just before they were in view of the school Euan took her in his arms. "I do love you. Honestly I do." He stroked her damaged cheek, kissed her gently and walked briskly away. With great weariness she dragged herself the rest of the way. Ahead of her was an evening with George.

Promptly at 6.30, he walked into the living room.

He was immediately solicitous and kind, which in its way was almost more unnerving than when he was angry.

"Drink darling?"

"Thank you" she said dully.

"First of all," he said, in unctuous tones, pouring a drink and handing it to her. "First of all I want to apologize deeply for last night."

She looked at him in shock. George never apologized.

He went on, "I was wrong to treat you the way I did, terribly wrong."

For the first time that evening he looked at her bruised face and then quickly looked away. She hadn't tried to hide the bruises with make-up and her appearance was pretty gruesome. He settled down opposite her. "You have to understand, I am not a violent man, but it was all a terrible shock. I lost control and for that I am deeply sorry."

Celia sipped her drink and said nothing as George launched into what sounded to her like a prepared speech. "I know your life here hasn't always been easy Celia, and I am aware that I haven't always been quite as helpful as perhaps I should have been." He paused, adding with a thin smile, "I fear I have been irritable when I should have been more patient." Celia remained immobile, too exhausted to speak but finding his smooth tones sinister. George leant back in his chair and continued, "Since returning from the States, I have had a great many pressing problems to deal with, which I didn't want to worry you about." Celia made a mental note to find out from Wal just what the problems were. She suspected he had lost a mistress and there was probably some sort of scandal involved. If so, it was no wonder George had been so agitated. To lose both a wife and a mistress would definitely dent his image. George droned on. "Yes. I should have been far more patient with you, I realize that now. You were such a young little thing when I married you, only just out of your teens and you'd led such a sheltered life." His expression changed. "However I did find your rejection of me so early on rather hard to bear."

She couldn't let that pass. "But George, the reason for my rejecting you, was because I found you with another woman."

He sighed, "Celia, Celia, you are such a child about these things. As I think I told you at the time, it meant nothing to me, just a trivial incident that's all. My marriage is what is important to me. My marriage and the school."

He moved over to sit beside her on the sofa and gave her hand a little pat. She stiffened. It was as if he were talking to an errant schoolboy. A vision swept over her, of Euan and her making love in the sand dunes of Iona. She quickly closed her eyes and tried to bring her thoughts back under control. As she opened them again she saw George looking at her rather anxiously, so she gave him a wan smile. Satisfied that she wasn't going to pass out on him he said, "We've got ourselves into a bit of a muddle, haven't we. But now it is out in the open, I think we can put this unfortunate affair with Euan Mackay behind us. I realize I have been no saint and I'm quite willing to be broadminded and forget the whole thing." Celia couldn't let that pass either. "George, there is something you have to understand. It wasn't just an 'unfortunate affair' as you put it. I happen to love Euan."

George looked at her, as if deciding what to stay. Then he stood up. "Another drink?"

She nodded and he walked over to the trolley. He was obviously making an enormous effort to control his temper. Once returned to his seat he regarded her sadly and his tone changed. "My poor Celia. You don't understand even now, do you? It's all over between you and Euan. If only you had told me about this involvement earlier I could have helped. I'm not such a bear am I?" She didn't trust herself to answer that, as George went on, "You have to understand that Euan Mackay is only interested in what is best for him. Believe me, I know the type well, he's ambitious and single-minded. They're all the same these grammar school boys who've had to fight every inch of the way. Nothing comes between them and their achievement and in many ways I admire him for that." He gave a little laugh. "I felt a bit of a fool storming over there last night. He had not the slightest intention of taking you away with him. Told me so himself. He's been offered a very good job in television and that is the only thing he cares about now. Nobody will be allowed to jeopardize such an opportunity," and he paused to give full effect to his words, "and that is exactly what would happen if he was named in a messy divorce case. No, no the affair is well and truly over. My only quarrel with the man is over what he has done to you." He gave her another pat on the hand.

Celia sat as if in a trance. George's half-truths were beginning to undermine what little confidence she had. She also felt a certain sense of betrayal by Euan. In spite of this she still managed to speak defiantly, "Whatever he said to you George, I know that Euan loves me." That unctuous smile again. "Well of course I can quite understand that he's very fond of you." Fond? Celia bristled at the word. "You're a very beautiful and stylish woman and Euan is certainly a social climber." She felt that was insulting to them both but there was no stopping George now. "You were never going to be enough for him Celia. I am sad for you but you just have to accept it. He's had his little fling and will now go his own way. All I can do is remain here and pick up the pieces."

He stood up, letting his words take full effect. "I'm not going to rush you darling. I have given this a great deal of thought. I think it might be a good idea if you went away for a little while, maybe even abroad. You just choose where, and I will make all the arrangements. Then, when you return, we will go away for a family holiday together, which is long overdue."

She sipped at her drink too tired to argue. "I want you to know that I have great confidence that we can make our marriage work. I am even glad for this little hiccup, it has brought us both to our senses. We can now make a fresh start. I know I have behaved badly in the past. Well I promise to remedy all that."

Celia drained her glass thinking grimly his mistress must have given him the boot, otherwise he wouldn't be making such rash promises.

George was looking down at her. "Perhaps the time has come for you to make an effort too?" By 'effort' he obviously meant she was to share his bed again. She must have looked alarmed because he sat down beside her and said with a little laugh, "Don't look so panicked darling. What a funny little thing you are. I'm not going to rush things. You just have to tell me when you are ready."

She looked down at his hands. They were fat and freckled. She hated those hands and the thought of them touching her made her feel sick. "I only worry about your welfare Celia," he went on, "you are very precious to me you know." She knew she had to say something, if only to stop him talking, so she murmured, "Thank you George."

He stood up again. "Good. That's all settled then. I'm glad you're being so sensible. Now off to bed with you darling. You're looking tired. I'll have your supper sent up on a tray." She managed to say, "I am tired George. I am very tired."

She started to leave the room but as she reached the door she looked back.

George was rubbing his hands together, a really pleased expression on his face, convinced he had won the battle. A shudder went through her.

Once in the safety of her room her sobs could be controlled no longer and she threw herself on the bed. What would become of her now?

Her life had become a battleground and she was being torn in two. George was determined she should stay, and Euan was determined she should leave, and both options seemed impossible.

Her tears finally subsided and finding the handkerchief Euan had given her earlier she wiped her eyes and went over to her desk.

After a moment she pulled out the black book, which Euan had returned to her without comment, and went straight to the account of her mother and Edward.

As she read it she thought, 'It now all makes sense. My 'parallel lines' theory has come full circle. I will never break away now.'

She slammed the book shut, put it back in the desk drawer and locked it.

Why on earth had she thought of the stupid theory in the first place? Why had she gone to Dr Strutter? Why had she fallen in love with Euan?

It had all gone horribly, horribly wrong. Now she understood why her mother had given up the struggle and stayed.

All that was left for her now was a life doomed to be spent with a triumphant George.

It was a long dark tunnel and there was no sign of any light at the end of it.

ELEVENTH SESSION   July 7th 1980

As I parked outside Dr Strutters's front door in Wimpole Street, it suddenly hit me that this was certainly the last time I would see him. The poor man would probably heave a sigh of relief at news of my departure, as I must have been one of his most erratic patients. Over the last four weeks I had cancelled two appointments and put him through a hysterical telephone call, the morning after the dreadful ordeal with George. I'd so desperately wanted to drive up and see him, but he had told me, politely but firmly, to make an appointment for the usual time.

So much had happened since that call, so many momentous events. And now here I was, a changed woman and what was he going to make of that?

Mrs Maitland gave me a strange look as I arrived. I immediately thought it was probably due to all those cancellations making a mess of her appointments book. And yet it wasn't a look of annoyance, it was more like sympathy, and as I walked into Dr Strutter's rooms he regarded me in the same way. For once he was the first to speak.

"I was so very sorry to hear about your mother Mrs Roxby Smith. Please accept my sympathy for your loss."

So that was it. They had both heard about my mother's death. But how?

As so often, Dr Strutter anticipated my thoughts. "I saw the obituary in The Guardian," he explained. "It was a very good one I thought. Sometimes obituaries can be so dry, but that really seemed to do her justice. I hope you thought so too."

I nodded. "There were several but that one was definitely the best."

He cleared this throat. "You seemed rather upset when you rang me last. I think it must have been a few days before your mother's death?

I felt a little embarrassed. "Yes, I do apologize for that call. The situation with George had turned unpleasant. I just didn't know what to do and needed immediate advice."

The good doctor regarded me with a kind expression but his tone was brisk. "In my experience 'immediate advice' is usually suspect, and I am not sure I would have been much help in the circumstances." He smiled, "Jung once said that good advice is a doubtful remedy, but of no danger since it has so little effect."

I smiled too. "Well that's probably true. I think I really needed someone outside my life to talk to. It was a form of panic really."

"What brought on this panic?" he asked.

I tried to explain as succinctly as possible. "Well, Euan gave me an ultimatum, making it pretty clear we wouldn't stand the chance of a life together unless I was free of George. He also advised me to wait until after the end of term before telling George I was leaving, so that he, Euan, wouldn't be around to muddy the waters." I shrugged. "Unfortunately George became so unpleasant I just couldn't stand it any longer. I told him I wanted a divorce and after that the whole situation spun out of control. George was physically violent and forced me to admit my affair with Euan. After that he became terribly angry and made it clear that he would make things as difficult for me as he could and would name Euan in the divorce. I knew Euan wouldn't want that, and worst of all, George threatened me with losing Natasha. I was being torn in two and it all seemed impossible. I kept thinking how similar my situation was to my mother and Edward."

I paused, "So when I rang you I was in a total despair."

Dr Strutter was frowning. "That was three weeks ago. And now?"

I lit a cigarette. "It was really my mother's death that changed everything. It's why I'm here today. I wanted to try and explain how something positive has come out of my parallels theory."

This caused him to smile. "Well, that sounds promising. Why don't you tell me about it?" I settled back in my chair.

"My mother's death came as complete shock. As far as I knew she hadn't been ill beforehand. They said it was a sudden heart attack and that was that. Consequently there was little time to organize anything and the funeral turned into the usual drab affair. Anyway, afterwards Dolly, my aunt, and I went back to the house and started to sort through Audrey's possessions. It was such a sad task, she had so little. A lot of it was already packed in suitcases. Suddenly Dolly said, 'Did you know that your mother was leaving Bernard?' Well I didn't, and I can tell you I was absolutely amazed. I asked Dolly if she was sure because I certainly hadn't heard anything. Dolly said it was definite, but added that Audrey had only recently made the decision. It made no sense. 'Why,' I asked, 'after all this time and after everything she had endured already?'

Dolly looked uncomfortable. 'I think she just couldn't take it any longer.'

I stared at her. She wouldn't return my gaze and I knew there had to be something else. Something had finally pushed my mother over the edge. So I took Dolly's hand and said severely, 'You have to tell me. I do have a right to know. What happened that made her decide to leave?' Dolly was silent for a moment. It wasn't exactly that she had aged, but the recent events had obviously taken their toll and her face had a sad, worn look.

At last she said with a sigh, "I suppose you're right. It would be wrong not to tell you. I was only trying to save you from...' her voice trailed away to a whisper as she added, 'the terrible tragedy.' Pulling herself together she blurted out, 'It was something Bernard did. I know he's my brother and I've always tried to find excuses for him, but this time I just couldn't.' She paused. 'It was all the fault of that wretched George IV biography. I'm telling you Celia, life around here had become almost unbearable and of course poor Audrey bore the brunt of it.' 'Why?' I asked, 'Was it the reviews that upset him? I know they were bad.' Dolly shrugged. 'It was partly that. After all it must have been difficult for him. Whatever else you say about Bernard, you have to admit he is a serious scholar. So it was terrible to have his work dismissed as a disastrous lapse.' She added crossly, 'I can't think what possessed him to write the stupid biography in the first place. Why didn't he just stick to his text books? I suppose some upstart publisher suggested it, knowing it would make money. I'm not even sure you could call it a biography, just a string of lurid tales. It's quite unbelievable when you think how thoroughly Bernard usually researched his work. But not this one. We all warned him against it. Tinker sat up night after night trying to persuade Bernard to have done with it, but to no avail. You know your father. It was almost as if he enjoyed being perverse.' I nodded grimly. 'Bernard soon became overtired, irritable and impossible to live with. Finally he finished it and we all heaved a collective sigh of relief. However, it was the disaster we had all predicted. I haven't read it and couldn't face it after Tinker reported it was all bosoms and bedrooms.' I smiled at this and admitted I hadn't read it either. One look at the reviews had been enough for me. I poured Dolly another glass of wine which she gulped down. She was now talking very fast. 'Oh, he'll make a lot of money from it. His publisher was right about that. One look at the lurid jacket and you can understand why it is selling out. It's even on the best seller list.' She sighed. 'To give Bernard his due, the whole thing has been a horror to him. I don't think he ever imagined how much vitriol would be heaped upon him, and from his fellow academics as well. It has completely destroyed his reputation as a serious historian.'

I tried to inject a positive note. 'At least he must be pleased with the amount of money he's making?' Dolly shook her head. 'I don't think he's even thought about that aspect of it. As soon as the reviews came out he embarked on a bout of heavy drinking, and as always on these occasions he became abusive and rude. But this time it was worse. He actually started to ring critics in their homes, shouting abuse over the telephone. He sent angry letters to the papers and even went on the radio shouting and swearing. None of us knew what he would do next.' She made a gesture of despair. 'In the middle of all this poor Audrey went down with 'flu. I think the illness, on top of the strain of Bernard's behavior, made her recovery very slow. Looking back on it she was probably far more ill than any of us knew, but she never complained or anything...'

Dolly took another gulp of wine. 'Then the most terrible thing happened. I don't think he knew what he was doing Celia. I really don't.' She looked at me and there were tears in her eyes. I could see she was struggling, so I took her hand and said gently,

'You must tell me Dolly. I have to know what happened.' She nodded and then burst out, 'He smashed up her studio. Wrecked it. Tore up all the drawings. Slashed the canvasses. Broke all the paint pots and paint brushes. There was nothing left.'

She paused and spoke more calmly. 'Audrey took me over to see it. She seemed unemotional and controlled. She just told me she would be leaving him and going abroad and that she wouldn't be coming back. That was all, but I knew she meant it.'

Dolly took out a handkerchief and mopped her eyes. 'I know he's my only brother and I've tried to make allowances for him, but I could understand why Audrey had no forgiveness left.' Her voice choked. 'The next day Bernard came over to say he'd found her dead in the kitchen. A massive heart attack the doctor said, all over in a minute. She wouldn't have suffered Celia. Apparently she had been taking heart pills for years and none of us knew.'

We sat in silence until finally I asked, 'Did Bernard know she was leaving?'

Dolly shook her head. 'I don't know for certain, but he must have suspected it. All her bags were packed and in the hall. She was obviously going away but I didn't see a note. There may have been one but I didn't ask. You can see the state he's in. He hasn't had a drink since. He asked Tinker to remove all the bottles.'

We sat on, silent and shocked. I stared at those suitcases and I wanted to cry, but no tears would come.

Finally I asked, 'Did you know about the Will?' Dolly replied that she didn't even know Audrey had made one. I said, 'Well she did. She left everything to me and at my death it is all to go to Natasha. Don't you find that odd?' Dolly sighed, 'I don't know what to think any more. But Bernard has quite enough to live on, especially now with the book.' I tried not to sound impatient. 'That's not the point Dolly. It's almost an insult somehow, not to leave him anything, not to even mention him. She must have been angry with him for a long time. That Will was made years ago.'

Dolly thought about this and said slowly, 'Perhaps, by giving you financial stability, she wanted you to have the chance of independence, just in case you should ever need it.'

I was about to say this was just what she had done, when Dolly started to sob as if her heart was breaking. I knew there was nothing I could say of comfort so I left her to it and went off to make some coffee.

A little while later, as we were still sorting through her things, I came across a trunk filled with odds and ends, and amongst these was a small packet of letters. I knew at once they were Edward's and I asked Dolly if she'd known about him. She leant back against the trunk. 'You mean her lover? I never actually met him but of course I knew about the affair. The whole family did. There were terrible scenes at the time. Somehow Bernard was never quite the same towards Audrey after that.'

I said firmly, 'She should have left him then.'

Dolly shrugged. 'It's always easier with hindsight. It was difficult to know what was best at the time. Everyone put pressure on her to stay with Bernard. Even I did, because I thought it would be best for you. Now I'm not so sure.' She sighed. 'In his own funny way I am sure Bernard was very fond of Audrey. I think his present grief is genuine.'

I felt a sudden surge of anger. "I feel no sympathy for him. He's suffering from guilt, not just for breaking up her studio, but for all the years of pain and anguish he put her through. Now we know she had a heart complaint I am sure the stress and suffering he put her through must have hastened her death.'

Dolly looked tired but she gave me a penetrating look. "Are you leaving George?'

I was surprised by this and then realized Wal must have told her but before I could reply Dolly said, "I did know you weren't happy with him, and I have to tell you I never liked the horrid little man. I wish I'd been around to stop you from marrying him.' She shrugged. 'But who knows? It may have been the best thing for you at the time and you do have Natasha. One should never interfere in people's lives. I've learned over the years it's best to let them make their own mistakes and then be there to help pick up the pieces afterwards.'

I poured out the last of the wine and Dolly asked, 'Will Euan make you happy?'

I smiled, 'I really don't know. I'm only certain of one thing and that is that I love him,' and I added briskly, 'Whatever happens with Euan, I definitely have to leave George.'

I picked up the packet of Edward's letters and stared down at the beautiful neat handwriting. 'Don't you find the parallel lives strange Dolly? My mother, Bernard and Edward? Me, George and Euan?' She just looked sad, 'I don't know Ducky, I really don't.' I said firmly, 'It has convinced me of one thing. I'm not waiting as long as Audrey to make my escape. She left it too late.' I looked defiantly at Dolly.

When she spoke her voice was frail and distant. 'Life is very hard. I sometimes feel quite bewildered by it. There's Audrey and Bernard with all their years of suffering. There's you, about to embark on a new relationship. There's my brilliant Luke, sitting starved and squat-legged in the middle of India, having some sort of religious experience. I even feel sad about Wal. I know he's a clever and successful divorce lawyer, but he makes all his money out of human misery. It seems wrong to me, but then I'm getting old. Thank God for my Tinker. He was the best thing that ever happened to me.'

She patted my knee. 'So what are your plans?' I told her I would go abroad for a while until the mess with George was sorted out, and I added that my mother's money had made my life a lot easier as I now had enough to live on, although I would still want to find some sort of job.'

Dolly looked pleased, gave me a hug and told me I deserved it.

As I got up to leave she asked me if I was going in to see my father. I told her that I didn't think he would want to see me.

She looked shocked. 'Of course he would Celia. He'd be very hurt if you left without saying goodbye.'

For all Dolly's perceptiveness, she never really understood Bernard."

I broke off here and lit a cigarette. Dr Strutter leaned forward. "Did you go and see your father?" I blew the smoke out slowly. "I did as a matter of fact. Dolly went home and I went and knocked on the study door. As there was no answer I let myself in.

Bernard was sitting, still in his funeral suit, hunched and ill-looking, beside his gas fire.

There was still the same familiar smell of menthol, leather polish and tobacco that I remembered from my childhood. I didn't blame him for the fire. It had been a dismal day, grey and cold.

'How are you Bernard?' I asked.

He shrugged. 'As you see, I live.'

I removed some papers from the only available chair and sat down. 'Dolly tells me you have found a housekeeper.' He grunted, 'So I believe.' I tried to sound cheerful, 'Well that's a comfort anyway.' He gave me a withering look, 'Is it?'

He turned back to the fire. I felt I had to say something about his loss. 'I am very sorry about Audrey. It must have been a terrible shock.' His shoulders hunched even more and he mumbled something I couldn't hear. Suddenly he burst out, 'Your mother was a brilliant woman. Her death is a tragedy. I am not interested in a life without her.'

This annoyed me. It wasn't as if he'd appreciated her when she was alive. And there was not a word of comfort for me. After all, it was my loss as well.

He suddenly turned on me and said angrily, 'You couldn't hold a candle to her.'

I was shocked and managed to stammer out, 'I never tried to Bernard.'

He went on. 'No. You were nothing compared to her. Nothing.'

My God, I thought, he really hates me. He was mumbling again and then he said defiantly, 'She always put me first you know. All her life she put me first.'

She hadn't put him first in the Will I thought and I longed to shout this back to him, but I remained silent. He turned towards the fire. 'There's nothing anyone can do for me now, except leave me in peace.'

That seemed to be my dismissal. I stood up, but he didn't make a move. He just sat there, miserable and full of self pity. I didn't feel one jot of sympathy, just a dull anger. 'Well goodbye 'I said, and on impulse added, 'I think you should know that I am leaving George.' Without even looking up he said, 'You always were a fool.' I left then."

There was silence in the room and I was again aware of that ticking clock.

Dr Strutter was looking thoughtful. Finally he murmured, "How sad, how very sad."

He turned his glance on me and said, 'So tell me, what are the positives you have drawn from all this?"

I took a moment to answer. "Well, I think the best thing that has happened is that I am now determined *not* to make the same my mistake my mother did. I am going to break out of those parallel lines whatever happens.'

He smiled and nodded and I went on "You see, before her death I was being pulled in every direction and in danger of being of unable to take any positive action. I was frightened by George's threats, frightened of coping on my own and frightened of losing Natasha. Then, after her death, my whole outlook changed. I truly believe that even if my mother hadn't left me the money, those terrible, tragic events surrounding her death would have shocked me into realizing that whatever happened, I had to break free. Anything had to be better than the defunct and sterile relationship I was in.

So that is where I am now and I'm sure I can make my new life work - with or without Euan."

I broke off as a sudden thought came to me. "Oh, Dr Strutter, I've just realized we never discussed the dream I told you about, the last time I was here."

He looked at me in a rather strange way before saying. "I think you will find you won't be having that particular dream again."

I looked at the clock. "Well then, I think the time has come for me to say goodbye. Thank you again, for all your patience and understanding."

We both stood up and as I held out my hand he took it in both of his. He looked almost emotional and for one moment I thought he was going to kiss me, although I'm sure he wasn't. To cover my embarrassment I said, "To hell with the parallels. Yes?"

That made him smile. He asked, "Have you ever stood on a bridge overlooking a motorway?"

The man was still full of surprises, right to the end.

I nodded and he went on, "Then you will have seen the parallel lines of the road directly below you. However, if you look into the distance, you will notice that the parallel lines turn into a single line on the horizon."

I thought about this. "You mean the parallels of experience turn into the single line of life?"

He smiled and nodded, "Something like that," and then became aware he was still holding my hand and let it go.

I also smiled, "Are you advising me to look on my life from a great height?

He shook his head and said wryly, "If you remember I never give advice."

That made me laugh, "Nor you do."

At the door, I turned. "It did help you know, getting all those parallels off my chest."

He seemed pleased by that and said, "I doubt you will need to come back to me, but should you ever wish to do so, I am always here."

With that I left his room for the last time.

The sun was shining and dazzled my eyes as I looked up towards his window, but I could see that he was standing there and as I reached the car, he waved.

In some strange way, I really love that man. We've had such a detached relationship and yet it occurs to me that he is the first person I have absolutely and totally trusted.

The end of the eleventh - and FINAL - session.

Chapter 12

For the next week Celia occupied herself with organizing her great escape.

George, blissfully unaware of her machinations, seemed pleased with the way things were going. She had informed him that morning she would not be returning to Dr Strutter, which was welcome news indeed. He silently congratulated himself on his patient handling of her. His diplomatic skills had obviously paid off. The more he thought about it, the more it seemed to him that the row and subsequent talk had cleared the air. Celia certainly appeared to be in a far better humour, indeed almost cheerful, and now was busily making plans for her holiday. That had been a good idea as well, as long as it wasn't too expensive. He'd had to cope with rather a lot of legal bills recently. That apart, it was all turning out far better than he had anticipated. He made a mental note to give her plenty of space until she returned from the holiday. After that, if things continued to go well, they might even resume their sex life.

Yes, all in all, he felt he had handled it in exactly the right way.

Celia watched out of the window as George walked over to the school, noting his look of self-satisfaction, and she thought to herself that he wouldn't be wearing that expression in a couple of weeks, when the letter arrived saying she'd left him for good. George would be beside himself with rage, especially as there was nothing he could do about it.

Her only regret was that she wouldn't be there to see it.

Returning to her desk she looked at her page of 'things to do'. First on the list was the task of tracking down Edward. It seemed only right that he should be told of her mother's death. If she could contact his publishing firm the rest should be easy.

It was, and by lunchtime her sleuthing had paid off. She had spoken to Edward's wife in Florence, and from her learned that Edward was actually in England for the week. So she rang his London number. He knew immediately who she was and suggested a lunch the following day.

They met in a small Italian restaurant off Soho Square and as she entered Edward stood up and she liked what she saw. He was extremely tall, with an aquiline face, greying hair and rather piercing blue eyes under bushy eyebrows. She also noted he was elegantly dressed in a dark blue shirt and cream linen jacket, giving off just a faint whiff of Bloomsbury. A waiter conducted her to the table and Edward took both her hands in his. "Celia, this is wonderful. What a pleasure to meet you at last."

She said shyly, "For me too."

Edward continued to look at her until she turned away from his gaze. He immediately apologized, "I am so sorry. You see, I've only ever seen an old photograph of you and I was trying to match the photograph of the child, to the beautiful woman in front of me."

To hide her embarrassment she said, "You probably had a picture of a gawky teenager. I never was very photogenic." He smiled. "On the contrary, you had a potential beauty even then. Your mother was so proud of you."

Celia felt her eyes pricking with tears. She seemed to have misjudged her mother a great deal over the years.

They sat down and she said at once, "I am sorry I didn't find you in time for the funeral. It was so sudden you see." He shook his head. "Please don't worry. I wouldn't have gone. Too many years have gone by. I prefer to remember Audrey as I knew her, young, talented, vibrant and pretty."

They were silent for a moment lost in their memories, and then Edward said, "Let's order quickly, because I want to hear all about you and catch up on your life." He glanced at the menu, "There's a particularly good pasta I can recommend..."

And that's how the lunch continued. His manner was gentle and yet somehow he took charge of things without ever being overbearing. Over the next two hours Celia found herself telling him the traumatic events of the past year; the breakdown of her marriage, her falling in love with Euan, her sessions with Dr Strutter and her decision to leave George. She even mentioned the parallels, but left out the grimmer details of Audrey's life. She felt she should spare him that. Edward listened carefully, asking the occasional question, and when she finally came to the end of her narrative they had finished their meal and the coffee had arrived.

Celia looked at him anxiously. "I do apologize, I have completely monopolized the conversation and I really did want to hear about you. My mother told me so little."

Edward smiled. "No apologies needed. We have plenty of time to talk about other things later. For the moment let's concentrate on you." He paused and looked at her. "If you will allow me, I would like to suggest a plan that has been formulating in my mind whilst you've been talking." Celia smiled, "Of course. Please go ahead."

He took a moment, as if ironing out the finer points. "Well, you say you need a holiday. Could I suggest you come and stay with Francesca and myself in Florence? We have a small cottage on the side of our house where you would be completely self-contained. Natasha could come and join you when she breaks up. We also have a small farmhouse near Sienna where we go at weekends and we'd be delighted if you cared to join us."

He broke off and looked at her a trifle anxiously. "It's only a suggestion. I shall quite understand if you have other plans." Celia spoke quickly to reassure him. "I can't think of anything we'd like more." He smiled. "I'm glad, but I haven't finished yet. You also told me you are going to need a London flat and that you will then look for a job. Do I have that right?" She nodded and he said, "Well, I think I can help you with both." Celia gasped. "I don't believe it. Really?" He smiled again. "You might not like it as a permanent solution, but it would certainly give you a base while you are looking around for something else. I have a London flat, which I hardly ever use, so you are welcome to that. In fact it would be a relief for me to have someone stay in it when I wasn't there. I merely keep it on because I am still on the board of my company and very occasionally have to come over for meetings and so forth." He paused, "and that is where the job comes in. I am sure I could find you something in the firm's music department. I remember that music was always your great interest."

Edward looked a little apologetic here, "It might not be very grand and the pay will be a nonsense, but it could be a start for you."

Celia could hardly breathe. For so long she had been used to everything going wrong in her life, and now, in the space of two hours, it was suddenly all going right.

She felt like crying with relief.

Edward worried by her silence asked if there was anything wrong. She shook her head.

"On the contrary, I'm wondering if life is playing a horrible trick on me and that I'm actually dreaming all this. It's more than I ever could have hoped for."

He looked at her kindly and said in a gentle voice, "I'm just glad I could help. You seem to have been through so much."

This brought a lump to her throat. "You've worked miracles. I don't know how to thank you." He held up his hand. "Please, no thanks are needed. It's all been extremely easy." Celia looked at him shyly. "I can easily afford the rent. My mother left me quite enough to pay you that." He shook his head. "I wouldn't dream of it. As I said, you will be doing me a favour."

They drank their coffee and he told her about Florence and their farm-house near Sienna. His anecdotes about their Italian life were vivid and amusing and some of his stories made her laugh. She didn't want the lunch to end, but finally, with some reluctance she said she had to leave in order to avoid the rush hour traffic out of London.

On the way home she decided not to tell either Euan or George of this encounter. There had been an uneasy truce with both of them over the last three weeks and she was happy to let that continue. They had both managed to put her through the mangle, so she certainly wasn't going to let them off the hook just yet.

The next job on her list was to make an appointment to see Wal, so the following morning she dialed his office number. A receptionist came on the line with that sort of irritating voice with upward inflections that all receptionists seem to have. "Simmons and Woolcock, can I help you?" You could almost see the tight little skirt and scarlet finger nails. Celia said, "I'd like to speak to Walter Simmons please." "Who shall I say is calling?" She replied patiently, "Celia Roxby Smith." "Hold the line please."

There were a series of clicks while she waited. At least there was no music. In the background she could hear the little chant, 'Simmons and Woolcock can

I help you?" The wait continued. Just as she was about to give up, the receptionist returned to her. "Thank you for holding Mrs Roxby Smith. I'm putting you through now."

There were more clicks and then Wal's voice boomed down the line. "Celia! Sorry to keep you hanging on." She held the receiver a little away from her ear. "That's all right. You do seem extremely busy." Wal laughed. "Of course I'm busy. I'm a divorce lawyer woman. So what is it I can do for you?" She hesitated. "I wondered if I could take you up on that lunch?" The voice boomed again. "Of course you can. What about tomorrow? I've just had a cancellation." She told him that would be prefect and he gave her instructions to meet him at a well known restaurant, at one o'clock.

Although she made sure she was on time, Wal was already there, sitting at a table by the window. It was obvious he was a lawyer who liked to be seen. Indeed, it was difficult to miss him, as today he was wearing a flamboyant waistcoat, patterned with what looked like cabbage roses. He stood up to greet her. "My dear Celia, what a treat on the eye you always are. You're looking particularly wonderful today. Could it be love?" She made a reproving face as they sat down. "You are so excessive Wal." He disregarded this and waved an arm. "Do I order champagne?" She shook her head. "I think that would be a little premature." Wal sighed. "Very well, a bottle of my favourite Chablis it will have to be." He gave the order and then waved at several of the other tables. Celia was amused by the grand gestures. "Do you know everybody here?" Wal grinned. "Quite a few. It's a good meeting place you know, a sort of staff canteen." Celia raised her eyebrows. "It's a rather expensive sort of canteen. The divorce business must be a lucrative one." Wal looked down at the menu. "Let's say there is never a shortage of clients," he remarked dryly. Celia also studied the menu, which was long and complicated. It seemed easiest to choose something she knew she liked.

"A Dover sole and green salad for me please." Wal took longer, being torn between three dishes, but in the end decided to have the same as Celia, only with a more exotic salad. The waiter disappeared and Wal waved at some more people who had just arrived at the nearby table. Then he leaned forward expectantly, "Well?"

She smiled and decided to quickly put him out of his misery. "I'm leaving George."

Wal leaned back again, obviously pleased. "At last, thank God for that. How's he taking it?" Celia sighed. "We've only spoken about it once. Then he took it extremely badly." The wine arrived, tasted and was approved. Wal put down his glass. "George taking it badly is fairly predictable behavior in the circumstances. Of course, he hasn't got a leg to stand on. I can see to that. What are you going to do? Divorce him?" Celia hesitated. "I think so, eventually. Unfortunately he now knows about Euan and will try to make trouble for him, so I won't rush things. For the moment I am just going to get used to being single again." Wal gave her a searching look. "Was that Euan's advice?" She shrugged. "More or less. He made it very clear he doesn't want to be involved in a messy divorce case."

Wal stopped eating. "Celia, I'm now going to give you a bit of a sermon. Euan is a shrewd operator. I've known him for a long time and I think very highly of him. He's an impressive man. Of course he has his faults - don't we all - but Euan's main fault is a tendency towards selfishness. Euan will always do what is best for Euan, and as you already know, he hates scenes and messy involvements. I'm quite sure he loves you, more than I've seen him love anyone, but you won't last long unless you give him space. He's a writer and like all writers he can be bloody difficult. If he ever felt 'cribbed, cabined or confined' he'd be off like a shot."

Having said his piece he poured out more wine. Celia said mildly, "Thanks for that, but you're actually preaching to the converted. I think I've got to know Euan pretty well." She added with mild irony, "And I could actually do with a little space myself."

Wal now dived into his fish which he filleted with positive gusto. This was a side of her cousin she hadn't seen, but no doubt this passion for food accounted for his widening girth. The filleting completed, he asked if George would make trouble over Natasha. Celia shrugged. "Knowing George he'll make any trouble he can. But if he does start to get difficult I won't bother with the divorce, I'll just leave him. In another few years Natasha will be eighteen and independent anyway."

Wal frowned. "What happens if you want to marry Euan?"

She thought about this. "I'm not sure the question of marriage ever came up, if we want to live together then we just will, divorce or no divorce. It's very early days. I have to settle into my new life first. Euan has to settle into his. He has a job in television. I expect you knew?"

Wal nodded, "But to go back to the question of divorce, I have to tell you Celia your attitude worries me a little. Without a divorce or legal separation you are going to be unprotected financially. I don't suppose George is going to feel well disposed towards you if you leave him, and he could make things extremely difficult on that score."

Celia removed a fishbone from her mouth. Her filleting hadn't been quite as efficient as Wal's. "I am aware he'll try to make things as difficult as possible. That's what made it so hellish when I first threatened to leave. The financial side of things left me utterly panicked, George saw to that. I just couldn't see how I would ever manage. But the situation has completely changed now." She paused. "Did you hear about my mother?"

Wal dropped his knife and fork onto the plate with a clatter, and looked aghast. "Oh Celia, how absolutely dreadful of me, I should have said something. What a sad, sad business. It happened so suddenly and I'm afraid I didn't make the funeral, much to my mother's annoyance. How's old Bernard taken it?"

Celia shrugged. "Not well." She didn't feel she could elaborate on this.

Wal remained contrite. "I must write to him."

She still felt angry with her father so she said nothing. After a moment she asked,

"Did Dolly tell you about the Will?" Wal shook his head. Celia smiled. "Well this may come as something of a shock. Audrey left her entire estate to me. Not a single penny went to Bernard, in fact he wasn't even mentioned. After my death everything goes to Natasha." Wal whistled through his teeth. "How very strange, I thought she was devoted to the man. There could be no other reason for her staying so long with someone who treated her so appallingly."

Celia remarked dryly, "I think that devotion ran out some time ago," and she added more briskly, "anyway, I gather from the lawyers it's a considerable sum, added to which the royalties from her book illustrations will keep coming in. She was far more successful than I had realized. So you see I will have plenty to live on, without any help from George." Wal resumed his eating. "What a relief," and then he chuckled. "That must really be bugging him." Celia said quickly, "George doesn't know. He still thinks he can beat me into submission by threatening me with penury." Wal positively beamed. "How very satisfactory. Thank God for Audrey. Somehow I couldn't quite see you as a pauper." She laughed and went on, "I've got a job as well, and a London flat."

Wal looked astonished. "My God you are a cool one. How did you manage that so quickly?"

Celia felt pleased. It was gratifying to have impressed Wal after all these years. "It only happened recently. Did you ever hear about Edward, my mother's lover?"

Wal sat bolt upright and almost yelled, "Your mother's what?" One or two people glanced in their direction. Celia was beginning to enjoy herself. "My mother's lover. She nearly left Bernard, when I was about thirteen." Wal opened and shut his mouth like a goldfish. "You amaze me, you really do. Somehow Audrey and a lover just don't go together. So, what stopped her?" Celia shrugged. "Heavy family pressure I think." Wal sighed. "It's a pity she didn't leave Bernard, her life might have been a lot happier, and indeed yours as well." He leaned forward. "So tell me about this mysterious Edward then. What's he like?" Celia thought about her lunch with him. "He's totally charming, and rather elegant in a Bohemian sort of way. He has his own publishing firm and was the first person to take on my mother's work. That's how they met. I think he's mainly retired now. He lives with his wife in Florence and they have a farmhouse near Sienna, but he keeps a flat in London." Wal considered this. "He must be worth a bob or two then." She smiled. This reaction was so typical of Wal. "I don't think he's short of money," she remarked dryly. "Anyway, he obviously loved Audrey and wanted to do something to help. So he fixed me up with a job in the music department of his publishing firm, and has let me have the use of his London flat, which he almost never uses. I am going to Florence at the end of the week to stay with him and his wife, where Natasha will join me when she breaks up. I'm really looking forward to it. I've always wanted to explore that part of Italy." Wal whistled through his teeth again. "Well I'll be damned. Does Euan know any of this?" Celia shook her head. "Not yet, I'm seeing him tomorrow." Wal gave a short laugh. "You'd better invest in a good bottle of malt. The poor man is in for a shock." He looked at her. "Seriously, I am delighted for you Celia, nobody deserves it more."

The rest of lunch passed happily enough, mainly mulling over the past. Wal confessed to having many twinges of guilt when he recalled what a monster he had been to her when they were children. "If it's any comfort," Celia told him, "Luke was marginally worse. And I do know I must have been the most pathetic and annoying child." Wal grinned. "Who could blame you, with that upbringing?" And they both laughed.

Later that evening Celia sat at her desk. Now only three tasks remained. First she needed to put Euan in the picture, then she had to tell Natasha about all these developments and, most of important of all, she had to compose the letter to George. Wal had told her to send a draft to him first. After any corrections had been made, she would send the final version from Italy. It was a great comfort to have his expert advice. She hadn't had to deal with the travel arrangements either. Edward insisted on making all those. So everything was in order and she'd even managed to keep George happy. He had welcomed the news that she'd be staying with friends in Italy. It obviously pleased him that it would cost so little, added to which, he'd be rid of her for the whole summer. Celia smiled to herself. Little did he know that he would soon be rid of her for good. At the weekend she would drive up to Natasha and the following day she would set out for Florence.

She took the black book from her drawer and wrote, *Freedom heyday!,* at the end of the last session. Then she flung herself on the bed, happy but exhausted.

Saying goodbye to Euan wouldn't be easy, but after that, it was a new life. She had survived, and she felt a sudden rush of gratitude towards her mother. Thanks to her money, the road to independence had been made so much easier, and it was good to know that Natasha would also have that money after her death.

For the first time in her life she was looking forward with excitement, instead of dwelling gloomily in the past.

To hell with the parallels! She had fought them and won.

Chapter 13

Early the next morning Celia left a note at Euan's cottage saying it was important he met her at lunch time. She then drafted the letter to George and put
it in the post to Wal.

At midday she climbed up the hill and waited for Euan by the oak tree.

The wood pigeons cooed gently to each other and a summer haze lay
across the valley obscuring the village and school from view. Their oblitera-
tion seemed significant somehow. Now her thoughts turned to Euan. She
still felt rather bruised from their last meeting and uncertain too. He hadn't
given her much to cling on to, and there had been a certain 'cruel to be kind'
attitude, that she had slightly resented afterwards. But, to be fair, his shock
tactics had worked. That, and the events surrounding her mother's death.

She caught sight of him, emerging from the mist and she knew with absolute certainty, that she still loved him. That hadn't changed. As he neared her,
he paused to catch his breath and she called out, "You look like some ancient
warrior." Euan panted, "I feel like one too. I practically ran up here because I
haven't got long. What's so urgent?" She leant against the tree. "I wanted to
say goodbye."

He looked startled. "That sounds very final." She smiled. "Au Revoir
then." He gave her a peck on the cheek. "That's better. I thought I was in for
blast of Rachmaninoff and a scene from 'Brief Encounter'. So, where are you
off to?"

She told him Florence." He whistled, "Lucky old you. And then?" She
tried to keep the triumphant note out of her voice, "Back to London. I have a

job and a flat lined up for the autumn." His eyebrows shot up. "Bloody hell! You've been busy. I'm impressed. How did all this come about?" She smiled, remembering Wal's words of warning. "You'd better sit down Euan. There's a great deal to tell you."

Once settled she embarked on the whole saga, starting with her mother's Will and then the meeting with Edward, finishing up with her lunch with Wal. He listened intently and didn't say anything until she had finished. "Phew. That's quite a tale."

He looked at her, "I was sorry to hear of your mother's death. It must have been a shock. I thought of writing something to you, but didn't think I could say anything very helpful. It's always difficult with a parent's death. I remember with my father…"

He broke off, deciding not to take that particular subject any further. Celia gazed into the distance and thought about her mother. "The funny thing is," she said speaking slowly, "since her death I have felt much closer to her than I ever did before. She's become more real somehow, especially after meeting Edward." She added more briskly, "And it's because of him, and of course her money, that I have been able to change my life. I think my mother might have been pleased about that. I do hope so."

Euan was silent for a while. She couldn't tell what he was thinking. He was wearing one of his inscrutable expressions. Perhaps he resented her getting her mother's money and Edward's help. It meant that she wouldn't have to struggle in the same way that he had done.

He lit two cigarettes and handed one to her. As he blew the smoke out he said,

"I'm pleased for you Celia. I really am. You deserve a break. I know you've had it rough for a long time." She thought a little crossly that if he'd known it had been so rough for her, why hadn't he been more helpful? But she said nothing.

"So when do I next get to see you?" She told him the end of August.

He suddenly looked anxious. "Are you going to be all right?"

She said more brutally than she meant to, "Do you honestly care?"

He was taken aback by that. "Of course I do you stupid woman. I happen to love you and I'm going to miss you."

She relented. "I'm going to miss you too. And you are no good on the telephone. And I know you won't write. It's hopeless. Oh well, they say that absence makes the heart grow fonder."

This made him laugh. "And I'm sure 'they' are right."

He threw away his cigarette. "What are you going to do about George? Have you told him you are definitely leaving him?" She shook her head. "I've drafted a letter and sent it to Wal for approval and corrections. George will get it when I am in Italy. He can't argue with a letter and Wal is going to handle everything after that. So I should be a free woman by September."

Euan gave her a look of mock terror. "How bloody terrifying!"

Celia punched him in the chest and they both fell backwards onto the grass.

A little later he said, "I would come out and join you in Italy, except it might be difficult with the new job."

Celia sat up. "Tell me about the job. I've no idea what you are doing. George seemed to know more about it than I did, which in your language was 'fucking annoying.'

He gave a laugh. "Swearing suits your new independent status, you should keep it in. There's not very much to tell you about the job yet. It's early days, but I think it could be interesting. I'm one of two script writers working on a new classic serial, which we are adapting for television." Celia inquired which classic. Euan shook his head, "You wouldn't know it. Some obscure nineteenth century novel that a researcher has dug up."

He looked at his watch. "Celia, I must be getting back. I don't want to be in trouble with your soon-to-be-ex." She smiled and then took the black book out of her bag. "I wanted to give you this. I know you've read it, but I don't want there to be any chance of George snooping around in my room and finding it while I'm away. I'm leaving quite a bit behind, including my desk. I can send for what's left once I'm installed in the London flat. There's nothing else private, but of course this is." She handed it to him. "It's all up to date, I finished the last entry yesterday."

Euan took it. "I'll keep it safely until you return. Good excuse for you to come back to me." Celia kissed him, "As if I needed one." He kissed her back and then stood up. "Poor George. This is one round he hasn't won."

They started down the hill and he asked, "When do you leave for Florence?" Celia told him in two days, because she was going to see Natasha first. Euan looked at her.

"Will she be all right with all this?" Celia nodded. "She'll be fine. It was actually Natasha who suggested I leave George in the first place, and she's nuts about you."

He laughed. "I'm glad to hear it. Give her my love."

She was suddenly horribly aware that the moment of departure was upon them and found she could only manage silly banter, so she said, "Lucky her to have it."

Euan seemed to catch her mood and he murmured, "Stupid woman."

He took her in his arms and they stayed that way for some time.

Last thing that night Celia took a final look out of her bedroom window. The mist had thickened into fog so that she could hardly see to the end of the drive.

It wasn't that lovely a view anyway and she had no regrets at never seeing it again.

She turned back into the room. Her cases were packed, ready for her departure in the morning. Suddenly the buoyant feeling of optimism that had been with her since meeting Edward, began to fade and falter. Surely nothing could go wrong now?

It would be too cruel.

Mentally pulling herself together she thought instead of Euan. He had been lovely to her today and now the autumn seemed a very long way away.

In spite of falling into a deep sleep, she woke up early and looking at her watch saw it was nearly six. There was no point in trying to go back to sleep now.

With a feeling of excitement she quickly dressed, picked up her suitcases and crept out onto the landing. She walked quietly past George's room, down the stairs and out through the front door.

There was still thick morning fog, but not bad enough for her to worry about.

As she edged the car out of the garage and into the drive, her optimism returned.

She was free at last.

With a symbolic gesture she threw her house keys out of the window, turned out of the gates and onto the main road.

A day later Mrs Maitland came into Dr Strutter's room. She placed a newspaper in front of him. "Oh Dr Strutter, I'm so sorry. So very sorry."

He read;

"PILE UP ON THE A 11

Questions are to be asked in the House about the 3 mile stretch of the A 11 outside Norwich, scene of yesterday's appalling 40 vehicle pile-up in the fog.

Among the four victims killed in the multiple crash was Celia Roxby Smith, wife of George Roxby Smith, the headmaster of Civolds, the well known preparatory school…"

Chapter 14

Two weeks went by and then Dr Strutter had an unexpected visitor.

He opened the door, "Won't you come in and sit down?" He indicated the leather chair opposite his.

"You know who I am?" the man inquired. Dr Strutter gave a faint smile, "Yes, I do."

Euan Mackay was not quite as he imagined him. Younger perhaps and less well built. He looked at the tall, rangy man, with his fierce expression and, as he started to speak he recalled the mention of a faint Scottish accent.

"This was Celia's time," he said.

The doctor nodded. "You're quite correct. It was always Wednesday afternoons."

There was silence for a few moments. Then with an awkward gesture Euan Mackay pulled out the black book from his jacket pocket and placed it on the low table between them. "I came here today to give you this. It's the book in which Celia wrote her account of your sessions together. She wrote everything down, along with her thoughts and reactions. It reads like a book. When she went away she gave it to me to look after."

He broke off, "I never had the chance to return it. She died the following day."

He paused again. "Anyway, I thought she'd want you to have it."

Dr Strutter was taken aback. "Thank you. That is most thoughtful of you."

He too paused and then came to a decision. "However, I kept my own notes and I really think Mrs Roxby Smith would have liked you to keep it."

He pushed the book towards Euan and as he did so he made a study of the man opposite.

The face was pale and strained, with dark rings under his eyes. There was no doubt the man was suffering a deep grief. Sensing he was being scrutinized Euan started to speak again, struggling with the words. "I wanted to thank you. I mean, I know it was your job, but she really did seem to trust you. I don't think she would have made the break if it hadn't been for talking to you." He roughly wiped his eyes and his jaw was clenched in an effort to master his feelings. "It's so bloody tragic that she never had a chance to enjoy her freedom." Dr Strutter nodded in agreement.

There was another silence before Euan burst out, "I did love her you know. I can't bear to think she might have doubted that. But all her life she had been trapped into making decisions. I just knew this was one she had to make for herself."

He seemed very agitated about this. Was that due to a slight sense of guilt?

Dr Strutter stroked his trousers and his voice was soothing. "And I think you were right. The last time I saw her she was both happy and excited. Optimistic too I think."

Euan looked up. "I hope so. She certainly did seem that way to me as well."

Dr Strutter held his glance and offered what crumbs of comfort he could, choosing his words carefully. "Don't forget you gave her a love that she never thought she would experience. Her life changed when she met you."

A silence fell again but some of the tension left Euan's body. However, when he spoke again it was in clipped tones. "I thought I should mention that her husband has arranged a Memorial Service for her. It will be a very grand affair, in Oxford Cathedral. I shan't be going but I can give you the details should you want them."

Dr Strutter shook his head and murmured, "I don't think I will, but thank you for telling me." They looked at each other with mutual understanding.

"Ironic isn't it?" Euan burst out. George won the last round after all. Nobody knew Celia was leaving him. He just collects all the sympathy and condolences. 'Poor George,' they all say, 'Such a tragedy for him.' And I have to remember how it really was!"

Dr Strutter could understand his bitterness. The irony of the situation hadn't escaped him either, but he didn't feel that this was the moment to point out that George hadn't actually won. On the contrary, he had never managed to win Celia's affection or control her, and he knew only too well the contempt and dislike she'd had of him.

Euan looked across at him. "Don't you find it strange about those parallels? I never took them seriously when she told me about them. I just thought it was good for her to unload all that baggage. But now I can't get them out of my mind. There is something really eerie in the fact that both Celia and her mother should die, just as they were making their escape."

Dr Strutter seemed lost in thought for a moment, and when he spoke it was in precise tones. "It does appear strange I agree, but nothing more than a horrible coincidence I'm sure. And their situations were really not similar. Audrey Maddington was leaving at the end of her life. Mrs Roxby Smith was leaving because she had a new life ahead of her and was about to embark on an exciting future." He sighed. "As to the parallels? Well, we live in very small social worlds and it's therefore no surprise that certain events get repeated, and similar situations are experienced by successive generations. As you rightly pointed out, Mrs Roxby Smith was able to find a release through recalling these parallels and in the end it enabled her to take a positive step towards a new way of life. It is just a tragedy she didn't live long enough to enjoy it."

Euan was silent. He looked exhausted, incapable of saying anything more.

Abruptly he got up to leave. As he reached the door he turned and blurted out, "This grief is a terrible thing. I can't get her out of my mind."

The doctor held out his hand. "You have my sympathy Mr Mackay."

It was only after he'd gone that Dr Strutter noticed the black book lying on his desk. Euan had forgotten to take it. He glanced through the closely written pages but finding the contents unbearably poignant, he pushed it to one side.

Euan Mackay was right. Celia would be difficult to forget.

The next day the black book had gone, filed away by Mrs Maitland.

George sat at the breakfast table, staring at the letter in front of him. With it was an enclosed note from Simmons and Woolcock which read, "My cousin Celia had requested I send you the enclosed letter, after her arrival in Italy. In spite of her tragic death, I think it is only right you should see it, so I am now enclosing a copy.

Signed, Walter Simmons.

George read the letter through again and his complexion turned first an angry red, and then he went very pale.

So the bitch was actually leaving him. She'd had it all planned and never said a word.

It had been bad enough hearing about the fortune she'd inherited, but this was far worse and the implications of it began to dawn on him. If Walter Simmons knew, then soon a great many people would know, he would certainly make sure of that.

George started to sweat. This could be disastrous for him. He had gained some sympathy in the immediate aftermath of Celia's death, but if the news that she was leaving him got out, as now it probably would, then that sympathy would quickly evaporate. There wasn't even any evidence or mention of Euan Mackay, which would have mitigated him slightly. That meant that he, George, would be framed as a monster. The timing couldn't be worse. He had a difficult court case on his hands and it was likely that the scandal of that would reach the gutter press.

Another thought hit him. The governors would not be happy about this either. Celia had been held in high regard. This could put his job and indeed his whole future on the line.

Then there was Natasha. She, too, probably knew about her mother. It would explain her coldness to him at the Funeral. She had left the next day, for the holiday Celia had arranged for them in Italy, without so much as a word. How was all this going to affect the relationship with his daughter in the future? Was that to be ruined as well?

His greatest regret now was that he had ever met Celia Maddington.

Snatching up the letter he moved across the room and tearing it into small pieces he deposited it in the bin.

Damn the woman! Damn her to hell.

EPILOGUE

March 23rd 1981

It had been a long and tiring day.

Dr Strutter tidied up his desk and opened the top drawer to put his papers away.

And there it was, Celia's black book, just where he had put it away that morning.

Almost against his will he opened it again and started to read and this time he read it right through to the end. As he read the final lines he felt a lump rise to his throat. He re-read the words, "In some strange way, I really loved that man. We'd had such a detached relationship, and yet it occurs to me that he's the first person I have absolutely and totally trusted."

An image floated in front of him of that beautiful gold hair and her crushed broken body and he closed his eyes as if to shut it out.

There was a knock at the door and he forced himself back to normality.

"Yes, what is it?"

Mrs Maitland came in and reproachfully looked at her watch. "It's getting very late Dr Strutter, and your wife called and said could you remember to pick up the fish."

This was normality with a vengeance and Dr Strutter threw back his head and gave a great guffaw of laughter. It was totally out of character and Mrs Maitland looked startled. "Are you all right Dr Strutter?" He pulled himself together. "Yes, yes, quite all right thank you. I'm sorry it's so late. You get off home Mrs Maitland. I'll see you tomorrow." She left, shaking her head. His behavior had been odd all day. He needed a holiday. He really worked far too hard and she would suggest it in the morning.

After her departure, Dr Strutter looked at the book, uncertain what to do with it.

Finally he unlocked a side drawer, placed the book inside, and locked it again.

Perhaps one day he would send it to Celia's daughter. But not yet.

One last curious thing.

A few nights later, Dr Strutter was driving home after an evening function and idly flicked on the car radio.

It was playing her song, "Parallel Lines." He hadn't heard it since their first meeting.

"Breakaway. Don't stand behind the bars.

Keep reaching out, reaching out, reaching for the stars,

Breakaway, just breakaway, from those parallel lines..."

He stopped the car and listened.

When it finished he turned the radio off and sat in silence, feeling over-whelmed by a great sadness.

It was some time before he could continue his journey home.

ABOUT THE AUTHOR

After leaving the Central School of Speech and Drama in London, Jane McCulloch has worked as both a director of theatre and opera and writer for television, theatre, radio, and the recording studio.

She has devised and written more than thirty works for her own theatre company, and other writing projects include the book and lyrics for three musicals and the Christmas carol "This Christmastide," first sung by Jessye Norman. She has also published two children's books and four slim volumes of verse.

Parallel Lines is the first book in the Three Lives Trilogy, with the remaining two books, *Triangles in Squares* and *Full Circle*, to be published in 2015 and 2016, respectively.

McCulloch has four children and ten grandchildren and splits her time between a residence in London and a houseboat on the Thames.

Made in the USA
Charleston, SC
31 December 2014